NORTHWOODS PULP

Thomas Sparrow

Bluestone Press

Grateful acknowledgment is made for permission to reprint portions of:
CAREFREE HIGHWAY, by Gordon Lightfoot
© 1973 Moose Music Ltd.
All Rights Reserved Used by Permission
WARNER BROS. PUBLICATIONS U.S. INC., Miami, FL 33014
SUNDOWN, by Gordon Lightfoot
© 1973 Moose Music Ltd.
All Rights Reserved Used by Permission
WARNER BROS. PUBLICATIONS U.S. INC., Miami, FL 33014
ROLAND THE HEADLESS THOMPSON GUNNER, by David Eric
Lindell and Warren William Zevon © 1978, Zevon Music, BMI.
All rights reserved.

Library of Congress Catalog Card Number 99-63866

ISBN 0-9672006-0-1

Text design by Frank Mehle
Photography and photo concept by Molly O'Neill and Carrie Mohn
Cover design by Kim McAndrew-Spellerberg

Bluestone Press; P.O. Box 3196; Duluth, MN 55803
218.724.5806
Email: bluestone@duluth.com
www.duluth.com/bluestone

Thanks to Barrett, Kim, Frank and most especially Laurie, without whom this could never have been written.

TABLE OF CONTENTS

WHITE OUT

Buzzing:

Four hooded heads, four snowmobiles. Snow drifting down heavy, thick. Buzz, buzz, buzz….

Three Ski-doos and an Arctic Cat screamed full bore down an empty and colorless country road en route to a ribbon of orange tape Eddie had tied on a tree branch a few months before. He knew it was coming up soon. Then they would disappear into the forest and be gone before the cops even got shoveled out.

We're going to make it; we pulled it off, he thought proudly. So much white stuff on the roads you'd need a snow machine to get anywhere—and Johnny Law didn't own any. Eddie knew his little gig would change that chink in law enforcement's armor forever. After the Snowmobile Stick Up of '77, every cop-shop in the North would have at least one.

It was really a miracle that the whole deal went off. There were so many factors that had to be right for it to work; it was amazing how they all came together. When he proposed his plan last March, Eddie never really believed they'd get past the bullshitting stage. He'd been feverish, cabin feverish. Crazy from being stuck too long around too many bohunks. But he always believed it was a good plan and now he had proved it. There they were, zipping along a river bank with bags full of goddamn cash. Your fucking A it was a good plan.

This job felt different from the one he had pulled back in Louisiana; he wasn't as confident now that the gods weren't speaking to him. And they'd been silent for a coon's age. The first job was like some grand vision quest: He was young then and ripping off his employer for a hundred and seventy-five grand seemed like pennies from heaven. This time around, reality had forced its way into things. It wasn't for fun anymore, it was business—just business.

He was drunk the day he told the other three about it. Afterwards, they hugged and shook hands and bonded over their little scheme. He kissed Judy, and after over a year apart, it had felt strange. Strange to kiss someone you thought you were sick of and have it feel good.

Ernie Garrity didn't suspect anything was fishy as he squeezed the seat cushion between the heels of his motorcycle boots and grinned out from underneath his green ski mask at the tumbling white puffs, his brown eyes darting. Now and then he felt all warm inside, thinking about someone smart like Eddie being nice to him like this, letting him in on this gig as a full partner. That thought and a hit of crank he snorted on the way to the bank were keeping him nice and toasty. He felt no animosity toward Bovee anymore, in fact, he looked up to him. The fight with Eddie was a long time gone. Because of his little pal Bovee, they were rich now. They were both lucky to be free from Judy's clutches anyway. She just plain talked too fucking much. Christ, everyone knew that. Shit, give her a snort of fresh cat and she'd drive you up the fucking wall with her prattling on. It had been real nice stickin' it to her, though. But hell, she was starting to get fat now anyway....

Eddie saw the tape on the tree and raised his white-clad arm into the gray air. They slowed briefly. Eddie pointed at the marked tree, made a hard left turn, bounced over the ditch under a snow covered parasol of pine boughs and slipped into the darkness of the deep woods. The other three followed. The thickly falling flakes and the heavy carpet of soft white drowned all but the slightest whine of the engines. Four electric shavers faded into the dark and drifting forest. Off to the west, the very slightest hint of pink mixed in with the blue-black sky.

Bruce was content to bring up the rear; he knew the way. Only he and Ed knew exactly where they were going, so he could lay back a little, stay out of Judy's snow spray. Those three were kinda nuts anyway, always getting excited about stuff. Getting mad for no good reason. The only thing Bruce ever got mad about was if you tried to take his whisky—then you'd see mad. He really wanted a drink right now. But he could wait until they got to his Grampa's old hunting shack; there was plenty of liquor there.

The sky was losing its light. In amongst the dark, drooping pines, it was getting hard to see. The storm was slowing, but still coming down good: thinner flakes, more space in between them.

The four bank robbers whipped their machines up to the river bank and followed the meandering curves into the blackness. Eddie raised his arm again; he was stopping. He got off his machine and sunk up to his knees in snow. He spoke through the small oval in his blue ski mask: "We made it so far, we're doing good. We only got a little ways to go, about a twenty-minute run. We stay up high on the river bank here for a bit, then ah—when we get to a big swamp on the left, we're almost there. Everybody be careful along this bank, and pretty soon we'll be partying down like you've never done before." He looked around the forest as if in awe. "Now let's go," he snapped, as close to authoritative as he could get. Then he slid back up on the Ski-doo and buzzed off, leaving a swirl of blue smoke behind.

Three sleds bobbed along in pursuit.

Judy was a fucking mess inside, scared shitless. She regretted ever knowing these lowlifes, let alone going along on this fucking bank robbery bullshit. But she feared going to prison for her speed bust more than anything else she could imagine. She couldn't stand being closed up. No, never again for this girl. She knew she had to run. Ever since her mother used to lock her in the closet for hours at a time when she was little, she just couldn't stand being closed in—that's all there was to it. She'd start to sweat sometimes in the bathroom with the door shut—it was that bad. She wasn't going to end up like her Daddy, stuck down in that little room in the basement.... Have to run, have to make tracks.... The slamming of the Ski-doo was going to burst her bladder. Thinking about Eddie and Ernie: the way they came sweeping into that little bank—sawed-off twelve-gauges blasting away; white hoods and ski masks scaring everybody in there—makes her want to let it all go, relieve some of the throbbing down there. How good it's going to feel to get off of this infernal, buzzing, crotch-bumping bladder-buster. Get something to take the edge off. Hope those guys brought something.... Wow, enough money to escape to Arizona. Maybe slide down into Mexico, find a stud latino, stay loaded for a month. Jesus, why don't those guys be more careful, Ernie almost went over into the river—freeze to death in a hurry if he did.

Judy got revenge on her mother at age thirteen. She whacked the old bag across the back of the head with a bed slat. Put Mama in the hospital for a week. After the court hearing, poor little Judy had to go to the psyche ward of that same hospital for thirty days. Lack of impulse control, possible psychotic break, they said. The only way she made it through was the drugs that they gave her. She always wanted more drugs. Her frequent "night visitors" always gave her extra pills just to keep her mouth shut.

I suppose you might say that her mother and her hospital got her started on drugs. Once she got going though, she took care of it just fine, thank you. At least her mother never messed with her again, she took it all out on the old man.

Eddie Bovee slowed inside a hollow where the snow was stacked up in mounds of varying sizes, shaped by the swirling wind. He pointed to his left. The wind died down. Tiny white dots dropped from the sky, straight down and slow. Suddenly, Eddie rocketed full throttle down a hill and then bounced across a frozen peat bog. Ernie and Judy followed, Bruce about forty yards behind. Past scrawny, gnarled scrub pines at the edge of the bog, they popped into a meadow that ran open and uphill for about a quarter mile. A charcoal ruin of a farm house with a pillow of white frosting on the caved-in top sat on one side of the field. On the other side, darkness and wiry underbrush grabbed out at shiny popple trunks.

Eddie drove tight along the tree line. Ernie tried to make his snowmobile fly over the rolling bumps in the field. Judy tried to avoid Ernie. Bruce was thinking about how good that whisky was going to burn and how good that fire in the wood stove was going to feel.

Now was the best, even Eddie had to admit that. Made him about as happy as he could get, which wasn't that much. Joy was a distant memory, or maybe just imagination. Planning was his thing, and he was the one who planned the whole deal, every detail, down to the all-white, snow camouflage suits and the ski masks that he bought from a surplus store up in Duluth. He was the one who customized the machines. He clipped off the shotgun barrels with a pipe cutter, so they would be nice and smooth. He knew what days the payroll money—from both the lumber company and the mine—would be in the bank waiting to be snatched. Best of all, he knew how a snowmobile getaway during a huge blizzard—if it ever fell on one of the 'right' days—would be unstoppable.

He was always pissed that he needed those other bozos, but he had to have somebody like Garrity—with his drunken Irish capacity for physical aggression—to get the juices flowing. The others were necessary too, somehow….

He needed big dumb Bruce for his secret little cabin in the woods. And, Bruce being there kept Ernie in line. Eddie really dug it that one time when Bruce damn near popped Ernie's eyeballs out with one of his bear hugs.

Judy was along simply because she had delivered some crank to Bovee's house, and, upon Ernie's invitation, stayed on to party with her old friends. Eddie got so wired up he just blabbed the whole fucking deal, like he was trying to impress them. Judy was so fucked up, she said she wanted in. Once you were in, you were in.

Eddie always got a kick from outsmarting the dumbfucks. And he did get a thrill from the guns and the fear and the violence. Back at the bank when Ernie kicked that guy in the balls, he almost got his nut—right there in his pants—just like the time Jesse Ledoux gave him a hand job during a movie in eighth grade history class. He came to a stop, peered around slowly like a weasel on the lookout, then made a right turn between two giant spruce. Just ahead, at the bottom of a small hill, naked trees formed a dark circle around a tiny, gray patchwork shack. Behind the shack—up tight to the surrounding underbrush and second growth timber—was a forward leaning, single stall outhouse, a loaf of snow on the sagging roof. To the right, and slightly in front of the biffy, stood a "barnwood" garage which more closely resembled a lean-to.

Three machines putted slowly down the slope, eased across the yard and came to a halt under the least collapsed part of the garage roof. Bruce stayed up on the hill long enough for a piss.

Garrity climbed off his machine, pulled back his hood and lifted off his mask, revealing a grin a mile wide and long, curly, black hair like a pop star's. Ice crystals were forming on his thin mustache. "GOD DAMN THAT WAS SWEET. Did you see the looks on those fuckers' faces when we came bursting in there? I thought I smelled shit, like they was letting go in their drawers…." Smiling now, eyes twinkling. "Or was that you, Judy?"

Judy was struggling through snow nearly to her waist. She shot Ernie a brief sneer and kept on plowing toward the shack. "I should blow your nuts off, Ernie," she said, staring straight ahead. "And do the world one sweet favor."

Ernie rolled onto his back, laughing uncontrollably—adrenaline stoked, circuit overload. Bruce motored down the embankment.

Eddie popped the padlock on the cabin; Judy followed him in. They dropped white canvas bags full of money on the bunk by the door.

Judy pulled back her hood, lifted off her red mask, reached behind her head and tugged at the rubber band that held together her hennaed pony tail. She clicked small clumps of watery snow from her white boots onto the ragged, woven rug by the door. With her hair brushing against the tops of her shoulders, she was attractive, if slightly worn looking. *Just around thirty, feeling kind of flirty.* Men liked her. She knew it. If they hadn't always been that certain type, things might have turned out differently.

Bruce hovered maskless above Garrity, who was still lying on his back in the powdery white. Bruce's hair was black and slicked back. His eyes were big and kind and hurt looking.

Ernie sucked in huge breaths, huffed them back out into the rapidly cooling air and then grabbed at the little gray clouds of moisture drifting away from his head.

He flapped his arms and made a snow angel.

"Don't be getting too excited and acting crazy, Ernie," Bruce said. "You can have fun, but this is a polite place. My grandfather is buried around here and I don't want you disturbing him."

"Okay, duh... okay, Bruce. I'll try not to fart too loud when I'm outside pissing. Now hows about you and me go inside and have a drink. I bet you could use one about now eh, big fella? Just in case you wanta know, I've got some of that white stuff that keeps your eyes open and your dick in a vice, right'chere in my pocket." He poked at his chest.

"Speed kills, Ernie. You ought to know that."

"Suit yourself, Brucie boy. Pickle that oversize gourd of yours with firewater if you must. Suit yourself."

Ernie sprung forward on his hands and knees and began zigzagging through the heavy powder, snorting like a rooting hog. Bruce followed disapprovingly behind him.

Once inside, Ernie went over to the bunks closest to the barrel stove and peeled off his white duds. Underneath, he was the anti-white: black jeans and black Travolta shirt (Saturday Night Fever, not Grease) and dripping, black motorcycle boots, the kind with the metal ring on the side. A hunting knife—its deer horn handle sticking out the top of a black leather sheath—hung from his black leather belt with the shiny metal oval for a buckle.

Ernie popped a pack of Camels out of his shirt pocket and a plain silver Zippo from his jeans. He gripped the lighter between the fingers and thumb of his dragon-tattooed left hand and snapped it open with a quick jerk of the wrist. He fired up, took two quick, deep drags and blew out the smoke in a rush.

On the second hit he tried some smoke rings. "Whattaya say, big fellow? Come on, give me a hug," he said, making a mock sweet-face at Bruce and opening his arms, grin as wide as a mile.

"Lay off, Garrity," Bruce said, then he turned and trudged back outside. He waded over to a wood pile on the side of the cabin, brushed off the new powder and grabbed an armload of split wood. He started back to the shack. Easier to walk in the snow after you once made a path to follow.

Eddie fired up a stick match. Soon the flame of a kerosene lamp shimmied yellow in the stale cabin air. Eddie and Judy took the short shotguns from their shoulders and slowly removed their white gear, hanging the baggie pants and parkas on chairs and bed posts. Puddles formed on the warped wood floor as snow dripped from leather boots. Shadows on the walls wavered and shook. Bruce came in with an armful; Ernie mockingly held the door. Bruce put the wood down in front of the blackened metal barrel. Out from under a rickety gray table, he slid a cardboard box filled with newspaper and kindling. Scratching his eyes, he stretched up to his full six feet three.

"Start this fire, will you please Ernie, while I get the booze. Do you think you can handle it?"

"Duh… I'll try, Injun Joe."

"Hey you guys, lighten up," Eddie said. "We made it, goddamn it! It's time to fucking celebrate…" he rubbed at his sunken chin with a greasy hand. "Bruce, get the fucking booze. Where's the goddamn dope?" He ran his fingers through his wiry, wavy thatch of red hair and picked at the buttons of his blue flannel shirt. Then he squinted like a varmint, surveying the cabin's interior: Bruce was across the way, opening the brown plywood cabinet above the sink. Out came a bottle of Smirnov and a brown, half gallon jug of Windsor Canadian Whisky. Judy sat down at the table and lit a cigarette with a stick match. Ernie had the wood and paper crackling. Wisps of smoke seeped into the room. Eddie got up and started pacing around, grinning like he was about to make a speech. He threw his Marlboro on the floor and stepped on it. He plucked another one from the box on the table and lit it with a windproof, military-style lighter. Bruce set the vodka on the table, along with some tin cups.

"You got any ice, Bruce?" Ernie said.

"Yeah, Ernie, at the bottom of the outhouse. There oughta be a few cubes there, for you."

"Ooh, ouch, Bruce is trying to be funny. How cute. I guess I'll just have to do some of this here cat to take away my pain." He held up a knotted corner of a baggie, yellowish white powder inside; waggled it tauntingly at Bruce.

"Ernie, stop being such a fucking asshole," Judy said. "Just think about all the cash you're gonna have and leave Bruce alone. This is his place, after all. Try and be polite. Then give me some of that shit. That last one's wearing off."

Ernie whipped his sawed-off from the bunk and spun it in a circle in front of him like a macho majorette. He paraded around the room with his gun held high, gleefully shouting: "WHOO YAA. WHOO YAA. We Robbed A Bank. WHOO YAA. Did you see those fuckers? Did you see how scared they were? WHO YAAA. I showed them fuckers. WHO YA N

God fucking damnit! I haven't felt this good since I was cutting off gook ears in Nam."

"Come on Ernie, man, let's take care of bidness," Eddie said.

"Fuck you, business. I wanna feel the rush for a while, maestro. I'm about to get a fucking hard on, for the Christ sake. What do you think I do this kind of shit for, anyway? It's the rushes, Bovee... the fucking rushes. Don't you know that life is such a drag without the rushes, man? Feel it pounding inside you, man.... Ride with it brother.... Don't you know you're dying with every breath you take? Even if you're paranoid all the time... scared of getting caught... at least you feel alive. Not like the square-johns, man—Mr. and Mrs. Graylife—there just walking around half asleep praying they don't wake up and see how horsehit everything really is. This is our time to fly, Eddie my boy, so lift your heart to the lords of darkness." He put his gun down on the table and danced around the room shadow boxing. Shots of air hissed from his lips with each snapping punch. Once around the shack's interior—with punches thrown at every window and under every top bunk—was enough. Now he was tired, needing a little pick-me-up.

He bounced over to the cabinet by the sink and returned with a brown plastic dinner plate, on which he laid out lines of powder. He snorted one, pinched off his nose and wheezed. Wooh wooh.

Eddie smiled, a nervous light in his eyes. He moved close to the table, filled a glass and lifted it up to make a toast: "To the Fearsome Foursome, the best goddamn bank robbers in the fuckin' country."

They all filled containers and drank. Judy coughed. Ernie wiped his forehead; his legs pumped to some hidden beat as he huffed another row of noxious powder. Bruce smiled slightly, thinking about the next drink. Eddie sniffed some of the burning dust, then pursed his lips. "We should count and split the money first," he said, "before we get too fucked up. I reckon we can stay here until tomorrow night, then sneak back to our houses before anyone knows we were even gone. In this storm, nobody's going anywhere. But when the roads do get cleared, the pigs'll be crawling all over the place like fucking cockroaches."

Bruce lumbered over to the bunk beds near the door, plucked three satchels off the bottom bunk and lumbered back. He plopped the white canvas bags on the table. Dust squirted up, then floated slowly downward to the black, uneven floorboards.

"Jesus fucking Christ, Bovee," Ernie said, grinning and dancing around some more, throwing combinations. "You sure are business-like. Don't you ever fucking get off? How the hell can you do shit like this if you don't get a buzz, man? You don't even get off, you fucker. You're cold like a stone or somethin'. You should be happy here... now...."

"I am happy, Ernie," Eddie said slowly. "I just want to take care of business first. That's all."

Everybody grumbled, then pretty much said who gives a shit, and maybe we should split the money first and everything, no problem. Before we get too fucked up....

Eddie counted the money, putting it in five thousand dollar stacks. Final tally: $363, 778. That made $90,945 a piece, Eddie calculated instantly. The others all wanted to see it on paper.

"You can check it if you want; I know I'm right," Eddie said. He had always been good with numbers. Some odd recessive gene surfacing from out of the unknown DNA stew of his truck driving, Elvis-loving father, John; or his obese, cheap wine loving, mother, Louisa.

He didn't have to be good with numbers to know that his share of the take just wasn't going to cut it. Hell, he had had more back in 1970 when he rolled into Wisconsin for the first time. Back then, he had a hundred and twenty-five thousand dollars in a brown paper bag stuffed underneath some dirty laundry in the back of his VW bus. Cash that was still warm from his first heist: the Bayou Armored Truck Service, of Metarie, Louisiana—Eddie's first employer.

Seems Louisa's "good little boy" left the truck driver and an attendant tied up in the bathroom of a little combination store and service station where the armored truck made daily stops. Newspapers said he got away with a hundred and seventy thousand dollars, but nobody around Metarie believed snotty little Eddie "the Bayou Booger" Betancourt could have hit it that big. And they were right. It was only a hundred and fifty-five thousand. Still, a lot of money in 1969, and plenty enough to disappear on and reinvent yourself.

Eddie had lived in his farmhouse outside of Mintoc for over five years when the gods ceased altogether their whispering in his oversized, freckled ears. It had been a gradual thing. Fewer messages every year until they finally ceased altogether. Eddie felt abandoned. The fickle deities were giving him the finger. Sometimes at night he got panicky, started feeling so alone. Back came that oppressive dread of the same faces and places, over and over, day after day after day. Back came the desire to pull one over on all the fools. And, just as importantly, Eddie's money was getting uncomfortably close to gone. Drugs can get expensive.

His small engine repair business was unsatisfying, both financially and philosophically. His love life had recently taken a severe turn for the worse. He was at a loss for what to do about it this sad state of affairs until the bank robbery plan began to take shape in his head....

Ernie brought out more cat. His hands shook. The cabin was getting warm from the stove. They snorted the speed with hundred dollar bills extracted from the booty. The cabin got warmer. The Smirnov was drained in sixty minutes' time. Bruce started messing with a gray, plastic radio on the shelf by the window that you could see the outhouse from if it was light. A scratchy station came through.

"It's W-O-L-F," Judy said, "Leave it on."

"Why don't you bring it over here on the table, Brucie?" Ernie snickered.

Bruce did. Out came rock and roll, Led Zeppelin style. Something wild was sprung from its eternal prison, right there and right then: Ernie played air drums to Eddie's air guitar. Judy handled lead vocals, doing a passable Robert Plant impression. Ernie danced behind Judy's back making humping motions. Eddie joined him, lolling out his tongue and flicking it rapid fire—alien cunnilingus. Every time the singer turned around; the boys acted innocent, cute. This went on. They screamed themselves hoarse. Bruce sat and watched and laughed. Now and then he'd catch himself and cover his mouth with his hand, embarrassed about the missing teeth. When the song ended, the participants wobbled back to their chairs.

Ernie said: "Bruce give me some of that whisky here, I'm dry."

Bruce slid the bottle over. They all refilled. The radio station faded briefly, then it came back. A commercial came on. It was an ad for a finance company, HFC or something… then a local DJ:

"Hey all you snowbound Northwoods rockers…. This is Will Scarlett, coming to you from Hurley, Wisconsin, right here in the heart of Big Snow Country. We're rockin' with the flakes tonight and playing your requests. Get ready for one going out to Eddie B. of Mintoc. This one has a special dedication: For Judy, it says… Now here's Gordon Lightfoot." Pause—Static—

"Jesus Christ Eddie," Garrity shouted, bent over like an ape, arms hanging down to the floor. "How did you pull that off? What a great alibi." He sat back down and laughed, clasped his hands together between his thighs and stared slackjawed at nothing.

"I've called in requests there before. I know how long it takes them to get to your tunes. I can't believe the timing was this good though—I think it must be a sign from the gods."

Judy's face brightened ever so slightly as she leaned back against her creaking wooden chair and looked across at Bovee.

Bruce studied the woman with his soft brown eyes, tension flickering like aurora borealis.

The reception returned and a throaty, melancholy voice floated into the room:

I can see her lying back in her satin dress;
In a room where you do what you don't confess.
Sundown you better take care,
If I find you been creeping 'round my back stair...

Judy bit her lip and looked vulnerable. The radio went static again and then came back.

She's been looking like a queen in a sailor's dream;
And she don't always say what she really means.
Sometimes, I think its a shame,
When I get to feelin' better when I'm feelin' no pain.

I can picture every move that a man can make;
Getting lost in her lovin' is your first mistake.
Sometimes, I think its a sin,
When it feels like I'm winning when I'm losing again.

The sound turned to white noise. Gord faded in and out in the background....

I can see her looking fast in her faded jeans,
She's a hard lovin' woman, got me feeling mean.
Sundown, you better take care,
If I find you been creepin'—

Judy stared at the silver skull bracelet on her left wrist. She tapped her fingers to the beat. Four large rings—one on the pinky and one on the ring finger of each hand—rose and fell.

She stretched out her arms until the black turtleneck sleeves shoved out from under her faded denim shirt. Her wrists were thin and white. Then she stuck her hands into her jeans pockets and smiled like it was Christmas and Daddy had just came home. "Thanks, Eddie," she said. "Nobody ever dedicated a song to me before."

Ernie coughed and spit: "You fucking idiot, Judy. Those aren't nice things the man's saying."

"They ain't all bad, either, Ernie honey. At least the man shows a little respect."

"Respect?" Ernie sneered, "He's afraid of the bitch, probably keeps his gun loaded in case she comes creeping around his back stairs…. Fuckin' listen to it for the chrissakes."

"That's enough respect for this woman. And screw you, Ernie, the only song anyone'd ever dedicate to you is 'The Asshole from El Paso.' Or maybe, 'I'm a Loser.'"

"I ain't from El Paso."

"Too bad," Bruce said dryly, before taking a sip of whisky.

Everyone cracked up except Ernie; he stared at his fingernails and bobbed his head, eyes turned kind of inward—at least as far as they could.

Eddie said: "I always pay tribute to my former lovers—in some fashion…." Then his eyes darted off into space like he was watching a falling star. He had mixed thoughts about Judy Blue. He wasn't sure he felt anything anymore, for anybody in the world. He and Judy had been good for awhile: three and a half years. She was only the third girl he ever slept with. Third after sweet Melissa, back in high school, and that scrawny hippie skank who gave him the clap back in Frisco, in '69. He had felt things with Judy that he'd never felt before; somewhere deep inside he may have missed her. He wasn't sure; he didn't want to think about it. It made him twist inside.

The happy group talked real fast and real forgettable about shit they'd be able to buy with their money. They stared into space and said nothing. They smoked and drank and paced around the shack. They went outside and pissed on the snow. Judy used the outhouse, bringing out a dishtowel to wipe off the seat. They finished the Windsor in about an hour.

Ten minutes of staring and teeth grinding later, Ernie said: "Bruce, the way you gave up on that booze so easily, I know you got some more around here. Big lush like you... always got a stash."

Bruce grimaced, then pushed himself out of the chair and walked over past the stove, where he bent down on one knee, pried up a loose floor board and reached down into the resulting hole. Out came another quart of Windsor. Bruce held it like a prize.

"More Windsor, Bruce?" Ernie croaked, sarcasm dripping like sewage: "I didn't know Indians had such high falutin' tastes. You're a hell of a guy and I just didn't know it.... Didn't fucking know it."

"Lay off of Bruce, Ernie," Judy said, "or I'll tell everyone how small your dick is." She held up her thumb and forefinger about an inch apart, nodding and mocking with her dark eyes.

Ernie said: "Biggest one you ever had, unless you been fucking niggers. Which wouldn't surprise me. Shit, as loose as your pussy was, you probably been fucked by a horse." He whinnied. "Shit, more than once, now that I think about it"

Judy started toward her shotgun. Eddie grabbed her, held her around the waist.

"All right you two lovebirds, no more kiss and tell," Eddie said sternly. "We got to get along here for a while longer."

Bruce: "Yeah, Ernie, I told you to be polite at my grandfather's cabin."

"Maybe I'll go out and take a piss, then," Ernie said.

"Before you go, man," Eddie said, "I think we should all empty our shotguns and put the shells in a pile—away from the guns. Just so no one gets hurt."

Three agreed; Ernie shrugged and said: "I guess."

The sound of racking pumps chinked the smoky air. Shells made a sharp sound when they hit the floor. They stood the firesticks in the corner by the door. Eddie gathered up the shells and put them on the big bed at the back of the cabin with the ragged Hudson Bay blanket on top.

Time creaked by.

Judy stopped drinking. She paced around the room like a trapped polecat, smoking constantly, puffing furiously. Bruce went over to the little corner that served as a kitchen, leaned on the sink edge with a tin cup of whisky and stared out the window. Off to the north, stars were popping out. Ernie played rapid fire solitaire with one of the many sticky, worn decks he had found in a woven basket on a shelf against the back wall. Every now and then he'd get up and throw some logs in the barrel, Camel pinched between his lips. Eddie arranged and rearranged his bags and his money, again and again. He was remembering back to when he and Garrity had first met....

Ernie had shown him how to make methacatenone, or "cat," as they called it. Some of the best and cheapest crank Bovee had ever done. Amazing you could make something so powerful inside a Clorox bottle while you were driving down country roads toking badboys, shit just sloshing around in the backseat. Order up some ephedrine from a pharmaceutical warehouse, go to your local Pamida for a couple of your favorite household cleaning products... you're in business. That's why he decided to take the stupid Mick under his wing. The guy could make up some shit. No cooking, no explosions, no sweat. Lots of profit margin and cheaper than coke. Look at him over there, that Irish prick, playing solitaire like some fucking college kid. At least the fucker could say something once in a while, like for example how great the plan was, or something like that.

Eddie was scared of Ernie and his fists. They had been buddies before Judy came in between. Ernie punched Eddie out last year for slurring Judy's rep in public. Later, they patched things up—even hugged one night in the Stray Cat—but Eddie Bovee never forgave anyone anything—sometimes he just forgot for a little while. He would outsmart the ham-fisted Irishman Garrity, pay him back in spades for that broken nose.

As if on cue, Ernie spoke: "I'm getting fucking bored as hell, here. Fucking cabin fever. Cha cha cha... I gotta do something."

"Hey Ernie, let's deal some poker," Eddie said, chewing his lip.

"Nah, not poker. Maybe I'll just drink some more." He grabbed the bottle off the table with one swipe of his forearm, got up and started pacing and tilting back the jug.

Judy wanted to talk about her bust: how the Feds were such assholes. How if she'd done this thing or that thing, or not done this thing or that thing, or thought of this thing or that thing, maybe she wouldn't have been popped. How that weird Steve Nelson must have been the snitch. She always had a funny feeling about him. That night she was watching him in the bar, and the way he was twitching and looking around all nervous and going to the phone all the time... she knew something was wrong. Of course it could've been someone else, but you know about certain people, you know, you can just tell. Like this cousin of hers down in Rhinelander, always telling Judy shit and expecting her to believe it, but she knew, you know? Even at that young of an age, why, she was able to see right through silly Amy. Judy always thought she had this something special, not easy to explain, but she knew things, you know? Like this one time—this one reminds her of Steve Nelson, too—she was on a visit to Milwaukee, at her aunt and uncle's place in West Allis.... On and on and on.

Her trial was set for mid-February. She didn't plan on attending. The Feds came down on Judy for amphetamine possession with intent to distribute, back in July. They closed down her bar—The Stray Cat— and put signs in the window saying WARNING: This property has been confiscated by Federal Marshals for violation of blah... blah... blah... Underneath that a red, white and blue stick-on badge proclaimed: United States Marshall—NO Trespassing.

Eddie almost cared about her, the more he thought about it. Judy hadn't ratted him out, so she was good people. That's why he let her in on this deal. She hadn't given up Ernie Garrity and his clandestine cat labs, either, what the pigs had really wanted. She might be good for screwing again now that Ernie had dumped her....

An hour passed before you knew it.

All of a sudden there was a new vibe in the shack. It was quiet, but you could cut the tension with a knife. Eddie was at the table; he was the first one to speak.

"How about that poker game, people? Let's love one another."

Ernie said: "I'll play if Judy promises to shut the fuck up about whatever stupid shit she wants to talk about."

Judy had moved her chair against the back wall, next to a small window. "That's fucking it, goddamnit," she snarled. "Now I'm going to talk a blue streak about whatever I fucking feel like. Maybe I should tell the story of my love life, such as it is, this far along in my tortured existence. Or maybe I'll just gossip about my friends and former lovers...."

Ernie said: "You mean like the time I ate your pussy for three hours and you just fucking lay there like a dead carp? Tasted like it, too?"

"More like three seconds," Judy said, looking down at the floor. Then she jumped up, ran across the room and tossed the contents of her glass in Ernie's face. He gasped and sputtered, dove across the table at her. Grabbed a hold of her thighs and jerked her crotch to his face, grunting and snorting. She pummeled his back with closed fists, screaming obscenities. Bruce shot across the cabin floor, grabbed Ernie by the arms, muscled him away from Judy and back into the chair. Ernie didn't resist much; he was laughing too hard. Laughing so hard he fell onto the floor and lay there in a state near convulsion. Eddie sat grinning.

Judy was freaked. "Jesus, it was only icewater, Ernie," she said. "No need to get all worked up."

He grunted, sitting on the floor with his head lolling down towards his chest, chuckling strangely.

It got quiet again. Moods rose and fell like the tides. After a while, the tension began to dissipate. These people hung out together all the time, they were used to each other. Used to each other being drunk and disorderly, obnoxious and cruel. Most of the time, you forgot everything by the next morning. That was the way life was around here.

Eddie went out to his snow machine and removed a small leather satchel from the custom saddlebag. He returned to the cabin; he seemed refreshed. He watched Ernie dusting himself off and mumbling, flashing between anger and wild-eyed laughter. Bruce stood with his arms folded in front of him like a statue. Judy was lighting a smoke.

Eddie said: "Y'all got to lighten up in here, folks, we got to at least stay a little while longer. We're safe here, we just need to mellow out, that's all, get in a groove. The Man must think we skedaddled out of the state by now, or at least out of the goddamn snow belt. I got some reds here for y'all—us all—fucking whatever. And some great coke I've been saving since my last trip to Madison. We'll do the reds first, and then the toot. Judy, can you get anything decent on that fucking radio?

Maybe try licking the ends of those batteries or something, girl."

They swallowed some reds—at least Judy and Ernie did. Eddie only pretended to take his. He just laid them behind his lower lip for a while like a hunk of chaw, and when no one was taking notice he spit the whole mess softly down the inside of his white porcelain cup. A little while later, he skulked over to the sink and dumped the liquified sopor down the drain, where below, fated nightcrawlers and centipedes would soak up their ticket to the Big Sleep.

Bruce didn't want any reds, said they did funny things to him. He found that out one night up in Hurley, a few years back. Got in this bar fight up there with a bunch of drunken white guys, and the cops came, and then the ambulance people. It took six cops to hold him down while the paramedics gave him a shot of heavy downers and wrestled him into a straight-jacket. They put him in the back of the ambulance and ten minutes later he ripped apart the straight-jacket and kicked the living hell out of the inside of that ambulance. While he was doing his sixty days in jail, the doctor told him about his rare (less than two percent) reaction to barbiturates: instead of slowing him down, they sped him up, kicked in his adrenal glands.

The foul foursome became mellow in an ugly, owl-eyed, emotionally drained sort of way. They sat around the table staring at each other: smoking, drinking, snorting white powder. More white powder, and more again, thick like the snow outside. White snow, white powder, white trash. Now and then, one or another or three out of four (never all four) would lay down on a bunk and close their eyes while the depressants got a temporary leg up on the stimulants. Sedatives served as referee. Adrenaline, fear and alcohol laid back and watched the struggle, not too patiently waiting for their turn to perform. Tobacco, pot and wood smoke saturated the air. Outside, the stars were clear and bright.

Judy got sound out of the radio. In between static-laden songs they listened to the news about the daring bank robbery of the Mellon State Bank. The robbers were feared to have escaped the area undercover of the storm, the radio said.

Back in the world, the cops chewed their nails and waited for the plows to do their work. Sheriff Dennis Bennington was busy. Busy taking calls from reporters, cops and crackpots and listening to a lot of goddamn hysterical bullshit. He was trying to get through to the National Guard, and having a difficult time of finding anyone with the authority he needed.

Eddie was at the table shuffling cards; he liked the sound they made when you thumbed'em and flipped'em real fast. "What about that poker game, y'all?" he said. "In a few hours it'll be sunup, then we can crash out, take a few more reds. The cops must think we're in Missouri by now."

The other three crawled off the bunks like reptiles cracking through their eggs and slithered to the table: Judy's eyes stared downward, sunken in a death mask. Ernie was pale-faced, gaunt and grim. He twitched and laughed—a metallic, artificial sound—like a recording inside a doll when you pulled the string. Bruce was stoic and slit-eyed.

Judy was starting to crack. Her cheeks had no color and her eyes were big and round with little frightened pupils. "Look you guys, I gotta tell you," she said hugging herself and holding on tight. "I'm gonna leave town. I gotta get outta here, this whole fucking place.... They can't lock me up, put me back in there...." She stood up, facing down the other three. "I know we're supposed to go back to our lives and act like nothing's happened, but I just can't do that. Please understand." About to cry, voice trembling, hands wringing in front of her: "I'm going back to my place this morning, just before dawn. I've got my shit packed. I just gotta go, that's all there is to it—I just gotta leave, that's all, no big thing."

"You can't do that, you fucking bitch," Ernie hissed, snapping out of his slouch. "The deal was we stay around'n act like nothin' happened like you said. Now you're sayin' that yer thinkin' about fuckin' leavin'. The cops'll think she did it and track her ass down, won't they Eddie. She's a fuckin' bitch, she'll talk for sure if they catch her. She'll—"

Judy was pacing back and forth, hands jammed in her pockets. "Listen, you dumb fucker..." she rasped, "I'll speak slowly so you can understand. I GOT A COURT DATE IN FEBRUARY FOR A SPEED BUST, DUH, REMEMBER?" Now she was bellowing: "DON'T YOU THINK THAT'S A GOOD ENOUGH REASON TO LEAVE TOWN?" She took a deep breath and sighed, leaned toward Ernie, stared piercingly into his eyes and spoke with the calm of a frozen lake: "Or are you planning on being my fucking lawyer? If that's the case, I'll stay around for sure." She put her hands on her hips; her torso jerked like a run-over cat and her eyes tilted back in their sockets.

"Ernie has a point there, Jude," Eddie said calmly, rubbing his chin. "What if they chase you for jumping town? The bail bondsman will be haulin' after your ass, too. You stay around here you can probably beat this ol' drug rap thing. You got bucks now to grease yourself a solicitor—I think you should reconsider, honey."

"Reconsider honey, my ass. What am I supposed pay off the lawyer with… stolen fucking bills from these fucking goddamn bags? I can just fucking see it: Here you go sir, have a handful of twenties. Oh, you prefer hundreds? Just wait a minute while I go to my underwear drawer, I've got a shoe box full of hundreds in there. Why don't you have a seat and wait, it won't take a minute." Her eyes were narrow—red where they should have been white—saliva clung to the corners of her mouth. Hysteria and bowels-of-hell anger swam inside her voice: "You assholes don't UNDERSTAND. I CAN'T STAND BEING LOCKED UP. MY MOTHER USED TO LOCK ME IN THE FUCKING CLOSET—IN THE DARK. I'D SIT IN THERE AND SNIFF MOTHBALLS UNTIL SHE LET ME OUT. SOMETIMES, FOR HOURS… UNTIL I WAS TOTALLY CRAZY. DO YOU THINK THEY'LL HAVE MOTHBALLS FOR ME IN JAIL? DO YOU THINK SO?" Gesturing wildly now, random, arcing, slashes at the sweat-stinking air. "…'HOW MANY MOTHBALLS DO YOU NEED THIS WEEK MS. BLUE? THREE BOXES? OH. WE'LL GET THEM RIGHT AWAY FOR YOU'. YOU FUCKING BASTARDS! I CAN'T BE LOCKED UP. DON'T YOU UNDERSTAND? I CAN'T LET THEM… I CAN'T." She collapsed into her chair, sobbing, face in hands, fingers clawing at her hairline.

"Lawyers don't care where the money comes from, dear," Ernie said, condescending. "Shit, one could probably arrange for all the mothballs you could huff, if you played your cards right... gave him some of your famous naked hospitality."

"Maybe it'll be okay..." Eddie said, scratching the top of his head thoughtfully and trying to look relaxed when, in fact, his neck and shoulders were like steel bands. "Maybe they wouldn't go after you for the small amount of crank they found, but honey, you can bet they'd try and tie you to this job if you got caught. You could never comeback here. It'd be a sure thing they could prove the intent part if'n you was proved to have vacated the area with the intent of avoidin' ajudication."

"What do you mean, Bovee?" Ernie snapped. "You fucking little worm, you're starting to talk funny to me. Just look at her..." he pointed his thick, bent-up index finger. "She's a snivelly fuckin' mess. The cops pressure her at all she'll break like window glass."

Bruce, looking grim, not drunk: "You forget Ernie, that she didn't rat you out when she first got busted. And everyone in town knew that the feds were really after you and your speed."

"What fuckin' town is that you're talkin' about, man, Kickapoo fucking town? Out there where liquor is king and CLEAN is a dirty word."

"Calm down, Ernie," Eddie said. "We don't need no more dissension, here. Show some respect for the Native American. "

"How can I respect something I'm always seein' when I look down to take a piss?"

"You got dysentery mouth, Ernie," Bruce said, frowning and turning his head away from the group. "You should listen to what Eddie says."

"What is he now, Bruce? Your fucking new father? I mean, since your real old man is always shit-faced and sniffing after drunken white pussy, Eddie must be your new father figure…. Let me tell you something big fellow, he's not old enough, let me tell you that right now. You've had some better daddies in the past, even I know that. Maybe you should go and drag you're old boy out of the bar and tell him that Eddie is his latest replacement. I don't think Pop would consider Bovee a good influence on you."

Bruce was silent, tense, blood boiling. He turned and stared coldly at the offensive Irishman.

"Say… didn't you tell me your mother was a lush, Ernie?" Judy chirped in, composed now and rubbing her eyes with a red bandana, smearing mascara and sniffing. "You remember, that time we did acid out at my place and you started crying for your mommy? You remember now, don't you? The time you sucked your thumb and cried on my breasts…. A real Irish rose, I think you called her…. I thought I remember you saying that she'd bring Indian men home to your trailer when you were little—and how you hated hearing them together. I might of heard you wrong, though—you were crying so much, I mean. Huh, huh. I wonder if Bruce's old man ever fucked your old lady? Could've happened you know…."

"Shut the fuck up, you cunt," Ernie growled, his body coiling. "I'll cut off your tits and feed em to my dogs. You don't know a fuckin' thing about my mother. I'll cut out your fuckin' tongue and piss on it, you bitch." He jerked himself erect.

Bruce lunged over and slapped Ernie, sent him sprawling and dancing backwards across the room. He hit the wall and collapsed in a heap on the floor, laughing hysterically once more.

Eddie snapped: "Jesus you guys, this is bullshit. Y'all need to calm down, people. Like Judy, honey child, you shouldn'ta dragged ol' Ernie's bedroom secrets out like that, not in front of us men. That just ain't right. No decent woman'd ever drag a man's secrets out into the light like that, in front of his men friends. It just ain't right. A woman like that is just no damn good for anyone, you hear." He paused and looked around the room, jaw working overtime. "Everybody, please chill out, get into a groove," he said, his hands patting the air in front of him, palms down. "Just a little while longer and everything's gonna be alright. I got a big ol' bottle of special Cognac stashed. Just like the rich peckers drink. Now that we're all rich, I guess we should enjoy some-a that quality sauce, whattay'all say? It's gonna be heavy when the sun comes up, I promise you that."

"Just wait a fucking minute, Eddie," Ernie said, suddenly lucid and upright. "Your not going anywhere until you tell the bitch that she's not leaving here this morning."

Judy, composed again, pacing: "If I'm stuck here with you fuckers, Mr. Limpdick, I won't be home if the sheriff decides to make a check on my house, now will I? What registers in that hayfield you call a head about that little number?"

"What's he gonna think, Judy?" Ernie asked, sitting down. "You're out here in the woods bouncing your ass on the big totem pole over there? He doesn't know about this place does he, Brucie? Mean old sheriff Benny ain't gonna find us here, is he?"

"No, Ernie, he ain't," Bruce said. "But he might find you all beaten up some day, if you don't knock off the ethnic bullshit."

Judy: "I do love the strong, silent man. Everyone knows that I've always had a crush on Bruce—deep down in my heart."

"Deep down in your black fucking, empty heart, you got a crush on him, Judy?" Ernie laughed. "More likely down in the vast catacombs of your bottomless snatch."

Judy turned and faced him, no longer anything but defiant. "I'm really fucking sorry, Ernie, you know, if I was never good enough for you. You know what I mean, don't you? You know what I'm talking about. You were sobbing and sobbing for her to come home—remember? I wasn't enough for you then was I, honey? I can only wish…. Nothing I ever did was fucking goddamn good enough for you." The force of hysteria twisted her all up, her face a grotesque mask of pain, anger and rejection—years of hurt at the hands of too many people. She sobbed. Picked up the ashtray with a jerk of her arm and flung it awkwardly. Threw like a girl. The black plastic receptacle hit Ernie—sitting white-faced and stunned—flush in the chest, sending butts and ashes cascading down the front of his shirt. A fine, powdery, gray mist rose up around his face. He didn't move; his eyes just glowered deep and black for a few seconds like a treed badger. Then he laughed a hyena laugh.

"Shit, Jude, everyone here including you, knows you're just tryin' to get even with me," he said, smirking. "Nobody here believes that shit you're sayin.' Everybody here knows you're the town punch; the fucking blow job queen. We've all heard that story about you out at that biker party at Indian Lake. Bein' on your knees, and the waiting line and everything.... Everyone's heard that story. You're fucking famous around here."

Judy pressed her elbows to her sides and squeezed in furiously. Her teeth clenched together and her eyes bulged out, head tilting up to the ceiling. Out came a noise like a choked-off scream, so primal and so anguished you'd have thought she'd just watched her only child murdered. Wrenching sobs shook her and snot ran from her nose; tears poured out of wild, red beams. She fell off the chair and hobbled like a wounded cat over to the corner where she leaned her back against the wall and crumbled slowly down to the floor. She sat there for a moment slack jawed, sobbing softly, kind of blubbering, rubbing her nose with her sleeve. A funny thing though, the longer she sat there, the calmer she got. After a time, the resolve came back in her eyes. She took out that bandana and wiped off her face once more.

All the while, Ernie was looking around studying everyone, but pretending that he wasn't. Eddie was off in some special place of his own, chewing on his knuckle. Bruce paced around the room, tired as the world itself.

Silently, Judy rose up from the floor, dry eyed and tight jawed. "You guys..." she said. "You guys are something else. The only one who's nice to me is the only one I haven't fucked. Let that be a lesson for women everywhere...."

"The only reason Bruce is being so nice to you, Jude," Ernie said, "is because he hasn't. Don't you understand? He'd love to bury his Chippewa love sausage in your humungous wigwam."

Bruce picked up an empty bottle off the table and cocked it behind his ear, ready for a christening: "I'm gonna fuck you up, Garrity," he growled.

Eddie snickered. Bruce restrained himself, stood silent, hulking, staring.

"Come on man, ease off," Ernie said.

Judy couldn't let it ride; she put the pedal to the metal: "Being nice to you guys, that was my big mistake. You ain't never had a woman be nice to you before, have you? Any of you…. You don't know how to act, do you? I bet now you think I'm fakin' this or something. Shit Eddie, what harm did I ever do to you? I was a good lover. It was good between us. You were as soft and sweet as a woman Eddie, but twice as hard. I loved it between you and me. All I ever did was what you guys wanted. I even let Ernie call me momma when he came. Don't you deny it Garitty. You said lots of stuff that night. Want to hear some more?"

"Shut up you filthy whore! I'll kill you! I'll sell your ovaries to the meat market!" He whipped out the hunting knife and charged. He held the knife down low, his arm cocked back; blade pointing forward, aiming for Judy's crotch. Bruce made a move to intercept. Eddie kicked a chair out from under the table; Bruce tripped over it and crashed hard to the floor. Judy screamed and dodged to the side. Ernie buried the knife an inch deep in the gray wall. Then he turned around and looked at Eddie, grinned and gasped for breath. Judy pulled something out of her jeans pocket: Mace. She let fly.

Ernie fell to the floor screaming: "Bitch... cunt...." Rubbing his eyes.

Bruce was sitting on the floor watching intently.

Judy walked purposely to the table and picked up a brown Windsor bottle. She was just about to crown the writhing Ernie "Prince of Shitholes" when Eddie reached under his shirt and into the waist band of his jeans and lifted out his "little secret." He pulled the trigger on the snub nose thirty-eight: POP. Heads jerked. The bullet hit the ceiling above Ernie: CRACK. Chips of wood sprayed the floor and there was that sulfury smell from the shot.

Judy shivered. A higher power had screamed "CUT" in everybody's personal movie.

"That's enough of this scufflin, folks," Eddie said. "I ain't gonna fuckin' take it anymore. Judy, you sit down and shut up. This talkin' like a trashy whore is causing us all pain and suffering. You gotta keep a civil tongue in your head, girl. That ain't no way for a woman to act. Can't you see the trouble you're causin' here? Sometimes I think you're what the lord was talking about, I—"

"The lord was talking about me, Eddie?" Her head rolled wildly on her thin neck like an old wino. "What did he say about me? I'm anxious to hear. Just can't wait, don't ya know," she moaned, voice like a foghorn.

"You know, not to pick up fallen women... 'Leave them lyeth, something like that."

Garrity was convulsing—not from the spray now—but from laughter. He kept on mumbling something about "sleeping dogs," as he wriggled around on the floor like a lunatic—which he probably was.

Eddie stayed the course, holding the butt of the gun tightly against his solar plexus and smiling thinly. "I think y'all need to sleep," he said. "I've got just the thing to send us off to dreamland. Just what we need to get us back on the track. Bruce... hows about you grab that special bottle I left here just for the occasion. Maybe that'll soothe the ol' savage beast. Garrity, you get back to the table where I can keep an eye on you."

Bruce stood up and moved slowly into the kitchen, glancing briefly at the shotguns on the bunk. Ernie leaned his back against the wall and didn't move. Judy slumped into her chair. Any semblance of control she might have had was gone up the chimney, never to return. Her head tilted and swiveled on a rubber neck. Her jaw jutted in and out in and out to a manic, spastic rhythm, eyeballs rolling in sync with her head. She made a sound—pathetic and scary—an incoherent rasp that seemed a thousand years old. At first the rumblings were gruff and inaudible. Soon they became clearer: "He wants the whore to go to sleep, oh does he? He knows I've gotta leave. Can't stay here... Oooooh no... can't stay here. They want me to stay.... I never did anything... I didn't. I can't stay.... He knows it. Everybody knows it. Why can't I go? I'm the whore. I'm the slut. I'm the bitch. I'm the cunt. What'd I ever do? Just fucked 'em. That's all. Just gave 'em what they wanted. Shouldn't have... noooo... shouldn't have.... But I can't stay… noooo… gotta go. Really gotta go Eddie. Love to stay, you know, ha ha. He thinks I'm crazy…. Ooooh, yes… me. Ha… ha… me. Oooh no, you can't do that—can't do that, here, oooh nooo… heh, heh…. He thinks I'll tell it, doesn't he? Spill the beans, yes… spill the beans all over. Noooo, not me… I'm a good little girl. I won't tell, I—"

Ernie warmed up to this like a snake on a hot rock: "Tell what, Judy? You can tell ol' uncle Ern, baby. It's all right, now. Come on, baby, spill the beans to your old pal."

"Leave her alone, Garitty," Eddie hissed.

"Fuck off Bovee you little prick."

Bruce returned to the table with a bottle labeled: Courvasier.

Judy continued: "Ha, ha… me. Yes, me. Nooo, not me… couldn't be. Heh. heh, not me. Huh? who is that? Eddie? I won't tell, darling. You can bite me as hard as you want…. Really, it's okay. You can wear my underwear again too, I don't care… I won't tell. It's all right, baby—"

Bang. Bang. Bang.

Eddie shot her three times in the chest. The chair fell backward; she flopped twitching on the floor. Her body like a rag doll torn apart by an angry child. Pools of dark blood seeped out, pooling in her hair as it spread on the dirty floor. Eddie half expected her to say something.

Bruce bent over the body, touching her forehead, closing her eyelids, saying: "Jesus, Jesus," down low.

Ernie was sitting up straight now, whistling inward, head jerking.

Eddie looked at the gun and then at the body and shrugged, his ears ringing: "What the hell, she was just a bitch. You know? Ernie... Bruce... shit, now we got an extra share, guys. It'll be cool, you'll see...."

"You fucking killed her, man," Ernie screamed. "How could you fucking kill her? I never would have fucking killed her, I was just playing. Goddamnit how could you fucking kill her?" He started to rise.

Eddie took three quick, straight-legged steps, yelled "FUCK YOU GARRITY" and put a bullet through the middle of the tough guy's forehead. Surprise on his face and his brains on the wall. Then Eddie turned the gun on Bruce, who was standing over Judy, stunned. "Now it's just you and me, Bruce. I don't want to kill you, but you know I will if I have to. If only everyone had drunk from my Mickey Finn cognac when I wanted, this wouldn't have to happen. Those fuckers just weren't smart enough. They should have known better—and now they're dead and their bread is my bread. I'm gonna have to take yours, too, ol' buddy. I've got needs, you know? Now if you'll just swig some of this here ol' bottle every thing will be sweet dreams for a while and I can get on down the road, or river, as it were."

"Sure, I'll drink your crapola liquor, Betancourt," Bruce said grimly. "You won."

"Betancourt? Whattaya mean? You know who I am?"

"Yeah, Booger, I do. I was rummaging through your desk at the garage one night, remember? I was helping you work on an engine for one of your snow machines, you said you wanted me to roll a joint. When I found those clippings that you keep in that little folder of yours... I guess you forgot where you left them. You see, that's why I went along on this job. I thought you knew what you were doing, being experienced… that Louisiana job was sweet."

"And I did know what I was doing, didn't I? Now I got all the cash and I'm ready to dash—"

"Cause you're white trash," Bruce said in rhythm, chuckling softly.

Eddie clicked back the hammer on the snub nose and pointed it at Bruce's chest with an extended arm. He walked slowly toward the cognac bottle, keeping the dark pistol trained on the large man's heart.

It was a special bottle, enough downers in there to buckle the knees of a herd of elephants. But pachyderms were not Eddie's concern. Just one large Indian and the approaching daylight troubled him now. He had to get out of there fast, run the Wolf River down to where he had hidden his Wagoneer, on a forest road south of Woodruff, out of the snowbelt. He had to go soon, before sun up, because when the daylight hit the endless fields of snow, an airplane or a helicopter was going to spot their snowmobile tracks as plain as Mississippi mud on your mama's kitchen floor. Follow them right to the cabin about as easy as pie. It just hadn't snowed enough to cover them; and the wind had died down a long time ago. Bummer.

Eddie shoved the bottle over to Bruce: "Drink this, man, so I don't have to shoot you."

"You mind if I sit down, Eddie?"

"No I don't mind, you got a long way to fall from up there."

Bruce sat down, grabbed the bottle and twisted off the top. He drank heavily from the drugged dew. Eddie kept the gun on him and watched.

Five minutes passed.

Eddie said: "Take another hit Bruce, another one of your kind of swallows. How do you like it so far, big guy?"

"Kinda medicinal."

"I 'magine."

Twenty minutes later, Bruce fell forward onto the table, thudding heavily. Eddie kept one eye on him and stuffed the bundles of banknotes into a bleached canvas satchel. Then he couldn't wait any longer. He bolted out the door to the snow machines. A touch of blue-gray showed in the eastern sky. The air was crisp and clean and cold.

He started up the Ski-doo and putted slowly out of the lean-to garage. Suddenly, the shattering crack of a shotgun exploded in his ear. A slug smashed through the cowling and silenced the buzzing engine. Echo faded in the distance. Bruce moved steadily through the snow.

"Bruce, what the hell, you should be dead to the world. There was enough sopor in there to—"

"Yeah, Eddie, I should," Bruce said, coming toward the wounded snowmobile, shotgun pointed and ready. "But you can see me—take a good look. Right now man, I could chop a cord of wood, non-stop, no sweat. I could kick a sixty-yard field goal in a snowstorm. Did I ever tell you that I used to be a kicker? No? I could kick it along way, back when I was in high school—straight on—like Lew Groza. By god, I was good... something you should have seen... I tried out for the Packers one year—that was before you came to town, though. That can be something for you to think about, Eddie—after I'm gone. One of the sweet mysteries of life for you. And me? I'm sure you're wondering. But that will just have to be my little secret, too. And Eddie? I thought you might be thirsty, so I brought you the rest of your cognac."

Eddie whimpered and choked down the dosed-up liquor. Before long he was sprawled face down and drooling across the body of the Ski-doo, the tips of his boots hanging spastic and crow-footed in the snow.

Bruce LaFave—soon to be someone else—rode off in the Arctic Cat, singing softly to himself. He had always wanted to see Arizona, maybe open up a souvenir shop. Sell some turquoise and silver trinkets. Check out the roadrunners and the cactus and shit. Maybe start wearing a blanket.

Listen to him now, his deep and rhythmic voice—it's more Lightfoot:

> *Carefree highway…*
> *Gonna slip away on you… slip away on you.*
> *Got the morning after blues,*
> *From my head down to my shoes…*
> *Carefree highway… gonna slip away on you.*
> *Slip away on you….*

Those were the only words he knew, so sometimes he hummed.

HOLE IN THE WORLD

I was just passing through. At least that was my intent. But the car broke down outside of town and now I'm still here waiting. I'm trying to get up to the Great White American North—Hovland, Minnesota, to be exact. Going to meet up with my partner Stuart Moser and his wife Ginny, a.k.a. Virginia Burns, and pick up my final share of the take from the twenty-seven bank jobs that me and Stu pulled off over the last eight years—should be around eight hundred thousand.

Ginny and Stu have been up there for over a year now, laundering our money through the Indian casinos a little bit at time. They hang around and gamble for a few days and then cash in a big load on their way out. Works like a charm, they say.

After I settle up with them, I'm out of the life for good. Going to get me some nice wheels and travel around the country like fucking Jack Kerouac. Roll all over hell like a goddamn tumbleweed.

Damn, every time I call those two lovebirds at their brand new log home in the woods up there, I get the answering machine. I'm beginning to think they're not picking up on purpose. If I think about it too much, it drives me nuts.

I got myself an upstairs room in a boarding house because I just don't like motels. Maybe it's the memories of all the weird things I've done in motel rooms, hard to say for sure.

The good people of Larson Chevrolet Olds Geo have ordered the parts I need for the ABS system on the Olds 98 that I bought from an A-rab coke dealer back in Chi-town. He took it in as payment on an overdue account and sold it to me for four large, half of book.

This boarding house reminds me in some strange way of a place I crashed in down in New Orleans a long time ago; I'm not sure why. Maybe it's the old metal bed with the faded yellow quilt and the military style mattress. Or the paint-speckled dresser, or maybe the little yellow Formica table and the two squareback wood chairs over in the corner by the windows where you can look out at Ogden Avenue.

If you press your face against the window on the left and look down past the parking lot, you can see the top of a sign that says Mama's Bar. Next door to Mama's there's this little house with a jungle for a yard. ANTIQUES it says in black, hand painted letters on an old red serving platter nailed to a tree on the far corner of the jungle of a yard. I call the whole deal New Orleans Corner. In Wisconsin. In winter. And the weather ain't too bad.

They're taking too goddamn long with the car. First it was the diagnosis; then there was the wait while they sent to Detroit for a part. And now they tell me it's not going to get here until after the weekend. That one got to me. That and the answering machine up there in the woods. It's Ginny's voice, her dumb little bird voice: "You have reached 462-3952. No one can come to the phone right now, so please leave your name and number and we'll call you right back." After you've heard that a few too many times, you need a drink. But drinking always seems to lead to trouble.

Most of the time I just lay here on the bed staring up at the cracks in the ceiling, pretending they're lines on a map: the roads I'm going to travel down after I get my money from the Mosers. Sometimes I look in the mirror on the dresser and see too many gray hairs and too much flab around the middle. The eyes look tired. But how can you resist Mama's Bar? God knows I try. If there is a God…. I know the trouble that can happen. I just need to get out of this town, get out of this whole part of the world, and not start drinking and meeting people. I know what can happen, believe me. But you know, I just really need to meet Mama and feel the sting of alcohol on my tongue and the heat of it sloshing in my belly.

And what bad could happen in a place called Mama's? The more I think about it, the better it sounds, so I get my jacket and head down the stairs to the outside world.

I'm thinking maybe I should get some food, until I hit the pavement and catch a breath full of this stink like limburger cheese. A real god-awful stench that hangs thick in the air.

The sound of the answering machine keeps echoing in my head as I walk and the smell is so bad that I go quickly to the yellow concrete box that is Mama's Bar and Grill. I look through the little parallelogram window on the red door for an instant and then push my way inside.

Pink. Except for the obligatory Green Bay Packers poster and a couple of beer signs, the whole place is pink. The top of bar is mahogany or cherry wood—some nice stuff— with pink vinyl padding around the edges. Behind three rows of pink-lit liquor bottles is a mirror ringed in fluffy, padded, pink satin. The red walls have little pink dots and bows. A pink hue clings to the window trim, the faded pool table felt, and the vinyl tops of the chrome bar stools. Sugar sweet, like cotton candy.

I'm kind of overwhelmed at first, especially after I catch a gander of the aging, peroxide-silver, poof-haired blonde with Howdy Doody cheeks standing behind the bar in a shiny white pantsuit with pink powder puff wristlets; her lips as big and red as her teeth are big and white.

I sit down and try not to look too fucking mind-blown: order a shot of Wild Turkey and a Budweiser. The Bud comes in a can, the Turkey in a two-ounce shot glass about three-quarters full. Mama's perfume is strong and cheap.

I whack down the shot and shove the tin can to my lips for a wash. Goddamn. Son of a bitch. Those fuckers better answer that phone pretty goddamn soon. Cocksuckers.

Over to my left a couple of stools is an Indian guy wearing a wrinkled, blue-striped dress shirt: with swarthy, lightly pockmarked skin, heavy lidded eyes and some kind of Coca-Cola drink in a shorty glass sitting in front of him. About five-ten and a middleweight, he's checking out a fishing show on the wall tube behind my spinning head. His profile is exactly like the face on those old buffalo nickels. This guy's grandfather must've been the model.

I move to the next stool and turn around so I can see the TV.

A blonde, bearded guy in a flannel shirt is hammering the wall-eyes on some Canadian lake. I always liked fishing; my old man used to take me fishing. In fact, that's the last time I ever saw the asshole—the time took me catfishing, years ago, when I was eleven....

When you go catfishing in the summer time, you go at night. Build a fire by the river, boil a pot of coffee and throw out set lines with bells fastened to the rods so you can hear the fish take the bait: a glob of chicken livers on a big hook. We bagged a couple of nice cats that night. Eventually, I fell asleep by the fire on an old canvas chaise lounge. At first light, I woke up and my daddy was gone and one of the rods was busted, the line broke. At the time, I don't remember what pissed me off the most, losing the rod or losing ol' Bill. Couldn't say I'd miss the Saturday night slap arounds....

Ma was never the same afterwards, took to the pills.

So I'm sitting here watching the fishing show and trying to avoid looking at Mama. I mean, check out her white boots, they're too much. After a while, I'm getting a crick in the neck, so I stretch and turn my head from side to side. I come eyeball to eyeball with the Indian guy and he's smiling.

"You like fishing?" he asks me, friendly.

"I never caught one of them walleyes before, like that guy," I say, gesturing up at another 'nice fish' being netted. "I haven't fished in a long time. One of those fly-in trips up to Canada would be a kick."

"Shit, man," the guy comes back. "You can catch fish like that right around here, if you know the right places. Too bad there's not much going on now... maybe trout or salmon if you can get out on the big lake. It'll be better in a few weeks."

"Nah, I won't be around that long. I'm just here in town waiting for my car to get fixed—over at Larson's. I'm not staying around. That Lake Superior is something, though."

Then we get to talking about fishing and sports and all that for a while and I kind of get to liking the Indian guy. Even Mama ain't bad with time. She smiles too much and wears too much lipstick and makeup, but she's all right. After a couple more shots and beers, we order up hamburgers and fries that Mama cooks up to a delicious result. I'm feeling so good and generous that I pay for the meal and order another round. Mama (by now she's sipping pink wine from a champagne glass and insisting we call her Ethel) starts spinning yarns about her days as a stripper. Even brings out some yellowed old newspaper clippings with stories about her "dancing" at places called the Saratoga and the Classy Lumberjack and the Silver Slipper, under the moniker Ethyl Flame—sometimes Ethyl Fire. Her real name is Ethel Hawley. But what's in a name….

We carry on for a time like good-natured drunks.

At one point, Mama is down at the other end of the bar waiting on a couple of guys in blue coveralls, and the Indian guy asks me if I want to go outside and smoke a joint. He says it isn't that great, some home-grown, but it tastes good, and it's the least he can do after I bought dinner. So I say yes, and after we finish our drinks, we go out to the alley.

After we finish the jay, I pull a little chunk of black hash out of my pocket and inquire into the availability of a pipe, and he says: "Yeah, in my car but we better go inside and say good-bye to Mama first."

I say, "Fuck Mama."

He says, "I did once."

I laugh; he winks.

"I can't stand anymore pink," I say.

"Just a quick in and out," he says. "I need a pack of smokes."

I want a pack of Kools myself, so I go back in.

The place is overwhelming this time around. The walls are hideous. Mama's scent hangs everywhere like a lethal, tobacco smoke-laced nerve gas. My throat constricts and I can't breathe. I swear the picture behind the bar of Mama Hovland in fringe pasties is doing the shimmy. Sweat breaks out on my forehead. I walk fast for the door. As soon as I get outside, I'm all right. I smoke my last cigarette waiting, and then he comes out with a pack of Kools that he flips over to me. I say thanks and we go over to his beaten down old Lincoln and smoke the hash in a little pipe made out of a red stone he calls pipestone. He says that it's sacred to the Indians and leaves it at that.

Pretty soon, he says we gotta go find us some pussy. "You up for that, my friend?" he says. "What was your name again?"

"Don Enrico. What's yours?"

"Roy Hollinday. I already told you that."

"I forgot."

"How could you forget? Don't you remember, I told you what it meant… my original family name: Hole-In-The-Day? Remember, man? I told you—some school people changed it to Hollinday, a long time ago. Remember? Roy was for Roy Rogers. 'Cause my mother had this alarm clock with Roy and

Trigger on the face… they clicked back and forth like they were riding across the prairie. I told you all that."

"Now I remember. Before I didn't. Sometimes I got a lot of things on my mind." An Indian named after Roy Rogers—I should've remembered that. Sometimes I just ain't listening I guess.

Roy shrugs slightly and says: "No problem, Don. Whattaya say we sample the night life around here. It's the only life in this town."

"Yeah, I could do that," I answer. Guy has a way about him.

We cruise down to the main drag, hang a right and head toward what Roy tells me is the North End: bars, massage parlors, a closed hardware store, cab company and more bars. A few more bars and an all-night cafe.

Roy rubs his forehead and stares out at all the gaudy neon as we bump across the railroad tracks. In front of the Cove Cabaret, a burly bouncer type punches on somebody. Three chicks burst out of the darkness and dash arm-in-arm across the street right in front of us. Roy hardly slows. "Dykes," he says, smiling wickedly.

A flashing, Girls Girls Girls sign and an old bum vomiting on the sidewalk. People and cars moving by in a slow blur. I'm feeling pretty vacant but starting to think like something good is going to happen. The pressure begins to lift.

"I'm pretty fucked up," Roy says. "I think I need to stop before we hit the bars…. Just a short little stop, won't take long. It isn't too far from here." He seems so calm and sincere.

We U-turn in the middle of the block and head back south for a few blocks before making a right. I figure he's going to his dealer's place when we turn into the alley behind this strip mall from the forties: three, shingled, two-story buildings adjoining a brick corner drugstore.

Roy parks the ratty Continental. I just sit watching while he gets out and grabs a greasy canvas bag from the trunk and precedes to climb up the drugstore wall. The corners of the building are built with the bricks protruding about an inch and a half on every other row, and old Roy just scurries right up that convenient little ladder like a monkey to a banana stash. When he gets to the little flat area behind the second floor apartment, he takes out a small pry bar from his satchel and goes to work on a darkened window. He's inside in less than two minutes.

I'm freaking out. This fucking guy is burglarizing the place while I sit waiting in the getaway car. Me with priors and almost a million bucks waiting for me up in God's country. There's no way I should jeopardize that. I mean, I'm not running scared; I just have to get the hell out of this car.

I go over behind a dumpster where I can still see everything, and take a piss. He doesn't come out right away, so I sit down at the base of an old oak tree and fire up a Kool. The ground is wet but if I plant my ass on one of the tree roots I can stay dry. The ground has a pleasant, musty smell until the wind swirls and I whiff the dumpster.

Must be a half hour before that crazy fucking Indian comes sweating back down the bricks and hops into his car. I can see him inside there behind the wheel, bathed in blue neon, his head jerking all around. I know he's thinking: Where the fuck is that guy? Where'd he go—looking for a phone?

I time it so just as he backs out into the alley, I grab the door handle and rip it open. Only trouble is, Roy sees the door fly open and floors it. Damn near jerks my arm out of the socket.... A couple of yards down the alley, he realizes it's me and starts laughing his ass off, so I run up and get in. He floors it again like a fucking idiot and we go swerving and tire-spinning down the dusty trail. I'm sure by then that every house for a square block has punched 911.

"What the fuck were you doing back there, Roy buddy?" I say, none too pleased. "If it was anything illegal, I suppose I should say, what did we do back there? Because as long as I'm in this car with you, I'm an accessory. And that means I get to know what the fuck it was you were doing."

"Oh, nothing much, man, no sweat, not to worry." Roy says, barely under control, lips sticking to his teeth. "Just something I been thinking about for a long time."

"Whose apartment was that you just illegally entered?"

"That was my girlfriend's apartment."

"What's the matter, lose your keys or something?"

"Yeah, I did, a long time ago. I should say—my ex-girlfriend. We just broke up. Just now. Only she doesn't know it yet. I don't think she'll want me anymore, now that I've ruined her kitchen floor."

"Ah, man, what did you do, trash the place 'cause she's balling someone else or some shit?" I'm imagining all sorts of weird crap he might have pulled.

"No, man. I wouldn't trash a woman's place. I mean—for screwing somebody else. Nah, not me. It wasn't like that."

"What the fuck did you do then? Don't you think I have a right to know? One thing you need to know is—that I got priors… that's what you need to know. If I need to get out of this car to keep from getting popped, I expect you to tell me."

"I'm sorry, man," he says, eyes sparkling, burning. "I was thinking you might have done some hard time. That's what I was thinking back there at Mama's. I don't want to get your ass in a sling. Maybe you're right, maybe we should ditch this car. Take off the plates and—"

"It's still got registration numbers."

"Yes it does. But I never changed the title. Bought it from a 'skin off the rez—up by Bemidji. They'll never find that fucker. If they go looking, he'll just disappear into the woods. He probably stole the thing anyway. The plates though, are mine—off an old Pontiac I had."

"You haven't told me what you did back there, up in that apartment, Roy. You're a tricky one, aren't you."

"And your a persistent one, Mr. I-Got-Priors. I was going to tell you. But I want you to know one thing, yourself. I was an MP in the service and I fucked up a lot of tough guys when I was in. Some of 'em thought they were real fucking bad, too—before they decided to mess with me, that is. So don't think you can horn in on my action, here. I—"

"No, no, no, Roy. You got me wrong. This ain't no strong arm. I got plenty of action of my own that I'd like to get to without having to spend time in some jerkwater jail, that's all."

"Okay, Donny boy, then take a look in that bag back there and see if there's anything you recognize. Besides the burglar tools, I mean."

"Ha ha, very funny. You're a funny guy, Roy. So come on, tell me funny guy, what did you do back there in your girlfriend's apartment?" I snatch the greasy bag from the back seat and it's so heavy I wrench my back a little. When I look inside I have the answer to my question: I'm not sure how he did it, but the fifty or sixty bottles of colorful pills laying in the duffel tell me that the crazy s.o.b. hit the drugstore—hard.

"Jesus fucking Jenny," I say. "There's thousands of bucks worth of pills here. You got your Percodan, your Valium, your Dilaudid—some generic morphine, five and fifteen milligram.... Looks like some Brown'n Clears and some Green Hornets at the bottom here. I'd say you hit the mother lode." I take a nice deep breath and let it out slow. "So now that I've praised your work, can you let me get real far away from you?"

"Relax, relax, my man. There's no problem here. We'll be rid of this car and inside a bar in ten minutes, I promise you."

And he was just about right.

We drive into a rundown section of town—tiny, sagging houses all jammed together—until we come to a boarded up little number on a corner lot. Roy turns in the alley and jerks the big boat into the two mud ruts that serve as a driveway for the brown-shingled garage next to the dark little house.

Once under the sagging roof, Roy pulls down the squeaky, crooked overhead door and slides a rock over the strap at the bottom. Sheets of street light peer in through the sides. Roy pulls off the license plates with a Swiss army knife and we are soon out of there. He says the house is empty, used to belong to his uncle, but the city condemned it on some trumped up deal about the plumbing and the electricity.

We walk about a block and a half while Roy laughs about his sawing a hole in the floor of his girl's kitchen so he can drop down into the pharmacy below. How sweet it was, he says. Had it all planned for months, he says. Knew the perfect spot to cut... everything.

We come to a little parking lot at the rear of a bar and he tosses the now folded-up plates into a dumpster. We see the red and white Leinenkugel's Beer sign above the back entrance of the building and we stroll in.

I find out later it's called The Downtown Bar, but to me it's just another piss and puke joint with an asshole for a bartender and bigger assholes for clientele.

Roy and I take a booth in the back by the men's room. I notice that he is still carting around his satchel full of burglar tools and pharmaceuticals. I know right then that I'm slipping. Too many things on my mind. I'm just trying to get out of this town, and I run into this crazy motherfucker. But you know, I'm thinking, he's kind of fun. I kind of like the guy. And he has all those drugs.... I'm starting to feel like Jack Kerouac already.

I go up to the bar and order a shot of Jack and a tap beer for myself and a Bacardi Coke for Roy. The bartender is a skinny guy in a long-sleeved maroon shirt made of petroleum products. His black hair is greased down flat on his head and he's watching some talk show on the tube at the end of the bar: an Indian and a Black and a Hispanic having a panel discussion about race problems. The barman is fixing our drinks when he turns to his two cronies down the bar and says: "Them people just ain't as smart as white people, and that's a fact. They just don't have the same mental capacity."

The bald guy and the fat guy nod their agreement.

I'm thinking that these three white guys' IQs added together wouldn't equal a perfect score in bowling, if you catch my drift.

I get back to our table and there are two Percodan and a Brown'n Clear lying there waiting for me. Some kind of Green Bay Speedball, Roy says. This is not my usual modus operandi, but I'm remembering Kerouac, so I knock the pills down the hatch with the soapy-tasting tap beer.

By the time the Perc is gnarling and twisting at my stomach and the speed is crawling up my spine, we're on our way down the street to meet some "fine ladies." No car, you understand, we are walking. There's all these bars in this town, and they're all so close to each other. It's not a big town, either. Just a bar town, I guess. Easy to find some action, Roy says. I can't remember what I was worrying about anymore. Everything is going to be all right, I'm thinking.

So we're walking down the street, kicking at the trash on the sidewalks—seems like there are flattened plastic cups every-where—when Ray grabs my arm and pulls me into another sleazy bar. My tastes run towards the clean, well-lit drinking establishments at this point in my life, like the lounges at Holi-day Inns—shit like that—but I've spent my share of time in places like Marlene's. It's like, music on the weekends, drugs all the time. Good jukebox, nice-looking chicks, drugs all the time.

So there I am, all fucked up, don't know if I'm coming or going…. And sometimes I think Roy is walking us right into a police sting operation of some sort. Then the Percs wave through and he suddenly becomes this magical spirit merely showing off to impress me. Showing me how to find the Hole-in-the-Day and other indispensable lessons for a life on the road. Stuff you need to know to be free.

Time goes by, and I'm trying to have some fun, I swear to god. But I just can't get into it. These chicks that Roy is hot on are sisters; I thought they were Indians at first. Turns out they're Italian Jews, name of Stolten. Goes to show you never can tell. I get kind of interested in the older one (Ava) for a bit, but after about thirty minutes her drugs kick in and she goes from being stupid to moronic in an instant, and I feel kind of sick. Kerouac must of been in more interesting bars than this…. Pretty soon I can't take it any longer; shit is building up. I tell Roy to meet me outside without the women.

He gets out back and I'm taking a piss by the dumpster. You spend a lot of your time pissing by dumpsters in my style of life. "Roy, my friend," I say, shaking it off and sticking it back. "I need your expert help. And I'm willing to pay for it."

"Seriously folks," he cracks. "My fellow American, you have my ear."

"Roy buddy, oh mystical guide to the Hole-in-the-Day, I'm going to tell you something. No, never mind, I'm not. Changed my mind on that one. I do need a car though, Roy. Not your present sled, man. A car that no one's going to notice: Mr.

Workaday's car. I really need to get out of this place, you see. I've got some really pressing business just a few hours away from here. The fuckers aren't answering the phone. I need to get up there right away before they—ah, in case… something's wrong. What can you do for me, pal?"

"Why don't you just rent a car, Don? There's plenty available, even up this far north."

"I don't have any credit cards, my friend. Master Card and Visa run the world, partner, and if you ain't playing their game, you ain't renting no fucking car."

"Man of the world like yourself, Don, you don't carry any plastic?"

"Don't act so goddamn surprised. How many cards you got?"

"I had a bunch a few years back when I was working at the casino, but I'm afraid the accounts have all been temporarily severed from my possession. I guess they expect you to pay the money back."

"Yeah, ain't it a pisser—banks and their gall."

Roy sighs softly and stares up at the almost full moon. I watch a rat scamper underneath a shiny blue Chevrolet. Down the way a car horn bends its searing note to the intoxicated neon night.

All of a sudden, Roy says: "Shit…. I left my bag inside with Trudy and Ava. Those whores'll steal me blind."

He takes off for the door.

Being a thinker, I jog across the parking lot and down to the street corner just in time to catch the Stolten sisters hot-footing it toward the taxi stand. By the time Roy catches up, all sweaty and excited, his bag is safely in my hands and the girls are safely rolling away in the Yellow Cab. They were more than happy to give me the bag when I told them that Roy had a gun. I figure it was the best way to deal with a potentially dangerous and otherwise unwisely encountered situation. I mean, Roy's jaw muscles were working like locusts in a wheat field and his eyes glowing like the highbeams on a semi at four in the morning. Discretion was the better part of valor here, you know what I'm saying?

Roy eyes me suspiciously as if to say, who the fuck do you think you are, then he grabs the bag and shrugs. He shakes his head and laughs softly. "All right, you win," he says. "We'll go get a car now, Mr. Ex-con. I guess I owe you, now, huh? Anyway, that's what you think, eh?" He smiles some more, eyes bleeding red. Then he goes into some kind of weird Indian dance routine, I think just for my benefit. After he finishes that, he sings: "Okay Joe, we gotta go, me oh my-o," rattling it off with a hip–hop beat.

I just suck up some air and hold it in, praying for good fortune. Anything is better than waiting, I guess. I'm getting eaten up by this waiting. I just have to get to the Moser's.

We are heading somewhere on main street, Tower Avenue. My guy is walking fast, leaning forward, his arms swinging back and forth against the sides of his checkerboard-patterned lumberjack coat.

"What the hell, Roy," I say. What fucking hole in the world are you taking me to now?"

"We're going to Roy's own, personal used car lot. It's right down the block. Just you wait and see."

We cross the railroad tracks and come to this huge, gray

warehouse. Looks like it used to be one of those discount retail outlets that sprung up all over the place back in the seventies. Now it houses two bars—Starland and The Classic. A parking lot almost a block long and a half a block wide runs along the south side. The lot is full of cars, some of them way back in the dark where the pavement turns to gravel. Roy sure knows what he's doing, I'm thinking. Except we don't stop at the dark parking lot, we keep on walking.

Here we go again….

"Hey man," I say, lingering behind. "This place looks perfect to me. We can just wait out here until some drunk stumbles out to his car, then we cold-cock him and take his keys… 'nuff said."

"That's not the way I work anymore. Stealth is the key word for the wizened ones, my son. Besides, you haven't told me the story yet. What it is your so hot pants antsy about that you can't spend any time with the fine women I find for us?"

"Stealth is cutting a hole in your girlfriend's fucking floor? Flooring the getaway car down the alley is stealth? You're fucking crazy. You are a fucking lunatic. I should take a taxi up to Hovland."

"Hovland? You're going up the Shore? I was born up in Grand Marais. Actually Grand Portage—at the reservation there. That's close to Hovland. Yeah, I lived up there until eighth grade. Then I had to leave because I shot a kid in the ear."

"No fucking shit?"

"Yeah, that's correct, sir. Indian boy shoots white boy in ear with deadly arrow. Me and some other kids, who were all white—I'm the only 'skin there—were fooling around with this homemade bow one afternoon. Fucking arrow was just a stick with a nail in it. We were all shooting the thing, but it's me who fires off the seventy-five yard shot that hits little Jimmy Nelson square in the ear. Leave it to the 'skin boy to fuck something up."

"All's right with the world, I guess. But I never said I needed a driver, just a car. I think I can find my way by myself. I took a course in map reading—in prison. Always trying to better myself, you know."

"Man, there's shit up there that only someone like me knows about. Roads and people and rivers. The highway runs right along the North Shore of Lake Superior. There's heavy magic along that road. You need me. If your shit is bad, things can happen to you up there." He takes a toothpick out of his jacket pocket, sticks it in the corner of his mouth and starts grinding away.

"What do you mean, if my shit is bad?"

"If your spirit is struggling with the rest of you, or if you are weakened by a disease of the spirit."

"Sounds like a lot of happy horse shit to me. And somehow, you don't seem so spiritual—in the pharmaceuticals department, if you know what I mean."

"Shit, man, I'm on a first-name basis with every evil spirit on the North Shore. We're all old friends. They don't even bother with me anymore because they all ready fucked me over in every way possible." He pauses for effect. "Now don't try and kid me, Don. I know you got some kind of big dope deal going down or something. I ain't seen hash like that chunk of yours—not for a long time around here. Me no drive, then much sorry—no car for you, Johnny—'nuff said."

"Okay Roy, you win. You truly are a magical mystical motherfucker. You guessed right: it is a dope score. Coming in over the pole. How did you guess? So how about this for a deal? I'll give you a grand now for the car and two grand when we get back. Provided there's no more fucking around."

"You got a deal, Al Caponi. What type of vehicle do you prefer? Two door? Four door? Sport utility? Minivan?"

"How about something—how do you say? Unobtrusive. Low profile."

"General Motors unobtrusive, Ford unobtrusive or imported unobtrusive? Just don't ask for Chrysler. I don't do Chrysler. A man has to have his values intact." He turns his head slowly from side to side, scoping out the lot scene. "Tell you what Don, buddy, you watch my back and I'll go get us a real nice vehicle. Something your mother would be proud of. Got my handy dandy all-purpose used car converter right here in my bag of tricks."

He sticks his hand down inside the satchel and digs around at the bottom, squinting in the dim light. Out comes a six-inch diameter metal ring with about five pounds worth of car keys strung around it. He shakes it like a shaman's rattle. The sound is like Tambourine by Judas Priest. "I used to work repo for a Jew car dealer over in Duluth," he says proudly. "This was my severance pay." Then he sniffs a bunch of times rapid fire and disappears into the darkened rear lot.

I turn around and face the sidewalk, folding my arms across

my chest and rocking back on my heels a bit. By George, we're having some fun now.

So I wait about five minutes, and all I get for entertainment is this young college guy across the street, standing in the door-way of the flophouse Lexington Hotel, dry-humping and tongue kissing this old hag of a bar fly. I'm getting ready to yell at those fuckers and condemn their public indecency when I hear an engine start up behind me.

Roy is backing out of a parking space. He has his arm out the window waving me on. I run up to the black Cadillac Eldorado and jump in the plush charcoal-gray leather seats. Roy is snorting and laughing and looking at me proudly. Am I supposed to praise him? I don't know.

"Jesus, man, this is unobtrusive?" I strain for politeness. "This is stealth? We'll be riding down the highway to the Grey Rock Hotel in this goddamn pimp car."

"Calmly please, calmly. Let's think this out, Donny. This car is black. It is night. It is dark, or you could say, black, at night. We will fit right in."

"It's a goddamn almost new Caddy. Perhaps a bit ostenta-tious for an a—Native American—don't you think? I mean, no offense meant, but it doesn't seem like your people are ex-actly burning up the place around here. With financial success, I mean."

"Again my son, I shall say to you: The car is black. The night is black. The crow is black. Bear shit is black. We will be fine as long as I stay the speed limits. There's a lot of rich fucks from Chicago up that way now, staying at the condos. This car will fit right in, like I said, no problem. The cops up on the shore are usually too busy busting teen-age girls and then coercing blow jobs from them in exchange for leniency to be checking any hot list from Souptown. As long as you got the money, honey, I got the ride. Besides, I've always wanted to drive a car with the fabulous Northstar System. Whatever the fuck that is…. Look at the dash work on this thing."

"Cockpit City. I really need a drink."

He drives me back to the rooming house so I can grab a few necessities, and we're on the way. Before we leave town we stop at a liquor store and pick up a few supplies.

We are about halfway across this big bridge, the John C. Blatnik Bridge it says on a green sign, when I start to feel pretty good. I stare at the lights on the hillside of approaching Duluth, Minnesota. It isn't bad to look at when it's 1:00 a.m. All the drugs and stuff seem to have found some common ground.

Look, I'm not recommending drugs. In fact, I hate all that pharmacy shit: pills and capsules. It's all poison. If there's any kids reading this, I'll tell you right now: Stay away from drugs. 'Nuff said.

This is going to be one of those nights. The Great American Night: a fine automobile, a lunatic for a companion, a damn near full moon and the unknown lying just ahead.

The ride is a dandy: fantastic stereo, the most comfortable seats I've ever been in, and it moves like a dream. I look over at Roy and he's almost glowing: Chewing juicy fruit, popping the radio from station to station in search of the perfect song and smoking on a rum-soaked crook. The air system in the Caddy is good: sucks out that smoke real nice.

We cruise through Duluth and hook up with the Scenic North Shore Drive. There is a nice four-laner above it, but Roy says the winding two-laner is the way to go. The moon is putting a big glow on the inky waters of Gitchee Gummi. Roy told me earlier, that that was what the Indians called Lake Superior. I asked him what it meant, and he said he didn't know. All he knew, he said, was the lake had a power and a spirit all its own. Beautiful but cold. Alluring but frozen. Like a thirty-year-old virgin, I said, and he looked at me funny.

We glide along the winding road drinking cans of Bud from the two twelve-packs in the back seat. They are getting warm fast, so I have Roy pull over while I throw one twelver in the trunk. When I got back in, Roy hands me the weed and I roll a bunch of joints.

We smoke some. We aren't saying much. We cruise by houses with friendly looking lights inside. We roll by a few taverns and a store and cross a small bridge at the French River and then it is just blackness. We are fitting right in.

Roy says: "We're almost to Kaniffy River," about three times.

I'm thinking that's a funny name for a river, until we come to this fishing village name of Knife River.

I look at him funny.

A glowing neon "Smoked Fish" sign is our welcome. There is a closed general store, a used car lot and not much else. The river is wide and dark and running heavy. I open the window as we pass over and I can hear the water moving down below; a fresh smell rises up from it.

Rolling into the moonglow darkness once again, yearning for

something but I don't know what it is. Maybe its up here ahead, on this road, sign says: Two Harbors.

Christ, I'm getting fucking squirrelly. I got green money waiting for me. After I lock that shit up in my trunk, then I can be a poet. Right now I can feel all warm and fuzzy 'cause I got a 9 mm Glock pistol in my grocery sack in the back seat. That Glock is a smooth item: efficient and deadly and uncaring. Elegant and brutish. Shit, it's probably the sons and daughters of the Nazis making these guns. That's why they shoot so good.

That's right, I said I had the gun in a grocery sack. It's my luggage, my favorite brand, the good old brown paper grocery bag. If a piece is lost or damaged, you can easily find a matching replacement. Keeps the loggers in business, too. That must be something they do up here in Minnesota; sure is a lot of trees…. It's dark in those trees when you can't see the moon and you're driving along this snake of a highway….

Roy has the Eldor doing fine. There's a radar detector, so we're always pushing the road. The thing corners like a heavy cat but holds the pavement without too much sway. So Roy is flying up this steep grade leading to a blind left turn and suddenly we hit the turn and pop around the bend and there's Lake Superior, big and awesome, right on top of us, moonlight all over her like a funeral dress. I get the surest feeling we're going over the edge of this hundred foot cliff, so I grab for the safety handle on the dash as the Caddy digs into the corner.

Roy snickers. "These cliffs do that to people," he says. You're not the only one." Then he weaves us through the upcoming S-turn one-handed at about twenty mph beyond safe, me holding on tight all the while.

We speed northward, chased by the mocking moon through two bright tunnels and a place called Castle Danger. We stop to take a piss by the water's edge just outside of a touristy looking town name of Beaver Bay. I know it was Beaver Bay because Roy starts up about how he chased a lot of beaver around this area. I, like a dummy, ask him if beaver is good to eat, you know, because I always wondered what trappers did with the rest of the beaver after they skinned off the pelt.

Roy laughs and bobs his head, covering his mouth with his hand—merriment at my expense.

"I try to eat all the beaver I catch, don't you Don?" he says. "I mean, I like to eat pussy, don't you, paison? I always say, if you don't eat your woman's pussy, I'll steal her from you. With me you see, it's a passion. In the heat of the summer, man, I dream about opening up a Cunnilingus Center for Women. They would come in there and lay that thing down on the table and pay me to gobble it. I'd die a rich and happy man."

"If your face didn't fall off from diving diseased muff."

"Women love that shit, don't y'know. I had a girl friend once who was a dyke. I mean, you know, she went both ways. We had a couple of nice three-ways with a couple of her friends. She was the one perfected my technique—showed me a few tricks, and now I am the master."

"You were in three-ways? You lucky asshole. The only time I ever had a chance at a three-way, the bitches wouldn't let me in the room. Locked the door on me.   A couple of fucking whores I'd spent a lot of money on for Christ sake. I'd never have eaten either one of their pussies, I'll can tell you that. Ah…was that the same girlfriend whose house we just visited?"

"Nah, Jane was a while ago, in another town. I was down in Minneapolis then, hanging with the militants."

"That must have been a tough one to give up. All that hair pie, I mean. You must have been like a fat man in a bakery."

"I got sick of those fucking dykes being around, to tell you the truth. There was this butchy one, she was a stripper— called herself G.I. June—was always wanting to bang me up the ass with her strap-on. One night I'm lying on the couch in my underwear, just about nodding off on some ludes, when I see her coming out of the bathroom with her big rubber dick bouncing in front of her and she's carrying a big jar of hand cream. Woke my ass up in a hurry, I'll tell you. I moved out the next day."

"No shit. JESUS MAN, LOOK OUT!!"

Roy slams on the brakes and swerves into the oncoming lane to avoid a deer. Empty beer cans clank in the backseat; the tires screech; my stomach jumps into my throat.

After my heart beat comes back down to tolerable, I notice on the beautifully glowing dashboard clock that it's 2:45 a.m. The booze and the pills and the speed are like a heavy weight behind my eyes. The question is: Do I—we—drive up to the Moser's at this time of night and start this thing off on the wrong foot for sure, or find some place to crash?

I pose the question to my erstwhile guide and well-paid chauffeur, and much to my surprise, he answers by pointing to the glowing light of a small motel right up ahead. He, however, recommends some cabins a little ways further along, where we can park the car out of sight from the bulk of traffic.

I vote for the second alternative, and that is how we choose the Evergreen Point Resort and Motel.

Roy turns off the highway at the Evergreen Point sign; a green arrow points the way. It's a bumpy little road that crosses over some railroad tracks as it winds its way downward to the lake and then finally to a brushy point with a gravel shoreline that stretches out into the bay about a hundred yards. A series of small, green, old-time cabins stand among the pines and birch trees. Up ahead in a cul-de-sac, is a newer, but definitely not new, motel; OFFICE glowing above the door in red neon.

I get out of the car by the office and stretch. A small paper sign on a bulletin board informs us that we are to choose a room from the available keys on the board, place the fee in one of the provided envelopes, and drop it down into the slot on the door of the manager's office, which is closed for the night.

We take cabin number three.

Roy parks behind a barren, but tall enough, hedge at the back of the unit. I grab the rest of the beer from the trunk. Roy unlocks the door on our little cottage.

It's a little musty and damp, but the scent of cleanser and Lysol and ammonia from countless washings keep everything on the pleasant side. I put the beer in the faded, coppertone fridge and sit down on the brown hide-a-bed couch. Roy is pacing around, stretching and growling. "I'm a little strung out, I confess," he says, working his jawbone. "If I'm going to sleep tonight I'm going to have to reach into the ol' bag of tricks. Maybe I should just stay up all night."

"If you do that Roy, you won't be in any shape to guide me in the morning. That would mean you're not earning your pay. I'm afraid I'd have to dock you."

"Fuck you, dock me. I could drive these roads blindfolded and drunk in a snowstorm. I could stay up for three nights running, and still be better then the rest of these assholes around here. But you are right, boss, I should sleep. I'm getting too old for all-nighters on drugs. My god, the toll it takes."

"Just make sure you take your vitamins, Roy, and you'll be all right. You seem like the resilient type."

"I'll drink to that. Vitamin S it is then."

Roy reaches in his jacket pocket and brings out four red capsules and lays them on the red Formica table. Vitamin S: seconal. I take one; he takes two. We leave the other one on the table for the mice.

We sit there drinking beer for a time, waiting for the slumber to overtake us. I look over at him every so often, and there's this glowing ring around him, sometimes blue, sometimes red. He talks about living up in this country as a kid: how his father disappeared before he was old enough to remember much about him. Some said the old boy was a shape shifter. Others said he was just shiftless. In that paternal respect, Roy and I share an unspoken bond.

The shape shifter business kicks off a whole weird bunch of stories. Stories about weird shit that I don't believe for a minute, but I get all nervous inside anyway and stumble into the bedroom just to escape.

I wake up the next morning, face down in the pillow, with a feeling in my chest like my daddy has just left me again. My head pounds like mule kicks. My throat is dry as the desert but my gut is okay. I got a rock solid gut. When I look out the bedroom window, I see that the Caddy is gone. Suddenly, I've got killer heartburn.

The first thing I think of is my weapon, so I lurch into the living room and grab for the sack. I lift it up and the weight is there. I reach inside the bag; my fingertips feel the smooth plastic pistol and I relax.

He was just a car thief, I think to myself. Going to sell that sled up on the rez and I'll never see him again. Then I hear tires crunching up slowly on the gravel outside, and get a rush of paranoia thinking Roy dropped a dime on me and it's the cops rolling in. I whip out the piece and jack one into the ready position. I run over to the wall and sneak a peek out the window above the big old-fashioned sink. There is Roy getting out of the Cad with a couple styrofoam cups and a white bakery bag. I stick the gun back in the sack and set it on the red counter next to the sink.

"Coffee," he says a couple seconds later, grinning through the door. "I really needed some coffee. I got these cinnamon and caramel rolls, too. They're some of the best in the world. Baked up fresh everyday at the Grand Marais Cafe."

"They open all ready?"

"Already? It's nine-thirty, Mr. Dead-to-the-World."

"No shit, I thought it was just first light."

First thing I do after those rolls and all that coffee, is take one hell of a good dump. Then I jump in the tiny little tin shower stall and wash away the drug sweat. Afterwards, I'm walking out of the can with a towel wrapped around me, and there's Roy with my fucking gun in his fucking hand, and he's pointing it right at me. The bastard was just waiting for the right moment, I'm thinking.

"Nice piece," Roy says, turning and swinging the Glock toward the lake, which we can both see through the front window. "I used to shoot a forty-five, in the service. Couldn't hit the side of a barn with that hog. I bet I could do better with this little number."

"What the fuck are you doing with my fucking property in your hand, Roy? You ought to know better that to pull shit like that. In the joint, you could get a shank in the spine for something like that, man."

"Well, this ain't the joint, Mr. Heavy Dude. You see, up here, if you see a man's bag sitting in a puddle of water by the sink, you take it out of the water for him. And if the bottom of the bag is all wet and a gun falls through onto the counter, you pick it up and dry it off and give it back to the guy." He sets it down on the table and smiles, looking up at me like a contented crow.

"Son of a bitch…. You are a surprising man, Roy. You just keep me guessing, don't you. You doing this shit on purpose? Trying to flip me out? First the drugs and then the driving—and after that the fucking stories about shape shifters for the Christ sake. What the fuck is that all about? Then you take off—and then you come sneaking back. What the fuck is the deal here? I'm getting to goddamn old for this shit. I just came up here to get what's coming to me, not to get run through the goddamn wringer."

When I pick up the gun, I feel better again.

"I'm going to roll a joint," Roy says. "And speaking about what you got coming, how about me? Where's the thousand beans for the 'skin boy chauffeur. I haven't seen the color of your money yet."

"Yeah, Roy, you're right. I owe you. I guess I flipped out, didn't I? I'm getting too goddamn old for this fucking shit." I go into the bedroom and fish my wallet out of my pants. My clothes are in a pile on the bed: jeans polo shirt, sweater and the wool socks I bought in Superior. I feel like an asshole for going off like that, so I take eleven crisp Ben Franklins from my wallet with the intention of giving them all to Roy. I figured an extra C-note was a good way to apologize.

He wouldn't take it, he says, unless I deduct it from the two grand he has coming at the end of the road. I'm thinking that I never met a man this honest. Except myself of course.

I call Ginny from the pay phone outside the motel office, but it's the same old answering machine bullshit. It's an ugly day, the air's real damp and chilly. Big, watery snowflakes are flying by. The wind is blowing hard, coming in off the lake. I shiver and zip up my leather jacket. I wish I had something a little more suited to the weather than my jeans and Nike cross trainers. I have the Mosers' address in my pocket . I figure Roy can find the place for me before I ever get through on the phone, so I hop inside the idling black beauty, shove the Glock under the seat and motion for wagons ho.

Roy waits until we're out of sight of the motel before he floors the son-of-a-bitch and shoots gravel all over the place. Then he slaps his thighs and hoots like a stoked-up owl. He can feel the spirits stirring today, he says. Gitchee Gummi is kicking up something special for everyone.

I can feel my gut stirring. I'm queasy and that's strange, because I got a rock solid gut.

Back out at the highway, the flakes are thicker and there are more of them. The stuff is blowing straight across the road in front of us. White is building up on the shoulders, but melting when it hits the blacktop. Hundreds of pine trees do the rope-a-dope with the wind.

Roy says: "This will be sticking to the roads the farther we go from the lake. Up on top of the hill, I bet it's already starting to pile up. The lake being open and the wind whipping off it keeps the air temperature above freezing down here, and the snow stays watery. Where is this place we have to go, anyway?" He pushes down the accelerator, and we rocket northward.

"It says here, Hovland, Minnesota. Fire number 3397, County Road 13 off of State Highway 7. That sounds simple enough, don't you think?"

"Look in the glove compartment and see if there's a Minnesota map," Roy says.

"Well Jesus, Roy, I thought you knew the rivers and roads and spirits and all that, like they were your old pals or some shit."

There is no map in the car.

"I don't know every fucking little road around here," Roy shoots back, scratching his nose. "The forest service is building them so fast, they don't even know where they all are."

"This ain't no fucking hippie's geodesic dome in the fucking forest primeval were looking for, Roy. We're talking a $185,000 dollar home, here. Only a year old. The fucker's paid cash for it. Do you—"

"They did what? Paid cash—185,000? Up here? This is the forest primeval, man. I bet we could ask anyone for miles where that place is—and not only could they tell us exactly how to get there, but they would tell us the same story you just did, only with greater detail and embellishment. Place like that in the middle of nowhere is going to stand out just a little bit, anyway. But paying out cash like that, up in this neck of the woods, is nuts. On top of that you say they're pulling off dope deals? Might as well put up a sign saying Felonies R Us. These people have either got boulders for balls or rocks for brains."

"A little bit of both, I'm afraid, Roy. You see, there's no dope there. Only money. I lied. The hash has already been sold and I'm just here to collect my share of the profits. You'll still get your two grand, so don't worry. Now let's find the fucking house if it's so fucking easy."

Roy just shakes his head, sniffs a couple of times and drives on. After a few miles we come to a sign reading: Hovland, five miles. Roy says that a Hovland mailing address means nothing, just the closest post office, and he's not about to ask anyone in town, because they'd take one look at him and know for sure that those rich people in the big house are up to no good… Indians are going there.

A couple miles later, there's another sign: Minnesota Highway Number Seven is coming up in four miles.

About a mile or so up Number Seven, the snow is getting thick. Already a few inches on the road, and now it's coming down so heavy and wet and windblown that it's really hard to see. Roy says the Caddy handles nice in the snow. He's cool and relaxed. We got the heater on and the radio is playing "The Wreck of the Edmund Fitzgerald." I'm kind of digging it, except my gut is still nagging me.

We come to the base of a long upgrade, and you can see up ahead that the snow is even thicker yet. Then I catch sight of the county road 13 sign, so we know we have to go up the hill. Roy says he thinks the Cad has traction control, because we aren't having any problems.

Up at the crest of the hill, the trees are farther back from the road: about thirty yards of clearing on each side. The country flattens out a little. The snow is at our backs and visibility is a little better. It's a good thing, too, because just as I spot the turn-off, out of the gray-white snow cloud comes headlights. Four headlights. Two of them right in our goddamn lane and heading right for us.

Right there, I know I'm lucky to have Roy along. He takes his foot off the gas and doesn't even think about hitting that brake pedal. We aren't going very fast, probably forty to forty-five, but how he finds that shoulder without going off and rolling us over is beyond me.

A big, blue Dodge Charger with a white racing strip down the middle comes blowing by. The driver hits the brakes when he sees us, but it's too late. The front bumper of the Charger bangs into the back of the small Chevrolet it's passing, and both vehicles go sliding by in slow motion, turning circle spins.

I'm struck dumb.

Miraculously, the cars stay on the road and fail to hit anything, except when they finally come to rest, front bumper to front bumper, headlights almost touching.

Four young Indians come bursting out of the Charger: one's wearing a frontier era U.S. Cavalry coat and another one's got feathers in his braids and what looks to me like war paint on his face. The other two are generic in jeans and parkas. All four of them stagger toward Roy and me instead of going to the car they hit.

I push open the door and amble out to survey the scene, squinting against the stinging snow. Then out of the tan Chevy pops an angry, older Indian guy: heavyset, hair in a pony tail with a little gray on the sides. He starts coming toward us too. His wife is still inside the car and looking concerned.

The dude in the cavalry coat glares at me with bloodshot eyes. His long black braids reach down to the gold epaulets on his shoulders. "We don't need you here," he sneers. "You better leave." Vaporizing alcohol rides by on a gust.

"We're just here to see if everyone is all right and to offer ourselves as witnesses," I say, glaring back.

The older guy is stopping by me now, checking out these young hotshots. They're coming at me with what seems like ill intent when Roy steps out from behind me and shows himself. They all stop dead. I figure seeing me with an Indian has thrown them off course, drunk as they are.

Roy doesn't say a word, just looks at the two cars kissing and chuckles dryly to himself. The older guy starts demanding to know who is the driver and did he have insurance. The four young bucks kind of cower and grumble to themselves, but then they start cooperating with the old guy. Roy and I trudge back to the Eldor and go spinning off, shaking our heads and feeling strange, or at least I am.

You couldn't miss it, really. Not very far down County 13, right close to the road and standing there all shiny and new in the middle of a big clearing: a two-story log house of considerable size with big windows all around it—fire number 3397.

Roy hits the brakes and we slide past the driveway. He backs up and we turn in. There aren't any tracks there ahead of us. It's 12:30. Sunday afternoon. The oldies station plays The Name Game:

Ginny, Ginny, bo Pinny banana pana fo Finny, fee fi mo Minny… Ginny.

There she is, like sweet berry pie: Staring out at me from the huge picture window on the main floor. Cute little red cheeks like I remember them, only now without the tears.

She doesn't look happy to see me. Her arms are folded tight across her chest and her eyes have that frantic, helpless look I remember so well. I think, for a second, that I should leave Roy in the car, but I say to hell with that and invite him inside instead. Fuck the Moser's. If they'd been answering their telephone instead of using that fucking answering machine, it wouldn't have to be like this. Roy is my compadre now. We've been through some shit together. He doesn't have to know about the banks and all that, but he is going to come in and warm up—maybe have a drink if he wants, while I pick up the cabbage. Or is it lettuce?

Ginny has the door open before I even touch the fancy brass knocker. She gives me a hug that smells of brandy and nerves.

"Jesus, Donny honey. Am I glad you finally got here. Everything's falling apart, Donny… They got Stu. They—"

"Settle down Virginia," I say to her, in that deep baritone that used to calm her down. "You can tell me inside. I want you to meet my good friend Roy. He's been kind enough to drive me up here." Roy nods politely. "Roy, this is Ginny Bruns." She raises her eyebrows at me. "I'm sorry. Ginny Moser—now. I forgot for a minute."

"Hello," Roy says. "I hope you don't mind if I come in and dry off a while. We witnessed a little traffic mishap down the road and I got a little wet, standing out there in that weather."

"Of course," Ginny says, bucking up a little. "Maybe one of you can get a fire going. A fire does cheer you up on a day like this."

"Injun make fire;" Roy says, "white folks talk important business, organize things."

We go up a small set of carpeted steps into a huge living room with picture windows on two sides and dark, natural woodwork everywhere. I stand there gaping: A thick, dark-stained, wood staircase leads upstairs. It's an open ceiling plan, and the second floor has a railed catwalk that offers a view of the giant stone fireplace. There is a big skylight in the high ceiling, facing South. All I can see is snow coming down. Roy is bending over the hearth when Ginny puts her arm in mine and leads me into a den at a back corner of the house. We sit down in wicker chairs in a terrarium overlooking the forest. The painted eyes of a fake deer stare back at us from the puffy white yard. Before we even sit down, Ginny puts her arms around my neck and pulls my mouth down to hers. Her tongue works against mine and stirs up old feelings, so I push her away. Salty kisses again, mama.

She starts sobbing. "They got Stu, Donny. The cops got Stu in jail, in Nebraska. They stopped him for speeding and they found the money and guns in the trunk. What are we going to do, Donny? What are we going to do?"

"Hang on here, hang on. What was he doing in Nebraska? Why did the stupid cocksucker have to be speeding?"

"He was seeing his brother. Jamie was helping him wash some of the money and working on some of the guns. Fitting silencers and stuff. 'Cause Stu and Jamie are going to team up now that you're retiring."

"I told you that son-of-a-bitch Jamie was trouble. He's a' fucking alcoholic, for one thing. He smokes crack, for another. He's got no discipline—besides that he's a thief. I told fucking Stuart that I wanted all my money up here waiting for me. I told him that goddamn Jamie would bring us down. I fucking—"

"He wants me to go down and bail him out." She's still whimpering: "All I've got is cash. But it's all clean."

"You bail him out with cash, they're going to pop you, too."

"I talked to a lawyer back in Indianapolis that Stu told me to call. He said that as long as the money is clean there's nothing they can do to me. They might hold me for a night and try and sweat me, but they won't be able to keep me there. I got the name of a shyster in Omaha, name of Burton, I can call if they lock me up."

"How much cash you got here at the house, Ginny?"

My stomach is doing flip-flops. Out in the yard the snow is coming down harder and harder. The wind howls and whines against the glass. My fucking money isn't here. Goddamn fuck.

"Goddamn it Ginny, I want my cut. Is this some scam of yours? You and Stu? Goddamn it. You know… I really need to get far away from both of you. Okay then, tell me how much you got here?"

"Almost three hundred grand, I think." She dabs her eyes with a kleenex. "I'll need a hundred and ten for Stu's bond. They set it at a million one."

"Stu finally broke the million mark… one of his lifelong goals. But Jesus fucking Christ, Virginia, three hundred grand is not even close to what I got coming. Are you sure this isn't some sort of scam? You come playing me with tears and kisses, knowing how easy it is for you? Thinking I'm going to believe anything comes out of your pretty little mouth?"

She laughs bitterly and blows her nose and goes over to a bookshelf in the corner. There are no books inside. She takes a strip of newspaper off the top shelf and brings it to me.

Duluth News-Tribune, March 14 Edition: *HOVLAND MAN ARRESTED IN NEBRASKA ON FIREARMS VIOLATIONS— $1.6 MILLION IN TRUNK—POSSIBLE "OVERCOAT" BANK ROBBER, SAYS FBI.*

The shit really had hit the fan.

"The fire's going, folks," Roy says, leaning against the door-jamb and smiling peacefully at the both of us.

I can see the fear in Ginny and the panic starting to rise.

"Ginny? Why don't you get us all some brandy, or something nice like that. Roy and I need to talk over our plans. That snow is really starting to pile up. Boy, look at it come down out there.... "

"Must be over a foot on the ground already," Roy says.

"What would you boys like?" Ginny inquires, always the proper hostess.

"I'll have what you're having, Ginny," I say, looking in her eyes for something that isn't there.

"A Coke, for me, if there's one available," Roy says.

Ginny gets up and walks to the kitchen.

"Roy," I say, "we got to get the fuck out of here as soon as we finish these drinks. The guy that owns this place got busted. The local cops got to be on to it all by now. Do you feel like someone's watching us? I'm sure they're watching the house. Maybe this storm'll keep'em away.... Do you think we can make it out of here?"

He ignores my paranoia and tries to smooth things out: "It's pretty much all downhill from here to the lake. After that we'll just have to see what it's like. Sometimes it's warm enough down there to keep the snow from sticking. Melts when it hits the blacktop." He nods and scratches at his chin. "I can get us at least back to lovely Evergreen Point."

"Fuck that. I got to get back to my car in Superior."

"We will, then," he says, squinting. "Through rain and sleet and snow, always go with Injun Joe."

I shake my head and smile weakly and try to figure him out.

Ginny comes out of the kitchen with the drinks and we all go in by the hissing, popping fire. There's a couple big leather chairs, two couches and an antique-looking rocker that I bet Ginny picked out from a catalog. We sit down and stare at the blaze.

That first brandy burns a bit going down—Moser never bought top shelf booze in his life. But I feel so warm afterward that I let Ginny talk me into one more.

About halfway through the second one—which is bigger than the first—I start remembering how it used to be with Ginny, Stu and me when we first teamed up. Then I look at her staring at the fire and acting helpless. I start thinking it could be like the old days again, this time without Stuart. It's that thought that leads me into having another brandy, and before you know it, I'm feeling all that pain again, when I thought it was gone.

Roy pulls a joint out of his pocket and holds it up between two fingers. "Anybody mind if I smoke?"

We suck that baby down and we calm down some and Roy takes up Ginny's offer to go for a tour of the place. I get up and walk over to the picture window overlooking the road. It's a lot darker outside than it should be, I'm thinking. The snow flies by in sheets. Sweet Virginia: how I could ever forget her?

She and Roy come back down the stairs and walk silently back to the fire. Roy goes to poke at a dangling log and Ginny turns to me.

"Ginny," I say, thick-voiced. "Why don't you come with us? You and I can have a life away from this trouble. We can make a new start somewhere: new names, new clothes, new haircuts." Why did I ever say that? Damn. I wasn't going to start that shit.

Ginny turns away from the fire and looks into my eyes. For a second, I think she's going to say yes. I can hear the emotion caught in her throat: "Roy, you know I'll always love you." Tears float at the edges of her sweet eyes. "You know I remember how it was before—before what happened... before you...."

Then her face glazes over and I know I've lost her yet again. "But you and I both know that we can never be like that again." She goes on with the stabbing: "We've been all through this before. It's impossible, Donny, you know that. I'm going to stay with Stu."

"You'll stay with that piece of shit until you're both back inside, for Christ sake. What the fuck is the hold he's got on you?"

"Stuart and I are married, Donny. And I intend to honor the marriage vows, if it's the only decent thing I ever do in my miserable life."

"It'll probably be the last thing, honey." I couldn't ask her about the kiss. I knew. She can't help herself. I yell for Roy. When he comes down, I ask him if he can go warm the car while I say my final good byes. He looks at me knowingly, grabs his jacket and leaves, politely saying thank you and nice meeting you.

Ginny brings me down a set of stairs to the unfinished basement, rummages around inside a large food freezer and fishes out a seafood box with 278,000 dollars inside. She counts out a hundred and ten thousand for Stu's bail and sets it aside on the workbench, putting the rest in a plastic garbage bag and wrapping it up nice and tight for me. I ask her for a paper grocery sack; I could recycle it later, for luggage replacement, I say. She doesn't smile. From a workbench drawer, she brings out a packet of casino receipts and a wallet full of IDs. She hands them over.

Just call me Rick Tomasy: new name, new game. A few dollars short, but still on the outside. One just has to see the possibilities… the positive light, Roy might say. But first I have to check the freezer real good to see if there's any more cash that my old sweetheart may have forgotten. Part of me wants to grab her hair and twist a little—just until she yelps a bit—to see if there's any stashes left around that she might have conveniently overlooked. But I can't do that, not to Ginny. Unless maybe if I picture her sucking Stu's dick and laughing, 'cause she knows it won't do me any good.

That's why I'm going to leave clean. Say goodbye, Ginny, and walk right up the basement stairs. Grab my jacket and bang—I'm out the door. I'll prove how easy it is, believe me; because if I stay, I might kill her, I swear to God.

It's nice and warm inside the Caddy; Roy is a little bit antsy. The guy on the radio is finishing up the weather report: Big storm, he says, like we can't already see that. Maximum late winter blizzard, payback for the exceptionally mild El Nino winter.

"We better hope it's melting by the lake," Roy says softly, shutting off the radio. "This is bad. Almost need a four-wheel drive. At least reservation four-wheel drive."

"What in the hell is reservation four-wheel drive?"

"A big old rear-wheel drive American sled with about a thousand pounds of junk in the trunk. You get some decent snow tires— maybe posi-traction—you can go almost anywhere in one of those boats. We're going to be plowing snow in some places with this beast. … But, we'll make it."

I'll tell you right now, I'm nervous. This weather and all, out here in the middle of nowhere… it's like nothing cares about nothing up here. Christ, there's no one or nothing around forever…. I'm not used to it. Walking inside a nice clean bank in the morning, before it opens—that's more my speed. Pushing a gun barrel against the pasty neck of some guy in a suit—I can handle that. But this shit… you could die out here.

We roll by the spot of the accident, plowing snow here and there like Roy said we would. You can feel the car bog down.

Another mile or so closer to the lake, and Roy says it looks like it's going to be better up ahead. I say, "How can you fucking tell that?" The snow is blowing directly in our faces and the windows are fogged up. In a fucking Cadillac, you would expect better. I can barely see the road, let alone four miles ahead.

Then VAROOM, the derelict Charger comes roaring out of the dull nothingness behind us and starts to pass on the left. It's throwing out a cloud of gray-white mist, only the mist has weight and you can hear it hitting the side of the Eldor and you can feel it pushing us toward the ditch. My heart's beating fast and I'm thinking about the gun. Then they're by us and disappearing again into the blizzard, the raw growl of the exhaust fading quickly.

Roy says Fuck, and I breath a sigh of relief.

"We almost got sucked right off the road," he says. "You get caught in the wrong windrow, you're gone—see you when it's dry. The ditch devils drag you right in. Ah, but not to worry. We are home free, now, Don, my man, I tell you." Farther down the road, he says: "Why don't you roll a joint, man. The shit's in my pocket." He lets off the gas a little and digs his hand into his tight black jeans. "Grab the wheel, will you, Don," he says, digging further into his pocket and lifting his ass off the seat.

I grab the wheel and look at the oncoming blur. Then I see it.

"HIT THE FUCKING BRAKES GOD DAMN IT MAN!!! I scream, hands frozen on the wheel.

Slow motion, coming right at us. No—we're coming at it. They're not moving—they're stopped.

"BRAKES, MAN, BRAKES!!"

Sliding, sliding, sliding—Roy trying to steer out of it.

No room.

Big collision.

Pain. Neck and back. What the fuck? Where are those crazy cocksuckers? What the fuck they stop in the middle of the road for? Where are the god damn air bags? Fucking General Motors!!

Roy has a strange, haunted look about him; his face is vibrating, turning feral. "It's the name game, Donny," he says, grinning oddly. "Get ready to play…."

"You all right, man? Did you hit your head or something? I—"

Roy jerks open the door and jumps outside. An Indian punk

is coming at him from behind the Charger. Roy throws a short right cross and the son of a bitch crumbles face first in the snow.

I'm reaching down for the Glock, when through Roy's open door pops a twenty-two caliber, long-barrel pistol with a drunken Indian in a greasy blue parka on the other end. I straighten back up and squint into the swollen red eyes. His breathing is heavy and fast.

"Just sit there, asshole," he slurs, steadying the gun at my face. "Don't move."

In the middle of the road, the one in the blue soldier coat is holding a deer rifle on Roy. The guy Roy drilled is returning the favor by punching Roy in the back of the head and kicking him in the ass as they slog toward me. Steam billows from the Caddy's fractured radiator and the sick-sweet smell of anti-freeze hangs in my nose. Out of the blue, fucking Roy starts singing: "Donny, Donny, bo Ponny, banana pana fo Fonny," and so on. Then he starts up with Roy: "Roy, Roy, bo Poy, banana fana fo Foy," etc.

This is pissing our rifleman off. He's grinding his teeth, his gaze darting around between me, Roy, the two vehicles, and the great cloud of driving snow. The feathers in his hair shake in the wind and ice forms on his thick black eyebrows. The other guy is slapping Roy from behind and rasping, "Cap him. Cap the fucker. Cap the asshole, that'll shut him up."

While this is going on, the one holding the gun on me reaches into the glove compartment and pushes the trunk button. Christ does he stink.

Roy is still singing.

At the back of the Cad, the war-painted one lifts up the trunk lid and yells: "Take him out in the woods and shut the smart-ass city boy up."

The asshole with the rifle motions for Roy to move, and the bizarre threesome head off towards the woods.

"What's in a name, Donny?" Roy says, looking at me strangely calm. "It's only a label. Just a surface to be lifted and thrown away when you choose, eh, paison. Just play the name game, Donny my boy." He starts up the song again as they lead him to the woods, singing all kinds of crazy names like nothing I ever heard before.

Warpaint goes searching through the trunk. First thing he comes out with is Roy's satchel, and he brings it around to the side of the car to show his buddy with the pistol. His eyes light up when he unzips that motherfucker. His voice is thick with emotion: "Look at this, Lonnie. I told you they were drug dealers or something—car like this… heh… I told you." He sets the satchel on the roof of the Cad and goes back to the trunk. He lets out a whoop. Found my sack. The guy with the pistol takes a look back to see what all the commotion is about and I reach under the seat and find the cold plastic. Guy I bought the Glock from called it a sissy gun, said you couldn't knock anybody out by hitting them over the head with a plastic gun. I showed him I didn't need it for hitting—I broke his jaw with a straight right hand.

The Indian never knew what hit him. I put two in his chest so fast that he only had time to fall down. Then I hop around to the back of the Cad and Warpaint is off and running towards the Charger with my money sack clutched under his arm like the Christmas turkey. I steady the gun with both hands, squeeze away and put some lead in his back, about halfway up. He falls forward and the bag flies up in the air, bills scattering everywhere, flapping in the wind.

I'm frantically stuffing bills back in the sack when I hear the other two coming along, shouting and arguing. The wind must've drowned out the shots. I run behind a big pine tree and listen:

"Did you hit him, fucker? shouts one voice.

"Don't call me fucker, you little asshole," yells the other. "Of course I got him. Even though you were the one let him get away."

"He slipped out of my hands like he wasn't there anymore. And then I couldn't see for a second. Fucking weird. And, if you hit him, why isn't he on the ground in there?"

They stop dead in their tracks as they come upon the two bodies and the occasional snowbound treasury note. I jump out from behind the tree, run at them and cut loose. I hit the one with the rifle and he goes down screaming and writhing; crawling and dragging himself toward the ditch. He doesn't make it; bullets travel faster than flesh. The other prick is moving fast down the road. I do the same, in the opposite direction. It's the name game.

A little later, I notice how cold I am: Terrible cold. Terrible wet. Teeth chattering. Heavy duty shivers. Toes stinging. Got to keep moving and thumping. I can't look into the wind anymore so I have to walk backwards. It's hard to breath there's so much snow in the air. Where's Roy? Still no one comes by. I know this is a good thing—given the carnage on the road behind me—but still I crave for the sight of headlights or maybe someone on a snowmobile. Those things must be all over up here....

I don't have a clue how long I've been out here now. I am crawling on my hands and knees, head bent down to the ground, in the slushy, heavy snow. My knees sting terribly and my toes are numb. Am thankful for the wool socks I bought at the Holiday station. Sometimes I try and stand up, but the weight of it all pushes me back down. The only money left is what I could stuff in my jacket and pants, the bag long since jettisoned. I think the cash keeps me warmer, but it seems so heavy. I realize I can't go any farther without a rest, so I sit down and wrap myself up in a ball in the middle of the road, my back turned to the wind. I'm so sleepy... maybe if I close my eyes for a while.... Where's Roy?

I jerk back awake to a fierce growling that's coming from another world. But it's the same world, and there's a great big wolf standing about six feet in front of me, blood and bits of blue cloth sticking to the sides of his toothy snout. A beautiful creature, coat full and gray, almost white.

"Go away, or I'll kill you," I say weakly, reaching for the pistol. Something in the animals posture makes me stop. He growls some more, showing his impressive teeth.

"FUCK YOUUUUUGHHH!!!!" I scream.

Seems like it almost laughs at me, then trots on by. Up the side of the road and gone. A flood of adrenaline gets me up and moving. It isn't too long before I'm walking downhill and I can actually see a few yards ahead through the blow. I'm getting closer to the lake, on the final downgrade. I'm feeling giddy, home free, almost warm. But there's ice on the legs of my jeans and my ears are on fire and I haven't felt my legs in a while, now. Icy fire inside the ears.

The closer I get to the lake, the more numb I become. I just keep moving, no sign of an automobile anywhere. I'm walking upright now, my hands over my face, pinching and twisting the flesh. The road is just as impassible down here, but the snow is slushier and the pelting from the black sky is wetter. Do they call it row, or snain, or daggers from frozen hell. Every inch of me is soaked, except under the leather jacket. It's funny, because I'm getting hot underneath there. My thin leather gloves have soaked through long ago. I'm praying to what ever god or spirit or brain-damaged fool that might listen. Even Roy. He'll probably be right along now, in the Cadillac, all warm and dry, some good tunes pumping out of the radio; not that fucking "Name Game" shit. Shiver, Shiver, bo pivver, banana pana fo fivver... ah, Jesus. I regret the day I ever met that crazy fucker. He'll be the death of me yet. Ha Ha. You like that? Be the death of me yet. Ha Ha Ha Ha Ha fucking Ha.

Now here I am, at the highway to hell, aka Superior, Wisconsin. There's an ungodly roar coming off the lake. Maybe I should hitchhike, I'm thinking. There's been someone through here, I can tell... drifted over ruts in the road. They'd probably try and take me to a hospital or something.... I think my face is bleeding. I'll just keep putting one foot in front of the other.

Or one stump in front of another, come some sunny day if the creeks don't rise. Roy is due any minute….

You ever hear the sound of a crow on a mild spring day and think to yourself what a nice sound that is? How things seem more right with the world if there's a crow up in a tree, cawing down at you? That's the feeling I'm getting from that big black raven son-of-a-bitch up in that tree across the road. He's about fifty yards down and making the sweetest sound. The wall of pines afford some protection from the wind and he's perched up there, ruffling his feathers and flexing his wings. I'm think-ing I should take my jacket off and go after that crow. It's all of a sudden so nice and warm. But that can't be right. I don't know what I'm thinking about, I guess. Maybe the crow can explain all this….

When I get real near the tree, the crow takes off and spreads his shiny wings and flies down another twenty-five yards and perches on top of a mail box. I go after it again. Maybe I can throw salt on its tail, there's so much lying on the ground up here. A mail box? A driveway? A little further down, around the bend, there's a house. A big, warm house on a cliff over-looking the lake, with a light on above the front door.

I'm so thankful when I knock on the storm door. I'm saved. A little porthole in the door opens up, and I see the face of my savior, a decent-looking broad about forty. She takes one look at me and starts screaming her lungs out. I can hear her yell-ing, "Call the sheriff, Steve," behind the thick door. Then I hear a crow making a sound remarkably like the yuppie bitch's yelling. I see the bird perched on a railing alongside a stone stairway that leads down to the shore of raging Lake Superior.

I pick up a rock from out of the little decorator's row that runs around the front of the house and peg it at the crow. Not even close. I walk over and he flies off.

Down at the shore there's a dock with a big boat: a twenty-two foot Boston Whaler with a high windshield and a small flying bridge covered by a blue tarp. Two big, black, shiny Mercs on the back. She's lifted out of the water, but I think she'll probably go. Even got some downriggers, if I feel like trolling. Someone's been using it this year already; everything is shiny. I know boats. I worked on a fishing boat once, just outside of New Orleans. I was nineteen.

Water splashes on my feet as I check her out: The prop looks okay; nice electric winch setup keeping her dry. I push the green button on the control box on the cedar post and Lucky Lady settles down nicely, like a kiddy ride at the fair. I have to admire this guy's setup: protected little cove, nice little cliff-side abode—truly first-class permanent dockage.

Once she's in the water and rocking, I unzip the blue boat cover and jump inside to the controls. Sure enough the key is there. I give it a turn. Nothing. Again. Nothing.

I rip off the cover and fling it aside and dash to the stern in a frantic search for the battery. I find it behind a little door; the positive cable is unhooked. I put the clamp on the post, but it's too loose.

My fingers don't work any more; they are hunks of dead wood. There has got to be a wrench or a pliers somewhere… just calm down.

Look.

Slow down.

Goddamnfuckingsonofabitch. I see a little gray plastic box with CRAFTSMEN stamped on top.

Somehow, I manage to tighten down that clamp. Somehow, the engine fires up. Oh what a beautiful sound, exhaust spitting against the water. Somehow, I unhook the moorings.

Motoring slowly, I can feel the power of the lake building in my chest. Up ahead of me is some angry water. God how I don't want to leave the safe harbor. God…. There is no God. Ten-foot waves crash against the jagged rocks, roaring like the angry ghosts of a thousand drowned souls. Fear, Daddy, fear.

God help me now.

There is no God.

I push the throttle down and tug at the dark green rain suit that I found under the seat. If only there had been some dry clothes or maybe a blanket…. I keep it a little below half throttle and just aim at the center of the breakers. Straight on into the wind. First big one we hit, there's a heavy crunch and we rock. I'm thinking we're in trouble, but we hang tight. I just aim it like a torpedo and hold on tight and up the throttle just a bit. Words cannot describe the bouncing, pounding, gut wrenching, bile-tasting kick of Gitchi Gummi. What does the name mean, Roy? Bad Fucking Lake? Lake that never gives up its dead? Like the song says, you know. Well, I'm going to beat this lake. Must've been at it about an eternity already….

The water seems calmer now, maybe I'm in heaven. But no, it is calmer. I'm coming to something. The water is brown, dirty over here. Waves are only rollers now. I can throttle up a little more.

When I first spot land, I feel like Christopher Columbus or

one of them guys must've felt. So what if it's an ugly, red clay shoreline with a raging snowstorm going on and everything frozen but my gut, which burns like hell. It's fucking land, beautiful, marvelous land. I love land, don't you?

Two hundred yards from shore, the engines gasp and spit. They kick back in for another fifty yards and then quit for good. The boat coasts forward for a moment, then slowly turns and begins drifting. Drifting ever faster, inexorably returning to the middle of the raging, rocking death ride.

I can see the huge black serpents coiling and rolling in the dark water. I'm going back to that lonely, indifferent place.... I crank and I crank on the starter, but she won't go; the gas gauge is stuck on the big E. As the shoreline slowly fades from view, there's a rock in my gut. For an instant, I'm ready to jump. Grab a life jacket and jump. But I never could swim much. And the water looks so cold. I'm sick of cold. What is it anyway? This cold? This wet? This lake?

Somewhere the sun is shining, mighty Casey has struck out.

And now it's too late. I just need some sleep. All those drugs... Ginny... goddamn Stu....

It's starting to get going again out here; the black snakes are licking at the sides of the boat. Best thing to do is curl in the cabin and get some heavy rest. Just lay down and dream a little.... Maybe, come first light, my daddy will be there waiting....

THE DEVIL YOU SAY

It was a dry, dry summer, if you know what I mean. There had been very little rain since early May. I was living on food stamps and the last gasps of my unemployment. insurance. Like the water in the creeks, my cash flow had slowed to a trickle.

Due to my detrimental financial situation, I was forced to take a reporting job at the *North Country Tattler*: a weekly, so-called "alternative newspaper" published by a sleazy, disingenuous hustler named Bill Crocket.

Crocket had a thing about investigative reporting and exposing scandal—as long as those involved weren't going to be making him any money. He was an opportunist who wanted to make a name for himself by making someone else look bad. I figured I could help him out and make a name for myself at the same time, if I could break something big in his shitty little paper.

The *Tattler* had already milked dry the local mayor's problems with gambling and spousal abuse, so I had to find new chickens to pluck, new dogs to kick. And then it hit me like an all-day itch….

I was sitting around my small third-floor apartment one night drinking cheap beer and smoking Kool cigarettes and listening to old Doors albums, hoping for an acid flashback to ease the boredom. I reflexively grabbed a magazine from the top of a large stack of periodicals my girlfriend had left behind—when she left me. She ran off with some insurance salesman who actually had money and a nice car. I don't want to think about it because it still pisses me off.

So anyway, there I was, thumbing through the March issue of *The New Yorker* and trying not to think about Jan. I began to read this article about the search for ritual satanic activity in America: how thousands of such cases have been reported, but none have ever been substantiated, even though all levels of law enforcement—from local cops to the FBI—have worked on the investigations.

The thing that really struck home was that Jan, my ex, once told me a story about some poor, pathetic soul she knew who claimed to have been abused as a child in a similar ritual to those described in the article.

This girl's particular nightmare included everyone in town, from the mayor, to the librarian, to her parents and older siblings. Allegedly, all these people participated in frequent satanic sexual rituals that took place in the middle of the Wisconsin forest; huge bonfires reflecting off the red satin robes of the possessed participants.

So I got to thinking about Wisconsin, how I had always felt a little strange when I was there. I was in the habit of spending a bit of time there from May through October, and I knew that, at times, the vibes were little on the weird side. It was almost as if there was some kind of malevolent presence lingering unseen, or at the very least, a huge, yawning indifference that could swallow you up without so much as a hiccup.

After I finished the article, I emptied the ashtray, went to the can, grabbed myself another Old Mil and plopped back down on the sagging maroon couch. The next magazine in Jan's pile was *Vanity Fair*. I wasn't holding out much hope for entertainment there, but I started thumbing through anyway, in hopes there might be a sexy lingerie ad or a topless photo.

There it was again: *Vanity Fair* had a piece on ritual satanic abuse in America. I felt something change inside me and read the article as fast as I could. The stories and comments were similar in both magazines. This was going to be it—the breakthrough I was looking for. I could feel the pieces of the puzzle shifting around inside my head: Jan was from Wisconsin. Her friend was from Wisconsin. I visited Wisconsin a lot. There was something else… I couldn't quite grasp it at first. It was about these suspicions that I harbored: things that I felt, sensed. Instinct.

I knew I had to go there.

Memorial Day Weekend, 1993: I packed up a duffel bag with clothes, threw my tent and camping gear in the back of my rusty but trusty '78 Ford sedan and headed for the land that time forgot. I had a pocket full of food stamps, two cans of Miller Light and a hundred dollars worth of Shoreview Palace dinner certificates—my pay from the *Tattler* for my most recent expose: People Who Lie in Personals Ads. I was hoping I could trade the certificates for fifty cents on the dollar to the Wisconsinites, if things got desperate. Provided, of course, that the tradees had never sampled the fare at the Palace. Earlier in the week, I pawned my deer rifle and my golf clubs for two hundred and fifty bucks. I would have to live cheaply, that much I knew.

The following are the only legible portions saved from my journal, which was scorched in an unexplained house fire on October 31, 1993:

JUNE, 1993: I'm down here in Wisconsin. I can't reveal my exact location, for fear the wrong people may find out. I'm staying at a campground near several small towns, using it as a base camp. Am currently trying to light campfire without the use of charcoal lighter. Easy for you perhaps, but difficult for me.

Just returned from at evening at one of the many Dew Drop Inns to be found in the area, where I was entertained by the sounds of Accordian Agnes and the Raggin' Bitches. A "riot grrl" band these ladies are definitely not, but on any given night, they could easily blow the Oulo Hotshots off the stage. The finale, when Agnes rips off her fringed, denim shirt and dances on the bar while playing a grunge-reggae version of Lady of Spain, is truly something to behold. It left me speechless.

The night's frivolity begins to fade as I contemplate the weight of my mission. After all, this is Wisconsin— VACATIONLAND. Could there really be ritual satanic activity in God's Country? But then... maybe that's why they built all the churches.... Sometimes I feel foolish, but then I remember that Ed Gheen, Jeffrey Dahmer, and the Posse Comitatus all called the dairy state home. I often feel a chill, even when the night is warm. Sometimes it feels as if some-one is watching me, but when I turn around, I see nothing.

The fire is finally going, and I feel a little better now. I think fondly of Minnesota.

Something in the flaming logs seems to warn me of upcom-ing danger. I take a long pull off my bottle of Windsor and move closer to the flames.

Enough for now, as I must rest. Tomorrow I continue the search.

JULY, 1993: Finding evidence of the devil in northern Wis-consin is proving more difficult a task than I had imagined. This is truly a strange area: miles and miles of lonely, tree-lined roads winding by an endless string of taverns. I often reflect on what an old drinking buddy once told me: "There is a law in Wisconsin that mandates a minimum of one tavern for every thirty miles of roadway." In my travels, the statute seems un-broken.

Frequently, it seems as if I'm in some kind of time capsule where things haven't changed in years. But there is more than that: the world here is like no other. A life created in the middle of the great forest where the isms of a bygone era still linger and influence. Racism, alcoholism and religious fanaticism still dominate certain pockets of the Badger state. This is a volatile mix.

In a state that's known throughout the country for its persis-tent bigotry toward Native Americans, it's not uncommon to go out with your buddies on Saturday night, get pig drunk and abuse some Indians, then show up nice and pious for Sunday church.

You can be guilt-free by the second after service beer. Thankfully, there also are many good people here. It is upon them that my survival depends.

And oh yes, beer—the staff of life here. It is generally not considered boozing, I have learned, if you're only drinking beer. Usually commencing around noon—earlier on weekends—beer consumption is just a part of everyday life. Real, certified drinking doesn't begin until the cocktail ice tinkles and the jugs are opened. I've been fitting in quite well, considering that I'm from Minnesota.

Tales of satanic ritual under the towering Wisconsin pines, tales of bonfires and sacrifices and horror, tales of entire small towns involved in satanic conspiracies…. No one will discuss these things with me. If I bring them up in conversation, the natives only stare at me as if I'm a leper or a queer.

Does this kind of thing really exist here amongst the colby and the cheddar? Or is it just the stuff of kids' fantasies and the 700 Club's ravings? It's my job to find out.

I've got a trick up my sleeve that none of those big city cops or federal agents ever used. An old northwoods technique for finding predatory beasts—trolling.

I've set up two stout rods. One is baited with fresh roadkill, and the other sports a pentagram shaped Daredevil. I think I'll troll along until I find a place with one of those neon, martini glass signs and see if I can lure something up. You just never know. I feel something drawing me to it, and I must follow….

AUGUST, 1993: I have returned to Duluth exhausted and frustrated and feeling like I should give up. I have traveled from Rhinelander to Racine, Luck to Lucerne, Menominie to Montreal. I've spent hours in small towns and even longer in small town bars. Listening, learning and drinking cheap beer have been my disciplines. Trolling led to nothing. Questions got no answers. Many nights I screamed into the darkness, offering to trade my soul for twelve cold Heinekens or a nice-looking woman—but nothing happened.

My landlord just took all my money for back rent, and my unemployment runs out next week. My apartment is musty and full of mildew and there's an awful smell in the fridge. Perhaps those old crappie fillets....

My discouragement runs high and my energy runs low. I can only sit around and mope and battle with the curious malaise that has overtaken me like a bad case of the clap. All I can do is watch television and listen to classic rock radio. My friends say to me: "What's the matter with you, Elton? What's with all this Satan shit? We're going to come around at twelve with some Two Harbors girls that are just dying to meet you. We're gonna bring a case of wine and let 'em fool around—you know—like we used to."

And I wearily answer, in a low rasp: "It's been an endless stream of cigarettes and magazines, warm beer and string cheese, Brewer scores and pine paneling. But I must go back; that sly, slippery serpent Satan mocks my every step. I will not give up, despite the fruitless chase he's led me on."

At least not for awhile.

I can feel the influence of the beast growing around me, even as I rest and recuperate. The Great Prevaricator is casting his net ever closer. Here in Duluth, the school board has banned the wearing of baseball caps in school as an anti-gang measure. Only a demonic presence could be behind this. A child wearing a baseball cap is a symbol of America's greatness and the glory of the "grand old game." And I remember when the school board made sense. Seen but not heard, I think.

Elsewhere in Minnesota, women are holding hands and lying on the ground in groups and humming, in order to get back in touch with the earth. What kind of madness is this?

My throat constricts when I contemplate what's going on across the bridge in Superior. It is there, on Wisconsin's northernmost tier, that some loathsome creature has been trying to abduct kids in broad daylight. Fortunately, the kids have all watched enough violent movies in their lifetimes and seem skilled in the methods of escape and defense. Because no child was actually taken, you may think that Satan lost this battle—but you're wrong. Now the parents in Superior are frightened and make their kids stay inside all day. If that isn't hell, I don't know what is.

A thought... an idea... a destination... something is climbing to the surface of my brain. It's something I've felt for awhile, an ever-growing awareness. Something you might get if you read a lot of newspapers and remember things like I do. If you remembered a lot of little crime blurbs over the years... and after awhile you got to thinking it was kind of odd how such a small spot on the map could have so many weird and terrible things going on in and around it, over such a long period of time....

It wasn't too long ago that they found that poor little girl down there, lying in the ditch, beaten half to death. No suspect, no motive, no clue. Right around that same time, the feds popped a big amphetamine distributor, right in the middle of the bucolic downtown. And strike three: a friend told me he bought tennis balls in a tin can there, in that same downtown—in the '90s.

The name burns on my brain. I can see it there when I close my eyes like I've been staring too long at the sun: Shell Lake. I'm beginning to get strong feelings about the place. You may scoff, but the industrious among you can check the public records of the last twenty years—then you'll understand what I'm saying. Simply examine the name: Shell Lake. Take away the S—which could represent Satan—and your left with Hell Lake. Need I say more? August 28, 1993.

September rolled around and I had pretty much resigned my-self to defeat. I stuffed my journal in my sock drawer and left it there.

   Then one day I was over at my Aunt Ethel's little house north of town, mowing the lawn for a little extra cash. Auntie Eth always tried to help me out when she knew I was low on funds. It was kind of a little game we played, where she knew I'd mow the lawn and wash the windows for nothing, but she'd always slip me some money anyway. Then I'd give it back to her and say, no, no that's not necessary. Then she'd give it back to me, insisting, and I would put it in my pocket and give her a hug. I'd been thinking about pawning my stereo, but only a junkie would do that.

   So anyway, I was out in back by Ethel's withered, stunted corn crop, when I heard this voice coming from the middle of it:

"Go—and they shall be there… Hell Lake is the center. Go and they shall be there…."

Well, I knew I wasn't hallucinating, because I'd been straight for so long. So I kind of flipped out, went running out of there, got into my car, drove immediately to the office of the *Tattler* and walked right in on Bill Crocket as he was talking on the phone. I heard him say something about the paint on his BMW before he hung up and turned his attention toward me. He smoothed down his off white, tropical-weight suit with the palms of his hands. A big gold ring with a single diamond flashed on his left hand. He leaned back in his chair on wheels, put his right hand against his upper lip and eyed me warily.

I spilled my guts and my story to Crocket like a strung-out crack addict trying to cop a plea to a hanging judge. I begged him for an advance, so I might make one last foray into Cheeseland. This time I would corner the followers of the horned one; expose them to the penetrating light of investigative journalism. Elton Kirby had a mission.

Crocket looked at me like I'd been huffing Carbona and shook his head. "You haven't written a goddamn thing that's worth a shit all summer, Kirby," he said, opening up his humidor and pulling out a foot-long cigar. "That journal, or diary, or whatever the hell you call it, is kind of cute, but I need some real news. I need somebody's balls on the table where I can crush them."

"I think I've got something this time, chief. If I'm right, we'll have an entire town by the nads. The mayor, the librarian, the sheriff… we'll have them all. Please, this is big. Just a small advance…."

"The mayor, you say? The sheriff?" He waved the cigar in a big circle and his eyes grew moist. "That's more like it Kirby. I'll tell you what I'm gonna do. I'll give you fifty bucks cash and twenty certificates from Sun Seekers—these things are worth at least fifteen bucks a crack."

"Tanning certificates in fucking September, Bill? It's still fucking summer for the Christ sake."

"That doesn't matter. Hey, find some chicks, some wait-resses or something... they'll trade'em for food or drinks. Tell'em how much of a shame it would be to lose that nice summer tan of theirs—that'll get'em." He turned away from me, grabbed a plastic lighter off his large antique desk and began shuffling some travel folders.

I took the money and the tanning certificates and left.

The day was sunny and breezy as I rolled onto the Johnny Blatnik High Bridge. Although my sinuses were a bit clogged and my stomach was a little queasy, my spirits were high. I stopped at the Hammond Spur station for some of their chicken, my favorite fast food.

The rhythmic snapping of the red and blue plastic pennants on the fuel pump island bid me farewell as I dipped my fingers into the greasy meat and drove back out onto the street.

Soon I was traveling down Highway 2, rolling along with the sunny sky and the semis. Past the sweet corn sellers and the melon stands, the empty motels and the muddy Nemadji River. Past the rusted railroad bridge and the President's Bar in de-caying East Superior, and then on to the four-lane Highway 53.

A few miles down the road I turned off at the Spooner exit

and headed south. A more beautiful stretch of roadway you would be hard pressed to find. It just begs you to speed, and I obliged.

Really moving now, I rolled past the Middle River, the inevitable piece of road construction and the Lake Nebagamon turnoff. Cattails like Havana cigars and multi-colored weeds swayed and waved in the ditches. The Jayhawks sang from the radio as I hurtled by the junkyard at Bennett. The roadside became a blur when I blew by Stone Chimney Road and Smithy's Supper Club. Tires hummed on the warm pavement through Solon Springs and by the Village Pump and then the Douglas County forest—which resembles a telephone pole garden. Followed by the Poodle Inn, Gordon, Wascott, Two-Mile Lake, the Deer Farm Bar at the entrance to Walleye Land, the road to Dairyland, the Totogatic River, then Minong—the home of Link Brothers famous store and the highest rate of mobile homes per capita in the region. Back on the open road, I breezed across Stuntz Brook, the road to Lampson, The Little Silver Inn and a farmhouse made of stones.

The countryside began to change. Pines and sand gave way to rolling hills and hardwoods—I was in farm country.

By the time I came to the statue of the giant rodeo cowboy outside of Spooner, the chicken was lying in my gut like a tungsten football and my sinuses were so clogged I was snoring while awake. I decide to find a local pharmacy and seek relief.

When I plopped down the bottle of maximum strength Pepto Bismol and a packet of SudaFed Allergy-Sinus pills, the kid behind the counter at Pamida was grinning like he'd been freely sampling the amphetamine suppositories.

"Do you take plastic?" I asked in a nasal drone.

"Sure," he said, "Visa and Master Card."

"No," I said, "not credit cards, I mean these." I pulled out a handful of Bayfront Bluesfest tokens from my pocket and showed the pimply teenager. "These are collector's items— what can you give me for them? Maybe you want some tanning booth certificates instead. Good for the complexion, I understand."

"Those tokens are way cool dude," said the boy. "Are they from that festival up in Duluth where the colored people come and play old music?"

"The very same, kid."

"I'll give you fifty cents a piece for them."

After we concluded our deal, the clerk was still grinning and I was hurrying for the door. Soon I was on the road again.

A few miles outside of Shell Lake, a strong wind came up. Then I noticed an increased lushness in the roadside foliage, as if the drought had never touched anything around here. The corn was over five feet high and fat, while everywhere else I had been the scrawny stocks barely reached three feet.

About this time, the antihistamines started kicking in. What follows is a little hazy in my memory:

"Go there and they will come... Hell lake is the center..." the voice echoed in my head.

I was walking around in one of the prettiest small towns that I'd ever seen. Why was I here? Some half-assed, hair-brained idea about satanic cults and a voice from a corn field. I felt small, I felt foolish and I felt crazy.

The blue-green waters of Shell Lake washed soothingly at my feet as I stood on the closed and empty beach. Then I turned up toward Main Street and went in search of beer. The best way to get to know a town is from its bar people, I always say.

As I walked, questions floated in and out of my mind like lazy black flies: What was that odd monument in front of the new school? What was the "Shell Lake Advantage" being touted on all those signs? Why was the corn so fucking tall? Would the bar have Leinenkugel's?

Inside the Water View Lounge, it was clean, very clean. A pleasant-looking blonde woman in her mid-thirties stood behind the long oaken bar. At the table by the front window sat a lady of considerable girth wearing a purple bowling shirt. At the far end of the room near the pool tables and the bathrooms were three old-timers chewing snoose, drinking beer and staring at the big screen TV.

Having learned that drinking Bud gets you accepted in the bars down here, I ordered one. Then another.

About halfway through the second beer, I noticed a paper sign on the wall behind the bar that said: WE HAVE BLACK STAG! MADE LOCALLY—TRY IT! A hand-drawn rendering of a large stag leered out from above the copy.

"Let me try some of that," I said, pointing to the sign.

"You want to try some of that," said the bartender, her voice deeper than I remembered. "It's on special today, three shots for four bucks."

"Must be my lucky day." Shots? I don't do shots anymore. I used to have some bad habits, you see….

"Every Tuesday is Black Stag Day here…."

"Cool." Without my consent, my right arm came out of my jeans pocket and laid a fiver on the shiny bar.

The bartender bent down below the cash register and opened a cooler door. She lifted out a large, crystal decanter filled with an inky, black liquid.

Three jet black, two-ounce shot glasses sat full to the brim in front of me.

"People around here like to down all three, one right after the other. That is, if they're man enough," piped up the huge woman in the hideous bowling shirt. "We call it a triple."

A triple… how original. Man enough you say? Down the hatch number one: vile, radioactive licorice. Number two: cough syrup with a mule kick. And now for number three: What is this shit? I almost gagged, my face got flushed. I looked around and everybody was staring at me, then they turned their heads away.

Soon we were all friends. Fellow denizens of a small-town Wisconsin drinking establishment. A wiry guy in camo pants and his square-headed, jut-jawed buddy came in from the sunlight and joined the fun. We all laughed. When I snuck in questions about the crime and violence in the area, they brushed me off, preferring instead to spin tales of the Harper family— some kind of local icons or something. They all kind of smiled and nodded when the camo dude said: "Just about everyone around here is related to the Harper's in one way or another… it's true really… almost everyone…. Ain't that right, Julie…."
He looked at the bartender.

"My cousin Mimi is married to a Harper, so I guess I qualify," she said.

I was feeling so warm and fuzzy that I decided to be honest. Come right out and tell these fine people what the hell I was up to.

"You know,' I said beaming, "I haven't had this much fun in a long time." I felt like I could whip George Foreman and not break a sweat. "And to think I came to town here on assignment, trying to find cults and satanic ritual and shit...."

Suddenly the room started spinning. The stag on the sign pulsated with life.

I turned on my bar stool: the three deer in the outdoor scene on the back wall were dripping blood. The blonde bartender came out from behind the bar, and horror of horrors, she had the rear end of a horse. She was a fucking CENTAUR. The young men closed in around me. They were SATYRS. Weaving, spitting, SKELETONS approached from the back room. The fat lady was grabbing her crotch and howling like a bull elephant in heat.

My head pounded; my heart was in my throat. Sweat dripped off my face like a rain storm. Nausea gripped me and I was about to puke. The floor undulated as they surrounded me. The heat of their bodies was unbearable and the smell of their breath abhorrent. I was weak and my throat was so very dry. Then I heard it, hideous and horrifying… The Demonic Chillin' Choir shrieking in unison:

"WHAT DID YOU SAY, BOY?"

With a last gasp burst of adrenaline, I charged at the circle with my head down, ramming my shoulder full tilt into a toothless old harpie. She fell backward on her skinny ass and I went stumbling and crashing out the door.

The sunlight hit my eyes and I was reeling. Life on the street seemed normal as I staggered toward my car. I was parked in front of Tony's Tap, a bar that had recently been closed down by federal marshals for amphetamine trafficking. I was feverishly working my key in the lock when the front door of Tony's opened up and a tall distinguished looking man with light brown hair and a receding hairline stepped out. He was wearing formal clothing, like a butler or something:

"Just in time for happy hour, sir; we have Black Stag on special today. Won't you join us?" He smiled. His teeth were brown decaying stumps.

The door lock popped up and I jumped in and jammed the key in the ignition. Unlike the movies, the engine started immediately. My intestines had a life of their own as I squealed out of the parking space and hot-footed it out of town.

I was running scared down the highway at eighty miles an hour when I popped over the crest of a small hill into a construction zone that I didn't remember being there on the way down. About thirty yards in front of me, a big, red Mack truck was pulling out from a side road on the right. Another large, red truck was bearing down in the oncoming lane, doing about sixty and throwing up dust like a stagecoach on "Death Valley Days." All I could see in the rear view mirror was a large, gold grille and the word MACK. They had me boxed in. My mortality was as real as a February morning in Duluth—right here, right now.

I swerved to the right, hurtled off the bank, flew twenty feet in the air and slammed hard onto the new roadbed. I fish-tailed and got her straightened out. Gaining speed, I rocketed off an up-sloping piece of hardpan like a four-wheeled Evel Kneivel, flew forty feet in the air and hit the old highway with tires spinning. Behind me, dust filled the air and my tormentors could not be seen.

All those big red trucks got me to thinking: I wondered if the color had any significance... nah....

The road ahead was clear. I sped on. Five, ten, fifteen miles. I had the thirst of a thousand slaves and a headache that a crate of aspirin couldn't touch. Then I heard a siren.

I pulled over for the cop, figuring I had no choice. He seemed like a normal small town officer: slightly paunchy and slightly sleepy. He walked slowly along the shoulder as I rolled down the window.

"Your driver's license, please."

I showed him my license.

"You know you were going pretty fast, Mr. Kirby. What's the hurry?" His dark aviator sunglasses hid his eyes.

"The devil made me do it."

"Speeding is nothing to joke about, sir. What is your business in this area?"

"Just visiting the Harper family, in Hell—er, ah—Shell Lake, sir."

"Oh... I see... well then, you may go. Have a nice day." He gave me back my license, turned on the heel of his jackboot and went back to his patrol car.

It's so good to be on the road again…. I was singing, yeah, but my skin was the color of a lily pad and nature was making all of its calls at the same time. I needed a roadside rest, and—as if by magic—one of those blue signs appeared ahead of me. I angled off into the oasis and pulled up next to the facility.

After I disgorged, I was walking out of the little toilet shack when I saw two geeks standing next to my car. One was wearing an orange Sunkist T-shirt and a matching, sweat-stained baseball cap, while the other had on a grease-stained, gray work shirt and a blue cap. Both wore blue jeans that sagged below their pot guts. Beavis and Butthead gone to seed. I could see no vehicle anywhere.

"What the hell are you doin' here, you long-haired, big-city faggot?" they croaked in unison like a two-headed lamprey on PCP. "We don't like your kind around here. We're gonna mess you up."

I jammed my hand through the open car window and grabbed a hold of the Penthouse magazine I had purchased at Hammond Spur for those lonely moments. With a quick flick of the wrist I sailed the skin mag onto the grassy area by the john. My two friends raced and dove for it, while I jumped in the Ford and got the hell out of there.

What seemed like hours but was really only minutes later, I began to feel safe. By the time I could see Lake Superior, the whole thing seemed like a dream. I'm still not really sure what happened….

Is their ritual satanic activity in Wisconsin? Probably not. Nothing organizes this demon, it thrives on emptiness and mind-numbing boredom. Lack of love is its siren's call. Does the devil live in Dairy Land? I really can't say for sure, but if the Packers make it to the Super Bowl, ask me again.

EDITOR'S NOTE: The Green Bay Packers went to the Super Bowl both 1997 and 1998, beating New England in '97 and losing to Denver in '98. Also in the late nineties, one of the largest internet child pornography rings ever investigated was traced to a man who lived just outside of SHELL LAKE, Wisconsin.

SOCIAL CLIMBING

In an age that is utterly corrupt, the best policy is to do as others do. — Marquis de Sade, 1788

"Three, please," said the mayor of Hammond politely, as usual.

I thumbed the cards off the top of the deck and slid them across the smooth, shiny surface of the round, wood table. Mayor John McKay took them gracefully and settled back against his straight backed chair, spreading his cards out slowly like a fan as he always did. Then he took a white-tipped filter cigarette from the pocket of his tailored white shirt and lit it with a silver Zippo and a flourish of his long-fingered, almost feminine hands and blew out the smoke in a slow upward moving cloud.

I figured he must have hit on his pair.

"I'll take two," said large-headed and balding Nicholas Cross on McKay's immediate left. He squinted, then tugged on the bridge of his previously broken but nicely set nose as if a fly was up there. "Make it two of the same kind if you please." He grinned strangely at the rest of the players and pulled at the loose skin around his Adam's apple like the fly had found its way down there. After taking his cards he made a quick swipe across his forehead with a hairy forearm and sat back.

I looked over to my left at the ever-grinning mug of Sam Cross, Nick's younger brother. His index finger was jammed in his ear and the rest of his stubby hand wiggled with gusto. The other hand rested comfortably against his slight paunch. A good-sized pile of chips and several empty beer bottles formed a barrier around his neatly stacked cards. He had opened right off the get-go and then drawn two.

The Cross brothers were cheating and I knew it. But it only seemed to be working for Sam. Nick had been losing big all night long and was down to writing IOUs. And the jing wasn't only going to his sibling, he was spreading it around.

Tom Geno, a slick haired dago from Zenith City had a few of those IOUs and also a gigantic collection of chips stacked up in odd-sized piles like rice cakes at a vegetarian picnic. And him the compulsive degenerate gambler that everyone loved to play against. Him the big fish from the bright side of the bay where the streets are a little cleaner and the sun shines a little brighter. The boys from Hammond always enjoyed cleaning that fish but this night the finner was having the last laugh. Yes sir, the Mayor of Zenith City was showing those Hammond boys a thing or two about poker… letting them know he's not the sucker they think he is. Tom took one and slid it in his hand and mixed them up slowly, one card at a time, without looking. Having the last laugh on these assholes would definitely be frosting on Mayor Geno's cake.

I was laughing myself—on the inside where it counts. Me—

hanging with the rich and influential. Just a punk nobody finally old enough to grow a decent mustache and there I was in on the "fleecing of the elite" as Sam Cross had called it. But the brothers were fucking up their scam right in front of me. It was going to be better than I thought.

The night before the game, I had told Sam that I wouldn't deal seconds or off the bottom of the deck to him and Nick like I used to in the old days. It always gave me a queer feeling, even back then.

The old days were four or five years ago when I ran a card game for Nick out of a little shack in the north end of Hammond near the warehouses. Nick or Sam would give me the cash every month and I'd pay the rent on the house (using a false name) and keep the fridge stocked with beer and provide fresh decks of cards when needed and deal with the delivery people if somebody had food sent in during a game. I took the house's ten percent rake out of every pot and was also the bouncer but we never had much trouble. I could usually talk my way out of tight situations and people—even drunken losers—usually liked me. At six-foot-one and two hundred pounds, most guys thought twice about me but every now and then you'd have to put the hand on someone. I never liked it much. Worst I ever got hit was by a three hundred pound broad. Big, mean, fat thing smacked me hard in the mouth one night and chipped a tooth. All because I had to escort her skinny little wimp of a husband out of the place for being drunk and obnoxious. What the hell you going to do, hit a woman? Broad like that—next time I will.

Occasionally there'd be a bunch of drunks that the Cross

brothers felt like ripping off and then I'd get to practice my little games of deception with the pasteboards—the tricks that I learned in my senior year of high school, the several months I was laid up with a broken hip. I crashed into a goalpost during a hockey play-off game in early March, I think it was. The goalposts didn't move in those days, driving the net took guts.

Always a shitty month, March. I mean, just the word: March—think about it…. That's what they say to you when they want you to go someplace you don't want to go: March upstairs to bed, young man. March up and take that machine gun nest boys. I put the down-time to good use though; I learned to handle a deck of Bicycle Brands like Bret Maverick at a suckers' convention.

And so it was that the Cross brothers began to exploit my talents like the bloodsuckers that they were. On occasion the boys would throw a big "Las Vegas party" for a bunch of high rollers and part of the hype was "professional dealers". That was always me and some other douchebag dressed up in fancy shirts and green plastic visors. I guess people don't mind getting ripped off if the rippers seem upscale enough. Boy could I do some things. Only once did anyone complain and he was a lawyer so what do you expect. Nick gave the guy his money back and told him if he ever came around anymore he'd be sorry. And that was the last we ever heard from the lawyer.

It was good fun and decent money for awhile and you got free beer and met some interesting characters that helped keep your mind off what you were doing. Then one night the cops busted the place while I was outside in the backseat of my car trying to get some kind of a job—be it blow or hand or whatever—from this tart I picked up in a bar that very afternoon.

Nick lost everything in the house that night—around a grand—and blamed me for a while so we became estranged. A year later he realized he would have lost it all anyway—no matter if I was in there or not—and at least his pal Keith didn't get popped, he says. What he was probably thinking was that I would have ratted him off if they'd gotten me. He must've figured he was lucky in at least one way.

One thing about Nick, he would do anything to protect his holdings. The string of low-ball rental properties, the two dive bars and his precious antique store gave the fat man a nice cash flow. But still he continued to invest in his little brother's quick money deals. I guess Nick couldn't help himself; the more he had, the more he wanted.

Sam's personal capital was born out of a whiplash scam that he pulled off a few years back. He used the insurance money to set up a very lucrative sports book. Book as in "bookie". He was also good at investing his brother's money in drugs and having some sucker like me do the retailing for him.

It was a natural progression for me to start selling, I guess. I was just going along with the flow. At first it was weed and that was no big deal—like I had a history with that stuff. Getting a student loan and using it to buy weed was common practice when I did my stint in college.

Everything was going along all right there for a while and then a ten-pound load I'd fronted out got popped and I was suddenly a maximum debtor to the brothers Cross. And when you owed money to them, you were the collateral. They owned you and they made you feel it. You were on call twenty-four hours of the day just to keep up with the interest. No job was too small or too large when you were into the Cross's pockets.

What choice did I have? I just went along with what they said. They knew guys who would break your knees with baseball bats for a few bucks.

What do you do if you're in debt? You up the ante.

So I started dealing cocaine, the new drug on the block.

Then I got into real debt.

Next around the poker table was a Greek sailor name of Miko: small wiry guy with tight black curls and long thick sideburns and a bushy coal duster mustache. He wore a thick blue denim shirt worthy of a first mate on a ship docked in town, which he was. A last-minute replacement for the captain of the ship who had begged off to tend to some late-breaking emergency. Or so it was explained to me by the bunch from Hammond, who brought the Greeks into the game in the first place.

Miko tapped his cards on the table and brushed away my offer of a draw. The stand-in was standing pat.

They were playing draw poker, Jacks or better progressive, trips to win. This meant that every time a hand was played where no player possessed three of a kind or better, the cards were reshuffled and a new hand dealt. As long as you didn't fold you were still in the game. The pot carried over and kept growing from hand to hand. It was one of Nick's favorite games. He always waited until near the end of the night when most everyone was half drunk; then he'd request the game. This night he was scrambling to find any game that might bring a large pot— big enough to recoup his losses.

We were like, eight or nine deals into this one and I think we were on Queens to open. It's pretty unusual to go that long without a winner, but some nights the cards just shut down for a while. There was a small fortune in the pot. Nick and Sam were betting and bluffing like lunatics and going through all these crazy tics and scratches and movements of body parts like they were warming up for a third base coach impersonating contest. Nobody else seemed to take notice and this made Nick even more brazen. One time he raised his right eyebrow so high on his forehead that it almost blended in with his receding hair line.

The next and final player was Peter McKay, brother (or half-brother as Sam told it) of John McKay and also Deputy Mayor of Hammond. He was a tall one with close-cropped, sandy hair and big ears that stuck out a little more than average. He had a square head like G.I. Joe and was wearing an ugly green polyester sport coat with a darker green turtleneck underneath. A heavy gold watch flashed on his left wrist and a gold ring with an emerald green stone sparkled from his right hand. He fingered the ring while he studied his cards.

The guy made me nervous. He had a pushy, prying way about him like a cop or a high school principal. . His eyes were cold when he smiled. I guess I just wasn't used to high society. I think he was starting to get wise to Nick Cross and his spastic routine. He grimly asked for two cards.

Sam Cross fingered a chunk of chips—the smile still on his face and a Marlboro dangling from his lips. A small flake of ash rested on his oily brown beard and he looked like a pudgy Bob Dylan. He took a hundred-dollar bill from the pocket of his baggy seersucker trousers and wrapped it around fifty bucks worth of chips and pushed it all into the mix. "A hundred and fifty beans," he said.

Mayor McKay called, then looked at his watch.

Nick raised it fifty and all the while he licked the left corner of his mouth and looked over at Sam. That was the scam, see. According to Sam they had done this when they were kids. He said they had some sort of psychic connection on account of they were so close as children that they could almost read each other's minds. These signals they were exchanging were supposed to communicate what cards one possesses or doesn't possess and other things I never really understood. They had to keep some secrets, they said. Remind me never to play with you, I said. They already knew enough not to play with me.

At that point of the evening even I could read Nick's mind: *If you fuck this up Sam you'll never get another cent from me as long as you live you scabby little cockroach—which may not be very long if I don't win you fucking dirt bag.*

Tom Geno folded, much to Nick's distaste.

Miko sucked hard on a Camel squeezed between his first two fingers. The smoke curled around a tattoo on the back of his right hand: some kind of fancy sword in the middle of some flowers. There was at least a thousand of his cash in the pot already, from my guess, and a lot less than that in his shrunken pile. He counted his chips carefully, fingered them softly one at a time and slowly slid all but one into the pot.

It seemed for a second that Sam Cross was going to lay them down and give us the old read-'em-and-weep. But suddenly the Greek chirped up in an accent as thick as the syrup in baklava:

"I would like to make a raise," he said, "but I have not enough cash. May I write a marker? This I have for collateral…."

He slid back his high-backed oak chair, glanced briefly at the bogus Tiffany light hanging above the poker table and bent over at the waist. He pulled up his wide, blue denim pant leg and reached inside his soft, black calf-high boots. He brought out a small handgun and set it on the table for us to appraise. Nick looked nervous.

"And what is this value for a marker? Any takers?" he asked, his voice rising anxiously.

"No markers to foreigners," Nick Cross snapped.

John McKay grimaced and glared over at his brother Peter who grinned thinly and put his hand to his upper lip to cover the oncoming sneer.

"Let me see that," said Sam Cross. "I've always wanted a little gun like this, I—"

"You'll blow off your putz with that thing Sammy," growled Nick sourly, chewing on a cigar.

"This is Walther PPK," the Greek said and put his palm down on the table next to the finely crafted pistol. "The 007, James Bond… he use this to kill many communists. Is least worth seven hundred American…."

"I'll give you two bills—two hundred—for it," Sam said, waving casually at his considerable winnings. "But if you want to buy it back, it'll cost you three—whether it's tonight or next week. Savvy?"

"Is not enough. Is worth seven hundred."

"Take it or leave it pal, the clock is ticking," Sam reached across the table and picked up the gun. The Greek eyed him suspiciously.

"Yes, please do," said Mayor McKay, his tone superior and weary. He stubbed out his cigarette in a square glass ash tray. "If I would have known you were bringing a gun I certainly would not have given my okay. Peter, did you know about this?"

Peter shrugged his shoulders slightly and straightened up to the full effect of his large torso. He smiled benevolently at his brother and the rest of us: "I'm sure Miko feels a little worried about carrying a large sum of money in what to him is a strange town, thousands of miles and an ocean away from his homeland. Hammond can be a little threatening in some sections, late at night. Something my brother and I firmly resolve to change. Isn't that correct brother John?"

"That's correct Peter. But we are not here to discuss work. Do you think Miko can take care of his business now and get on with the game? You don't know how Evelyn can get if I'm too late getting in."

"Relax, John," said Tom Geno, chuckling to himself. "You still got time to get some lipstick stains on that nice shiny shirt."

Miko's brow furrowed and frowned until his thick eyebrows met in the middle and formed a single row of bushy black hair. He glared across at Sam. Sam had his back turned away from the table and was busy aiming the gun at the chandelier and the overhead fan and the numerous antiques lining the walls and shelves of his rich sibling's rec room. Truly a child at play.

"Okay," Miko said. "Two hundred. I take it. I win hand and buy back tonight." Then he hid his mouth with the back of his hand and leaned over toward Tom Geno and muttered a barely audible: "Must be Jew."

Mayor Geno coughed and almost did a spit take with his Seven-and-Seven. Me, I was laughing on the inside again where it counts.

Sam put the diminutive weapon into the pocket of his worn sharkskin suit coat and counted out twenty ten-dollar chips. As soon as Miko got his hands on them they were tossed into the pot. Then the rest of his pile and a fifty-dollar bill.

A four-bill raise and it was the little guy. He was shoving it back at the politicians and the business men and the crooks. There you go American assholes…. There you go… I sell my gun—only protection from the crazy drug sick maniacs you have here. And I have reason to fear. Some of you know. But I shall win this game and return to ship with pockets stuffed and there I will stay until business is done and I can return home.

Peter McKay's chips lay on the table in neat little equal size stacks and his gaze was fixed on the Greek. He was trying to look into his eyes. Miko turned his back and got up and walked over to the leather-covered bar against the back wall. He poured himself a shot of Petri Brandy in a stubby glass. Fucking Nick always bought rotgut liquor for these games. Old Pete pursed his lips and made a noise in his throat that sounded like AHEM and held his cards close to his body. After studying each player with his prying eyes, he slowly counted out enough chips for the call and slid them in the pot. He peered around the table once again.

Sometimes I swore the bastard was fixing on me. All night long when I eyeballed him he would have this weird glazed look on his pasty face. It seemed like he was checking me out. But I suppose that made sense, because I was the dealer.

Sam picked an unopened Marlboro box from the table and tapped it three times hard against the palm of his hand, then removed the cellophane. He tore a hole in the bottom of the box and shook out a cig and left the flip top unopened. He rolled the unlit cig in his fingers and stared at the pot and purposely avoided Nick's gaze. He checked his cards. Then he brushed the ashes off his beard and counted out four hundred bucks and quietly called.

Nick's face was red, matching fifty percent of his plaid L.L. Bean shirt. Maybe some gray hairs were popping out. He rubbed his temples like there was an aneurysm. I wasn't sure if it was one of his signals or the onset of a stroke.

Mayor McKay said: "Too rich for my blood I'm afraid. Even though I had trips—I'm done. The cards were bound to loosen up. That's the last hand for me gentlemen." He flopped his cards over to me then sat back and sighed.

Nick—who seemed to be about to swallow his tongue—gripped tightly at the front of his shirt and glumly slid in his four hundred pesatas. "Call," he rasped weakly.

Miko was back at the table in his dark captain's chair looking like John Barrymore waiting for the right dramatic moment. His chest seemed to swell as he looked around at the remaining challengers and proudly slapped his cards down. Aces over eights, full. "Full house," he beamed. "Beat this, if you can."

"FUCK," Nick screamed at the top of his lungs. "An ace-high flush and I fucking lose. GODDAMN IT!!" He threw the cards in Sam's direction—they fluttered and spun through the smoky air and dropped onto the table. Nick got up and stormed across the room to the bar and chugged straight from the Petri bottle. He was swearing to himself.

"Beats me," Peter McKay said. "I'm afraid it's a bad end to a good evening." He flipped his cards over toward me, turned his head and looked smug.

All eyes went to Sam Cross.

Sam could hardly contain his glee. His body jerked with suppressed laughter as he plopped down his four sevens. Little bursts of air squeaked out the sides of his tightly pressed lips as he raked in the monster pot with both arms. Ain't it funny how the lucky ones stay lucky and the rest of us keep losing.

Miko groaned. His body went limp; he sank down into the chair in utter defeat.

Nick screamed: "YOU FUCKING ASSHOLE," across the room.

Peter McKay glared and blinked his eyes several times. His benevolent pose returned.

John McKay got up from the table and walked slowly over to the leather couch by the brick fireplace and picked up his brown cashmere topcoat. He glowed yellow from the flickering flames as he said a perfunctory goodbye and left the room. A moment later I heard the outside door open and close.

Sam couldn't hold it any longer; he broke down into a giggling mess. Tom Geno grinned along with Sam—that night he could afford to.

Miko regained a little composure after he finished his brandy but still had the look of a stunned rat.

Nick screamed again—at all of us this time: "OUT. ALL YOU ASSHOLES OUT OF HERE. THIS IS THE LAST

FUCKING TIME I DO THIS FUCKING SHIT. GET OUT… GODDAMN NOW!!!" Then he raked his hand across the top of the bar—sending bottles and glasses and ash-trays flying—before storming upstairs and slamming the door behind him.

I think that gave us all something to smile about as we showed ourselves out into the blustery March night. I needed a laugh bad. It was cloudy and there wasn't a star in sight. I shivered. The hawk was blowing from the North and the dampness went right through me. But it was more than the weather that had me shaking. Things hadn't turned out very good. My whole life was really the shits. I was in debt to the brothers for ten grand and after that performance in there I felt sure Nick would soon lose all patience with my financial delinquency. *You don't throw good money after bad*, he always said. And after I didn't turn the cards his way, I definitely qualified as bad.

Things were worse than I knew. It's funny how you can get started into patterns without realizing it and before you know it you're going down some road leading somewhere you don't even want to be. You don't know where you're going till you arrive and later when it's too late you're not sure how you got there. And for the life of you no matter how hard you try you can't find the way back. That's the way it was for me.

The love life was also the pits—too many classless, ignorant bar flies with a marked propensity for procrastination and sloth. I read that last part on a bathroom wall somewhere. But what do you expect from a divorced guy for Christ sake… church socials and discussion groups?

My ex-wife Loraine and I were flower children sweethearts

in the sixties. Then after seven years of marriage she caught me in the car with a topless twenty-year old and kicked me right out of the house. Losing Loraine wasn't too bad though because by then we really had nothing in common—even the sex was stale. All she wanted to do was go bowling and eat while I according to her only cared for drinking beer and "staring at little chickie's chests." The fact that it was imported beer never seemed to make an impact on her. Sometimes I miss the early days when she loved me still.

Despite the wind's nip, Sam was flying high and still laughing about his luck with the cards and his brother's tantrum. He invited me along for a drink and a blast or two off the silver bullet with him and Miko. He was going to buy the Greek a lot of drinks and try to make the guy like him and I had no stomach for the bullshit. I declined the invite and turned in the direction of my rusty 1965 Olds. Then I noticed Peter McKay coming up behind me.

"Mr. Waverly," he said, "hold up for a moment, please."

I did and when he caught up he pressed a twenty-dollar bill into my palm and gave my forearm a little squeeze with his other black-gloved hand.

"Just a small tip for your dealing tonight, Mr. Waverly," he said. He looked me up and down and smiled a little. "I did well, in spite of the rather bizarre group we had assembled. Thank you. Do you do this sort of thing often?"

"Not much anymore, I just owed Nick a favor—from the old days. Me and Nick go back a'ways."

"I see—uh huh. Well, maybe I can use you some day."

"Sure, anything," I said, nodding my head like a puppy eager for a bone. By that time we were at my car door so I climbed in and cranked her up while Peter trudged off to his dark green Mercedes diesel. I buttoned up the front of my brown corduroy Marlboro Man jacket and drove away.

*   *   *

It's clear to me now that the card game was the catalyst for all the sordid events that followed. It was a night where Fate came in and shoved all of us into the Big Mixer and threw in some glue and some nails and pushed the puree button. But the beginnings of the story go back a little ways more. Back to earlier that winter, one night when I was wheeling hack for Minnie Green and her Blue and White Taxi Company….

It was late January of 1978. Football season was over and the lights from all the Christmas trees were out. Approaching the John D. Haavik Bridge, I could see the yellowed ice of the bay stretching out to the mouth of the St. Louis River. They call it the St. Louis River but it's a long ways from Missouri.

The ancient Arrowhead Bridge and a rusted railroad trestle watched silently in the cold distance as I rolled toward the concrete and steel span that would get me across the water to the other side. *Break on through to the other side.*

Way back on the left, huge grain terminals loomed darkly behind rows of faded empty boxcars. On the edge of the road dark, naked branches stretched out like arthritic fingers, straining for a warmth that wasn't there. The wind blew hard off Lake Superior, pushing and shoving at the taxi's aging suspension.

The heater was on full blast—icy drafts whistled in.

I was headed to the Wisconsin side of the bridge and the north end of Hammond—a low spot on the geological survey where the losers, the lost and the sexually disenfranchised washed up like flotsam and jetsam. A place where strangely, I felt safe. Felt like there was nothing to prove and somehow that was a good thing.

Sure Hammond had its good people and its quiet neighborhoods like anywhere else but there was also something strange over there. Something peculiar—a feeling that lingered on the edge of comprehension. It was a place where you might find someone as indifferent or as desperate as you. Someone just as willing to go crazy, attempt suicide or commit a crime. Someone just right.

The first thing that comes to mind when I think of Tugtown is alcohol. Booze. Liquor. Firewater. Rotgut. For guys like me who grew up on the other side of the bridge, Hammond was a place for first-time experiences. Maybe your first drink in a bar. Maybe the first time you bought beer with a fake ID or had a pool cue broken across your back. Maybe your ear bitten off in a fight—could be anything. A town where anything *could* happen if the stars were right.

From the top of the bridge the three-story skyline spread out before me: dark, decaying and slightly greasy like in a 1930's version of a Dickens' novel from an alternate universe. I could see U.S. Highway 2 as it wound its way toward a barren, gray, frozen wasteland of snow and pine trees and the occasional country bar or small town.

Wisconsin—Devil's Country: Endless miles of two-lane roads and a population of outlaw bikers second only to the great state of California. Birthplace and home of Ed Gein and Jeffrey Dahmer.

Dahmer was probably busy grilling up his neighbor's cat about the time I turned right onto North Fifth Street, the primary gateway to the strip clubs and massage parlors, gambling joints, rock and roll bars, whorehouses and bad restaurants that were the pulse of Hammond's erogenous zone.

Wisconsin's legal drinking age was eighteen, recently brought down by the state legislature from twenty-one, and the party was always on. The town's funky old saloons were filled with raucous hordes getting drunk and doing drugs and raising general hell. The cash flowed as fast as the liquor as the wild-siding kids poured into town like beavers to a birch tree farm.

I cruised by the Wisconsin Steak House and a little seaweed green wooden garage in an open field with a hand-painted sign on the door advertising: "Hubcaps For Sale." As the sun began to sink below the horizon, flophouses and greasy spoons and blockhouse bars cast dark silhouettes.

Passing on my right was the Viking Bar, famous for drinks as cheap as a boat whore and strong as a trucker's breath. Then came the Nickel Street Saloon and the High Times and the Heartbreak Hotel. One Harley leaned on its peg in front of the High Times. At Beaner's Boulevard Lounge on my left, the strippers sold cocaine between dances and pussy after hours. I was thinking maybe I should stop in after my shift is over. I drove on by.

Next to Beaner's was Johnny's, where once a three hundred pound customer killed his drinking buddy by jumping onto the poor slob's chest and crushing his heart. Then came Tony's Cabaret, the Twin Port's only gay bar. Behind Al's Waterfront Lounge, huge ships rested on the frozen bay like bathtub toys for giants. Up ahead past Tower Avenue, Fifth Street hit a dead-end at a big mound of dirt and a sign that consisted of three long, black-and-yellow striped boards bolted to some metal posts in the ground. Past that, a bleak flat area stretched out dark and endless. Dead, brown weed stocks and piles of coal flecked with snow lay next to rusty railroad cars and the ghostly hulls of semi-trailers. A phalanx of railroad tracks spider-webbed around a metal hangar and led out of town toward better places.

I turned left on Tower and headed uptown. The streets were pretty empty, as it was still early.

Away from the waterfront the bars went upscale. In Hammond this meant they were cleaned once in a while and had bouncers. At least a few of them did. I drove by the Cave Cabaret, featuring The Zenith City Gloom Band, and past a "Girls, Girls, Girls" sign at the Castaway. In a blur of neon and exhaust came the Casablanca, the Brass Rail, Zanuzowski's, Yellow Submarine, Tommy Byrne's, the Poodle Lounge, Dugout Bar, the Capri, the Lamplighter, the Androy Hotel, the Elbow Room, D.T.'s, the Anchor, the Douglas, Betty Boop's, the Kro Bar, the Trio, the Classy Lumberjack and the Red Lace Massage Parlor.

At John Avenue—appropriately famous for its three whorehouses—I turned right and drove down past Bob's Chop

Suey House. One block later I parked underneath the glow of the Port Town Hotel sign that was fastened to the wall of the dark brick flophouse. Across the street was a laundromat and a closed cafe—DINAH'S KITCHEN on a faded sign.

I was five minutes early for the pick-up so I pulled out a Kool from the pack above the visor and fired up with some matches from a book that said: Jasmine's Lounge, "Where You Always Have A Good Time." I flipped the button on the transistor lying on the seat. Jagger was singing about love in vain. About that I thought I knew. Then something crossed through the glare coming from the naked bulb in the pea-green hotel door-way and I turned to see two good-looking girls strutting toward my cab. I remember thinking it was my lucky night.

I feasted my eyes on a tall, dark-haired, clean-faced beauty in a long brushed leather coat: dark tortoise shell sunglasses, hair stuffed up inside a floppy brown felt hat and a black silk scarf tied loosely around her neck. The other girl was a short blonde with long straight hair—cute in a baby doll sort of way. She wriggled inside a bird's egg blue high school letter jacket with a white W on the front. They got in the cab and were followed closely behind by a rush of cold, fresh air and sweet perfume and alcohol and chewing gum. I was putty in ten seconds flat.

I drove them over to the Castaway and the only thing I could think of to say was: "You girls from around here?"

The blonde answered yes and the brunette said no. Then they laughed and stared out the windows. I did the same and still tried to think up something clever to say and had no success. The town looked gray and dirty and the few people on the streets, ugly.

I parked in front of the Castaway and the chicks shuffled through their purses for the fare. I figured they must be exotic dancers. Why else would a chick go to a strip bar? Unless maybe they were lesbians. That would be all right, too. They sure were pretty.

I was just about to ask them their names and maybe their phone numbers—at least the tall one's anyway—when this scrawny punk of a guy came scrambling out the side door of the bar and started running through the parking lot like the devil himself was chasing. The dude's shirt was torn up and there was blood and spit all over his face. I knew the guy—Harvey Dornan was his name. A small time dealer/hustler who anybody with any brains steered clear of. He'd been missing from the scene for a few years but recently I'd seen him back on the streets and in the bars.

Shortly after Harvey went ricocheting by, two big guys in oxblood red leather jackets came busting out after him. They were pointing and yelling and running, then a third guy—sandy haired pompadour, short leather jacket, sadistic look—jumped out the door of a brown Lincoln and dished out a forearm shiver to the throat of the running hippie.

I jumped out of the cab and yelled, Hey! across the roof but they didn't pay me any mind. I started running to where Harvey was down but one of the husky dudes pulled a huge black gun from under his jacket and pointed it in my direction. I needed only that one hint. Harvey was fucked up anyway.

I ran back to the cab and jumped in and looked back to see if they were coming my way. Much to my relief they threw the kid in the back of the Continental and drove off. Then I realized the girls were gone. Three dollars for the fare lay on the front seat, along with a dollar tip. I lifted up the bills and put them to my nose to see if the ladies' scent was still on them. It was. I made a mental note to go to the Castaway for a show real soon and then got the hell out of there.

I was a little shaky so I drove back over to Zenith City and sat outside the Norshor Theatre for a few minutes to calm my nerves. "Close Encounters of the Third Kind," it said on the flashing marquee. My nerves didn't calm down at all and even though I could have used a few more bucks I drove to the Blue and White office and checked out for the night. I didn't tell Al, the hawk-nosed phlegm factory of a dispatcher, anything about the incident; I just said I was a little ill.

Wasted no time getting back over the bridge.

I slowed down in front of the Castaway because I couldn't stop thinking about that girl—the dark-eyed one—but still I drove on by. I was a little short on cash, you see.

I pulled around back of the gray-shingled barn-like duplex that had been my home for three months and parked the Olds in the circle of light cast by a sodium lamp in the alley. I walked up the faded wooden stairs past the empty cases of Leinenkugel's and the old paint cans and put the key in the lock of the ugly Aqua Velva-blue door.

My roommate Mick was passed out on the couch in the living room kicking out jackhammer snores. A beer bottle balanced on his slightly rounded stomach; the thumb and forefingerof his right hand held the bottle upright in a nocturnal death grip.

I settled back into the weakened springs of the old easy chair. A black and white movie droned on the tube. Daniel Webster was getting seduced by the devil. People and shapes and dis-embodied voices were trying to pull Daniel over to the dark side. Jesus that shit was eerie. Webster must have had a hard time making his dictionary with those fuckers on his ass.

I got up and turned the dial. There was a Kojak rerun on channel eighteen and Kojak made me feel secure. If Kojak was your daddy, man, and you ever got in trouble—you can fucking bet he'd get you out.   But I never liked that dude who played the sidekick so I shut off the TV and went to bed.

 The next day a biting Alberta Clipper roared into town and I was in no shape to wrestle with the beast of winter. It was shut-down-dead-stop-grinding-to-a-halt cold. The kind of cold where the car exhaust is pressed down low to the ground and the wind is all the time trying to get inside your face and rip your eyes out. The sun has no warmth and cars don't start and furnaces break down and water mains burst. You can feel the cold pinching in through the windows and underneath the doors in that kind of weather. You need some kind of routine to get you through. You need something solid in your life to hang onto. Me, I had myself a motto: Do what you have to do and stay drunk the rest of the time.

Fate seemed to have it in for me and I didn't have a lot to be thankful for except that liquor was cheap in Hammond—real cheap. That helped, being I was off the coke. In my own way I was going through rehab. I provided the castigation.

Slowly my obsession with cocaine started to lift. The drug

makes you selfish and greedy and all you care about is drugs and money and sex. After being clean for a while I started thinking about others again, like my wife and son....

Poor Loraine was getting fat and so was little Mike and I blamed her. If only I could've seen the kid more often I could've straightened him out. But Loraine told him I was a no-good character and that made it hard, if you know what I mean. Then she moved back in with her Jesus-freak parents and I only got to see the kid when she brought him to the bowling alley with her. And I hate bowling. Truly I hate bowling. Bowling alleys aren't so bad though, except all me and Mike used to do is eat greasy food until he started to look like a pregnant seal. I thought of a seal because of the way Loraine slicked his black hair down and this sound that he made that annoyed me. I guess eight-year-old kids do that sort of thing but sometimes I think she put him up to it. It was also pretty tough because I was living in Hammond and he was across the bay in Zenith City. It wasn't that far but I only spent time in Zenith when I was driving cab or working at the porno store and those are no places for a kid. It's important that you know about the divorce because it was, I think, one big reason I got deeper involved with the Cross brothers. After the break-up things started going downhill for me in a gravity-fueled spiral. Success was failure and failure was success and who could tell the difference.

Then one hung-over February afternoon I was sitting in the living room reading the morning paper in the waning light of a bitter day. The Gong Show was on the tube. Mickey was bartending at the High Times and dishes were stacked up in the kitchen and my room was piled-high with dirty clothes and all the beer was gone and I was getting thirsty.

MAN FOUND MURDERED
IN HAMMOND CITY FOREST

kind of jumped out at me from the newsprint. It was the number two story of the day and told the sad tale of a Caucasian male found lying face down in the snow. Shoulder-length light brown hair, five front teeth missing and three large bullet holes in his head, it said. Harvey Dornan, alleged police informant, it also said in black and white right there in front of me. Body partially eaten by wolves was also there.

Harvey had finally pissed off the wrong people in his short miserable life. Maybe if someone had fixed the poor kid's teeth a long time ago things would have been different for him. It was only two weeks before that I saw him running out the back of the Castaway with thugs in pursuit. I didn't do a thing to help him then—but you never can with guys like that.

All these bad premonitions and free-floating anxieties swarmed inside me like a cloud of locusts. Did I mention before that I get flashes from the future? Mostly bad premonitions like when you feel like something horseshit is going to happen and then it does.

The more I dwelled on it the worse it got. But later that night after a few drinks I got to feeling better, you know how it is.

Then time passed by routinely for a while. Days of high snow banks and low life. I made enough money to get by but not enough to make any progress on my debt. The only lesson learned: Time passes quickly when you dread the rising sun.

Cross is What My True Love Bears

February faded into March and I hardly knew the difference—still gray, still cold, still windy. I guess it was getting warmer though because the boats were coming in through the locks out East and steaming down our way. Here at the Head of the Lakes we depend on the boats for a lot of things. A lot of stuff moves through these Twin Ports and a lot of locals make their living because of shipping. It's one of the first signs of spring, even though there never is much of a spring on this end of Lake Superior. Most years you're craving it by Valentine's Day anyway.

Winter wears away at you until your innards cry out for relief. The warm weather and sunshine you so dearly want is cruelly held back, day after dreary day. Your eyes burn from the unrelenting grayness; the weight on your chest and the tightness in your neck are facts of life. It works on your sanity. Bad shit happens in this part of the world come March. Boozers drink more and druggies do more drugs and the well-off go South and the crazies go over the edge.

When Sam Cross invited me in on his poker scam I jumped at the chance like a condemned man in a hurry to the gallows. He and his brother wanted me to do my little mechanic number to kind of augment their other scheme, he said. I knew right then that I wouldn't do it, cheat that is, but I didn't say anything at first. My big break had finally come, I figured. I truly felt that it was going to lead me up the ladder somehow—hanging with the rich and influential like that. The right connections you know—something was bound to fall my way. I wasn't going to jeopardize my position with high society by cheating. Because that's what you need in this world—connections.

Sadly, my only connection remained the same after the game as before—Sam Cross.

One of Sam's bookmaking debtors was paying off his markers in wholesale LSD and I was given the job of turning them into cash. Three bucks for the red pyramids and five for the green. Take a little trip on the cheap. It was a good ride and you could drink a lot more when you were doing the 'cid. It was good for the town's economy, I figured. I'd sample the wares now and then myself and hit a few bars and usually blow the profits on drinks.

Several days after the big poker game had come and gone, the first sunny spring-like day of the year hit town. And wouldn't you know it man, I had to work at the fucking Wabasha bookstore....

About ten-thirty on a Saturday night and things were pretty slow. I had the glass front door propped open a crack to let in the soft night air. The juices were beginning to flow again and I was feeling pretty good. I leaned back on the rear legs of the hard, uncomfortable chair and sensually fondled a Dunlop red stitch softball. My eyes flicked restlessly around the brightly lit room. All the gash and dick and plastic genitalia burned the mucus on my eyeballs. I couldn't rest my gaze.

I was rubbing my eyes with the my knuckles when Sammy Cross walked in, arm-in-arm with a gorgeous girl: about five-six, medium-length auburn hair, a gorgeous slinky bod and dreamy brown eyes. The kind of girl that made your dick hard and your heart soft and turned your brain to mush—just the way I liked it.

My mouth must have dropped open or something because Cross and the girl both grinned when they looked at me. Then the light bulb went on in my head and I knew it was the girl from the cab and the Castaway and my dreams. This time without the shades.

"Sam—what are you doing here? And who's your friend?" I was suddenly embarrassed by my surroundings.

Her blue-painted eyelids were at half mast. A cigarette dangled from her long thin fingers. She looked me over with an appreciative smirk. My heart thumped like a big bass drum. Surely she must remember me... but she didn't let on.

Cross grinned like a satanic Teddy Bear. "Keith... " he said, "Let me introduce you to Mary." Always had manners, that guy.

I said, "Hi..." and a thousand worms wriggled in my gut.

"Hi," she returned with a sexy half-smile.

She took a walk around the shop, checking out the fuck-and-suck rags in a wave of perfume and tobacco smoke. I couldn't keep from staring. Her expression remained the unreadable half-smile. Crimson nails, a silver and turquoise bracelet on one wrist and no rings. Breasts pushed firmly against a thin black sweater—ass moving sweetly in tight flare jeans. Some funky platform shoes, an oversize Levis jacket—the picture was perfect like I'd seen in a dream or maybe on an album cover.

"Jesus, Sam..." I whispered. "Where did you find her?"

"Right over in your back yard, Keitho my friend. She's a peeler at the Castaway, in Hammond."

"Jesus… she is the one. She was in my cab. You're dating her then?"

"I'm trying to—but not tonight—she just dropped in over at Delaney's with a couple friends while I was sitting there having a few pops. I've been trying all night to get her to go to this big party with me. She says she won't go with just me alone. Some unresolved issues of trust, I'm afraid. The little girl is not as easy as I had hoped—and after all the cash I've stuffed down her g-string…." He peaked up at me for a reaction and got none. "No, I'm kidding," he said smiling, "really what the deal is, is that she's got two friends with her over at the bar and we thought you would be the perfect escort. Yeah, I bet Carla and Charlene will think you're dreamy."

"Fuck you. What do these other chicks look—"

"Why do you work in this place?" Mary asked—wide-eyed now, and innocent—upon her return to the front of my perch.

I was up on a raised platform, two feet above the rest of the floor, sitting behind the cash register and a small lectern. Everybody had to look up to me to pay for their smut. There was a sense of power in that chair. If the customers were feeling guilty when they looked up to you, you were like the High Priest of Porn about to pass approval on their sins. This girl had somehow turned the tables on me.

"Cause I know the manager and the pay is good," I said. I felt my race reddening.

"How much do you make?" she asked, still with the same expression. I loved the way her hair swept back.

"Five dollars an hour."

"But minimum wage is only two and a quarter."

"Well, actually I get three bucks an hour, but I ring up at least a ten dollar no sale every shift and put it in my pocket. Hell, the cops could walk in and bust me at any minute—I deserve a little hazard pay. And besides, this place is owned by Ferris Alexander—I should steal more...."

"Yeah, Waverly is a real prince," Cross chimed in, putting his hand on the girl's sexy shoulder. "See what I told you, Mary, have you ever seen such an innocent, honest, trustworthy boy as Keith. Just look at that boyish face—or should I say goyishe face? Why, the boy won't even steal *too* much from Minnesota's pornography king— who's so rich he shits quarters. What a guy you are Wavo."

Just then two men in worn trench coats came through the door. At the sight of Mary they tensed up and began to paw around the room like water buffaloes at an occupied water hole.

I lowered my voice: "What's this party you're talking about, Sambo?"

"Over in Hammond at Tony's Cabaret. Then a private bash at Peter McKay's digs. Big party. All the hipsters will be hanging."

"Are you kidding me? Tony's Cabaret is a gay bar. And fucking Peter McKay, what's his deal? And how did *you* manage an invite? He didn't look too enamored with you after the poker game, if I may say so. In fact it seemed like he wanted to bust open your wise-ass skull—if my perception was at all accurate you low-life son of a bitch."

"That maybe so. That maybe so, Keith, my man, but big Peter has seen the error of his ways. I'll have you know, we are now business associates. Time moves along, my son. By the way, he mentioned you—said you should come to the shindig, if I saw you. Said he might have a few ideas for you." He paused and stared at a huge plastic vagina hanging from a pegboard on the west wall. "Uhm... ah... y'know, Nick is getting a little anxious to see some kind of positive sign from you, if you know what I mean."

"Fuck Nick," I said, and looked down at Sam. A party given by the powerful Peter McKay; beautiful women at my side.... It was the start up the ladder I'd been waiting for. Nothing was going to bring me down.

"Big talk," Sam said casually.

"Fuck you," I said.

Mary cocked her hip to the side, rested her hand on her waist and lifted the heel of her boot off the ground. "We have to get the girls, don't forget Sam," she said, but she was looking up at me with those fascinating, heavy-lidded peepers when she said it.

"How could I forget those two," Sam said as he took Mary's arm and sashayed out the door.

"I'll be there in fifteen minutes," I shouted after them. "Don't leave without me."

The clock said 10:45.

"You'll have to make up your minds, guys," I said to the water buffaloes as they relaxed and approached the desk "We're closing in five minutes."

"I thought it said midnight on the front door," said the guy with an oval head like an egg and a soft-boiled look about him.

"Yeah, we just got here," whined the other one. "I've got a

whole pocket of quarters here for the movies—" He lifted up the side pocket of his gray overcoat and jangled it at me. He had long dirty fingernails.

"Boss has to come in and do inventory tonight, guys.... Sorry."

"Well, all right then," said the guy with the fingernails, looking around, "I'm gonna buy a magazine. You wait a minute."

He picked out a spectacular color photo collection of extra-large-breasted women entitled "Big Mamas." I rang up No Sale and set the ten-spot on the counter in front of the register. Fuck Ferris Alexander, a man needs a few bucks in his pocket when he's going to be with a lady.

After the dudes left and I locked the door behind them I turned around the CLOSED sign and pulled the curtain down. I was supposed to take a mop and a bucket of suds and swab down the floors of the movie booths and the surrounding area. If done correctly the job took thirty minutes.

I grabbed the Pine-Sol bottle from the cleaning closet and shook several drops on the inside of each cubicle and a steady stream on the floor and swished it all around with the mop at high speed. The job was complete in ten minutes.

I cashed out the register and put the money in the metal box and slid it underneath the gay magazines like you were supposed to do. Then I left and locked the door behind me. Walking down the busy sidewalk towards my car I felt like the eighth dwarf, name of Sleazy. *Hi-ho, hi-ho, it's off to work I go. I've filled the world with lots of smut, Hi-ho, hi-ho.*

* * *

Fifteen minutes after arriving at Delaney's and choking down one drink, I was back out in my car driving to Hammond. Sam had opted for the strawberry blonde duo of Carla and her mother Charlene. He took the two identically-coiffed and identically-dressed sweeties into his worn down Bonneville, laughing and giggling all the way. Mary and I got in my pitiful sedan. I'm not complaining mind you but I was as nervous as a spider on a barbecue grill. Thank god that drink was a strong one—tequila sunrise with a shot of gin thrown in for good measure, just like the Rolling Stones were drinking. They called them GTOs at Delaney's.

Mary seemed amused by the situation after I reminded her of our previous meeting.

"Should I ride in the back?" she said.

"I'll have to charge you then—cabby's law."

She grinned and climbed in the front seat. I drove down a block, turned right onto Railroad Street and headed for the bridge at a good pace. Every time we crossed over a set of tracks we bounced up off the seats and almost hit our heads on the roof. Mary found a big roach in the ash tray and fired it up. On top of the several cocktails she'd already downed it got her talking up a blue streak. I don't remember how we got on the subject but she was more than content to fill me in on her background....

"My father used to work in the mines up on the Iron Range," she said. Her voice had a delicious lilt to it, like a light brogue with a booze thickened tongue. Put that together with the way she crinkled up the sides of her mouth when she spoke and you know why I was falling.

"Ever been up there on the Iron Range?" she said. "I was born up there, in Eveleth. And now I just got through working up in Gilbert, before I came here. Ever been up there?"

"I've been up to Eveleth quite a few times, for hockey games when I was younger. Never been to Gilbert—although I may have driven through there once, I'm not sure."

"I was dancing at a club called the Gladiator. Ever heard of it? They do live sex shows there... the locals call it The Glad-I-Ate-Her."

"You're shitting me."

"No, they do, really, but that wasn't the reason I left."

I wondered if she had participated in those performances. Pictures rolled behind my eyes.

"Why did you leave?"

She turned her eyes to the darkness outside and wrinkled her nose at the acrid stench in the air. "It was just too weird up there. What is that stink, anyway?"

"Superwood. Ever think wood could smell like that?"

"Hell no.... Some old friends heard I was there—at the Gladiator, I mean. It was just too weird.... And then I met Larry—he was the only guy who wasn't an asshole up there. I left town with him."

"And so Larry took you home and saved you from a fate worse than death?"

"He took me to a cheap hotel until his money ran out and his wife found out and came barging in on us."

Hmm—aha—so, ah, that was nice. How do you like that line of work, anyway? Dancing I mean. Isn't that what everyone wants to know? I mean... I've always been fascinated by strippers—ah, ever since I saw them at the state fair when I was a kid. They used to stand outside on a stage while this guy hustled the crowd…. So I had to ask…."

"Well, I'd done it before, after I left my husband. I needed a job so—"

"Your husband? You had a husband?"

"Yeah. I was married when I was nineteen, almost twenty. Small-town Wisconsin guy—football hero and everything. I was knocked up—you know, the same old trip. I was ready to have the baby and live the small town life, y'know: the bowling alley, the bars and the ceramics classes and all that shit. PTA, Sunday dinners with the in-laws, Packer games—I was going to do it."

"What happened then?"

"I had a miscarriage. After that, I started to see things differently. And I started to get really sick of living in that shitty little house, him expecting me to be there every night in cute little dresses with dinner ready. We lived right by the highway, you could hear the semis rolling by. It really wasn't that bad of a house, I guess—and Doug wasn't that bad of a guy. But I just had to get out of there, y'know. You got to do what ya gotta do, y'know? God, there was this bitch that lived in a trailer across the road from me… used to drive me crazy. She'd come over all the time uninvited—sit around on her fat cheese ass and brag to me about her bratty kids or about how she had just got a new TV or stereo or something. Knowing that the only thing new that I ever got was a zit. God, I hated her. She stunk like cheap hairspray. She'd smoke my cigarettes and drink my beer—just stay there and stay there 'til I was going nuts. And she lived in a fucking trailer. Ooh, how I hated that thing—looking down at me from up on that hill. She even had old tires around the front of the thing, painted red and white with flowers in them. Can you believe that? I really wanted to burn it down."

"No shit?"

"I wanted to. I would have done the world a favor, getting rid of one of those ugly things."

"Yeah, I hear they're made out of old Hamm's beer cans."

"Real funny. So anyway, this girlfriend of mine was living up in Hurley, going to the junior college, or so she said. She always wanted me to come up and visit, so I did. Left poor Doug and his dirty laundry to fend for themselves. I packed up a suitcase and boogied up to Hurley, only when I get there, I find out that Shelly is working as an exotic—get this—to pay for junior college. One thing led to another, y'know, and pretty soon I was traveling the circuit and taking off my clothes, too. It was kind of fun, at first—partying all the time. There was always good drugs…. Got any more pot?"

"See if there's another roach in the ashtray."

Somehow I made it across the bridge and to Tony's Cabaret. Cars were parked everywhere but we found a spot in back of the bar by a big icy puddle. I was blown away but ready for a party.

* * *

THE SCENE: A packed bar room, smoky air—two floors of fun. Large dance floor surrounded by tables of all shapes and sizes. Gray and black walls and a life-size cardboard Marilyn Monroe sighing out at you from the end of the long wooden bar. Bass and drums and saxophone trio blew jazzy cabaret tunes. Sax player's mime make-up sinister. Eye shadow and mascara and burgundy lipstick on the androgynous bass player. A mass of bodies undulated close on the dance floor. Pretty girls held cocktails and cigarettes and coolly stared on from the sidelines.

I ordered two double Bacardis and orange juice from the fast-moving bartender and made eye contact with a chick across the way in a tight green-and-black-striped dress. She had great tits and had dark designs penciled around her eyes. There I was staring at some strange girl's chest. I guess my ex was right all along. Fortunately for me, Mary was too entranced with the whole scene to take notice of what the hell I was looking at. The only one whose attention I got was a skinny guy in a sweaty blue shirt. He asked me to dance. I said, "Later… much later," then turned around and caught a guy in purple pants and a sleeveless undershirt staring at my ass.

I was relieved to see Sam and his entourage sitting at a round table on the edge of the dance floor. He motioned me over. Carla and a blonde bimbo in black I didn't recognize were fawning over him. He must have broken out the nasal decongestant powder, I figured. Why else would anyone fawn over him? Both of the Cross brothers would fuck just about anything that paid them a moment's notice if they had the chance, but Sam always did better with the women, in spite of Nick's money. I guess you had to spend it.

We made our way through the swirling mass of humanity, me out front and Mary a step or two behind. We sat down next to each other at Sam's table. Mary smiled politely. I did the same. Sam paid us no mind. The unknown blonde prattled on about some shit as her red-nail-polished fingers posed a cigarette next to her huge dangling earring. Sam cut her off and looked at me. Then he looked away again and started spinning stories about what strippers can do with their pussies: like smoking cigarettes, playing the trumpet, popping out ping-pong balls—weird shit like that. The girls all seemed to enjoy it, some more than others. After he was finished Sam turned to me condescendingly:

"The big man has pronounced that we would be welcome upstairs at his little bash," he said, smiling from ear to ear. "You want to check it out? The ladies and I were just about to make the climb."

Carla smiled a hello to me. She looked wasted, but her hair was flawless.

"Hi, Carla. How are you?" I said. "Good to see you again. Where's your dear mother gotten off to? The powder room?"

"She and I had a little fight—she went home. It's not the first time, you know—she's always gets mad when I—"

"Ah, sure Sam, I'll go upstairs," I butted in.

"I'd be glad to go to the party."

Sam shouted: "Somebody grab that boy's arm and swing him on out of here before somebody kicks his ass for being too smarmy."

Carla swept over in a bustle of hairspray and perfume and took my arm. Her body was warm and she felt real nice against my hip. She gave my butt a little squeeze. I looked over at Mary for some kind of approval and she turned away indifferently. We hardly knew each other, after all.

Carla and I stepped and stumbled our way after Sam while he used his persuasive powers on the tall blonde. Mary was again a step or two behind, her hands in her jacket pockets, dark pool eyes surveying the scene.

We went outside and walked to the back of the parking lot and then struggled up about fifteen or twenty feet of wood stairway until we came to a well-lit porch. There was a green door with a brass knocker. Sam rapped on the thing and before too long a big, hairy, olive-skinned dude opened up. The guy nodded to Sam and waved us on through, all the while eyeballing the ladies.

The apartment covered probably a quarter-square block and filled the second floor above both Tony's and an abandoned hardware store. All the woodwork was dark and unpainted. The kitchen had dark blue walls and white old-fashioned cabinets that reached up to within a foot of the ceiling. Next to the kitchen was the huge main room: six-foot high windows on three of the four walls. Burgundy velvet black-out curtains shielded us from the lights of Tower Avenue, while the other windows were left uncovered. The view of Hammond's dirty back streets and darkened warehouses was very unspectacular.

A small group of people gathered around an upright piano. A white guy with an Afro played boogie woogie. The filtered glow from several Tiffany lamps shimmied on the shiny wood floor. A fish was carved on the side of a handmade portable bar where bodies mingled in the low light. On the far end of the room, more people that I didn't know but had seen somewhere before occupied a leather couch with a Mexican blanket on the back. Others sank into old-fashioned overstuffed chairs. Soft jazz came from a cabinet stereo. On one side of the room was a walled-in section with several doors and a long, dim hallway.

We stumbled over to the bar and ordered drinks. When the gaunt young man filled the order, Sam laid a twenty on the bar. The barman pushed it back.

"Drinks are on the house. Compliments of Mr. McKay," the bartender said.

We all kind of nodded to each other, as if to say this place was the cat's ass. Sam left a five-buck tip to show how classy he was. Then we just stood around for a while and talked about nothing and tried to act cool. Sam was trying to move on the blonde and Carla was none too happy about it. She clung to me a little and I can't say I minded. Mary was off in a world of her own that I wanted to invade, but I knew the value of a bird in hand.

Then I saw our esteemed host walk determinedly over to us like he's Max Von Sydow and it's a fucking World War Two movie. He was all dressed up in a brown suit and a dark brown turtleneck. His ears seemed to stick out more than I remembered and his nose was red.

"Hello, hello," he said to Sam, extending his hands in greeting. "Glad you could come to my party—and you've brought such beautiful friends."

"Well, you know me, General—always hanging close with the beautiful people. You know, if you be standin' close to the fire, you gwine get warm, brotha." Sam loved to spin out the pimp patois.

"Here, here," I said, trying to keep with the mood.

They all looked at me like I was an eel or something so I just stood there and slithered—on the inside where it counts.

"So, Mr. Waverly... we meet again. Sam here tells me that you are close to some influential people on the other side of the bridge."

Not only did I not know what he was talking about and could only imagine what lies Sam had told him, but the guy was sounding just like an old movie where I was the sucker and he was the con man.   And all I came for was the drugs.   Maybe I wasn't cut out for high society after all. I took a healthy slug of my drink and rocked back and forth on my heels and tried to think of something to say. "Oh, I don't know how close we are... not that any of them give a fuck about me," is what I came up with.

"So what else is it you do then, for a living?" McKay pried. He looked down at me like a Sunday School teacher. "Besides represent people who don't care about you."

"I'm ah... ah, manager of a bookstore. Over in Zenith City."

"I see, uh huh.... Which bookstore do you manage?"

"Um—the ah, Wabasha."

"The Wabasha..." he let the syllables slip slowly off his tongue. "I see, uh-huh." He crossed his arms on his chest .

"Pete, my main man..." Sam jived in. "This here is one fine

get-together. You are one hell of a guy, you know what I'm saying."

McKay, graciously: "Well, thank you Sam. I appreciate it." He slowly surveyed our fivesome, checking out each of us in turn. After a pause: "Why don't you nice people come back with me to the billiard room," he purred. "It's a little more intimate there. I like to call it the billiard room, but actually, there is only an eight-ball table. Maybe someday I'll get a billiard table. A lovely view from the skylight, though. And I have some things that you will appreciate Sam. There are also some things we need to discuss. But please come along, all of you beautiful people. There's all the liquor you could possibly need. What do you say then?"

"I say you are a prince of princes," Sam schmoozed. "Come on folks, let's go where the in-crowd goes."

And so we followed, like little black sheep who had lost their way.

We moved slowly down the hallway that ran alongside the rooms I had noticed earlier. We passed by three closed doors and McKay asked the ladies' names. The amber flames of kerosene lamps flickered on the dark walls. The hallway ended at a heavily-shined thick wood door, the kind of barrier that an axe might bounce off of for a few whacks. Genuine logs formed a wall like a real cabin in the woods. Inside, there was a pool table like the man said and a fantastic skylight. Miko was there, as well as another taller, Greek-looking dude who I found out later was the captain of the ship. The guy that Miko sat in for at the poker game.

A muscle-shirted kid with a dark complexion—probably one

of the local college boys—stood behind a leather-coated bar at the back of the room. Several dark couches sat flush against the beautifully paneled walls. A chandelier, made from the metal frame of a Conestoga wagon wheel with red, tinted lightbulbs hanging downward and a stuffed duck perched on top, hung from the ceiling by a long chain. Soft light streamed out of a small hurricane lamp behind the bar and a rectangular stained glass fixture above the pool table. Two old-fashioned oil lamps flamed on both sides of a steep set of stairs leading up to a sleeping loft, where a small ladder stretched up to the skylight.

"You people go back there and have Hector make you each a nice drink," McKay said, distracted. "He's born to serve. And my god, would someone please bring me back a snifter of Courvasier. I would be so grateful." He stepped over to the pool table and struck up a conversation with the seafaring men. My group short-stepped it to the bar. Hector did indeed look like he was born to serve.

He served us all drinks. Then a silver platter with lines of coke, neatly arranged. All the time he flexed his muscles.

I knew it wouldn't be long before Sam and McKay and the two Greek dudes were shooting pool for big bucks, and goddamn if I wasn't right.

Hector and the three woman went up to the skylight and chatted and smoked. I was up there with them for a while but they drove me fucking nuts with their endless chatter. Three cranked-up women was more than I could handle—figuratively speaking.

I went down to the main room where the nine-ball action

was going fast and furious. Miko was being taken for a ride on the end of Sam's magic cue. McKay and the captain—whose name I can't remember because it was hard to pronounce and I didn't listen very well when McKay introduced us—were playing backgammon at a small round table.

I fiddled with the radio (one of those built-in wall systems) drank the free liquor and watched Sam display a touch of artistry with a pool cue. I was gradually approaching the end of my rope. Since Mary wasn't paying me any attention, I thought about leaving. Then I noticed the two pool players were having a heated discussion. I could see Sam shaking his head from side to side, his mouth forming the words: "No way, man, no way".

Miko was gesturing aggressively, screaming about his gun: "Fuckin' James Bond gun. Fuckin' James Bond gun—man, I need it. Three hundred bucks was deal you said."

"In the first place," Sam said, turning away and lighting a cigarette with the burning coal of his last one and then dropping the butt in his nearly finished drink. "I don't have the piece with me, Miko," Sam turned back around but he didn't look Miko in the eyes, he stared at the floor. "And in the second place, the price is now four hundred. Time has gone by, my son. And time, as you may well know, is money."

I thought Miko was going to give Mr. Cross a little taste of knuckle sandwich but Captain Ahab came stepping over and put his hand on the mate's shoulder and said something in his ear. Miko thought for a second, then relaxed.

"Next week I have money," he said. "Then I buy gun back." His body stiffened. He stormed over and grabbed his dark blue wool seaman's jacket from the coat rack and stormed out of that place where particular people congregated.

Mary had come down stairs when the voices rose up, drawn by the possibility of violence, I suppose. I was on a bar stool helping myself to a bottle of Bacardi, mixing it with a dash of orange juice, trying to cut the edge from the outrageous coke McKay had doled out. Hector had long since abandoned the bar in favor of the attention of Carla and the other blonde, whose name I now knew was Joy. Captain Nemo and Sam had thrown down some money on the backgammon board. Our esteemed host Pete was getting a little ragged around the edges in spite of the fact that I never saw him do any blow. I guess that expensive brandy packed a punch to it because the guy's face looked like it was about to fall off.

Mary joined me at the bar and washed down a green and yellow capsule with the vodka. Might have been a Librium—I didn't ask. McKay homed in on us like a schoolyard bully on milk money day, weaving slightly and scowling as he approached. The friendly-host mask had totally vanished. He was agitated and tight and about to let us know all about it. Here was that mean streak I had sensed at the poker game rising to the front of the class.

Before he got close enough to hear, Mary put her forearm on my shoulder and said in a warm and husky booze whisper: "I think we should leave—you and me."

In normal circumstances I would have fallen off the stool at that. But I just tensed up and found myself staring at Peter McKay's huge, bouncing Adam's apple—my jaw set in a weird, off-center position.

"Enjoying our little get-together Mr. Waverly?" Peter was trying to regain his maitre'd' schtick. "And your friend here, Miss Ranford.... I trust she is enjoying herself." He almost winced he was trying so hard.

Mary swayed back on her heels until her elbow caught the bar edge. She grinned up at McKay: "Yes, I've had a wonderful time this evening. Thank you very much Peter. This was a real far out party. Definitely the best time I've had since I got to town, for sure. Best time I've had in this town, for sure."

"And where is it you come from, then? Are you a newcomer to our fine city?" McKay said, glancing over at Sam and the captain.

"Well—ah—from Michigan.... Yeah, the U.P—Wakefield." I knew she was lying but I didn't know why.

"So you are one of those tumbleweeds that come rolling in to Hammond from parts unknown, then," Peter said.

"Well, not exactly parts unknown, Petey," Mary snickered. "If you had a map, you could find it."

McKay ignored the comment with a slight arch of his thin, yellow eyebrows and continued: "My mother was from the Upper Peninsula. somewhere—that's where I was born." His voice was thick with liquor but there was an edge sharp enough to cut stone. "She died when I was young. Some kind of lung disease—but that wouldn't interest you, then, would it...."

Jesus, I was thinking, the guy is breaking down right in front of us.

"And how about you, Keith Waverly?" McKay said, rocking back and forth. "What is it that propels you? Card dealing? Drug taking? Hedonism? Any pleasure any time... is that it...

is that what you're about? Perhaps you worship a dark power because you think it's daring and rebellious…."

"You talkin' Satan? I'm not into that goofy shit. In fact sometimes I even believe in God, but the next morning I always write it off to the drugs."

Sam came bouncing up, not knowing what was going down. "Peter, why so glum?" he said. "I know just what you need. You need to lose a little more of that scratch of yours to a little Jew. That'll make you feel better I'm sure. I'll feel better anyway." Sam dropped his cigarette in an empty Manhattan glass on the bar and leered at Mary. He rubbed his sweaty hands on his baggy white pants and pulled at the front of his old-time wool Chicago Cubs jersey with the big grease stain under the C.

McKay's skin turned pale. He tried to smile but managed only a twisted grimace. He scratched his jawbone with his thumb and forefinger and breathed harder. He sneered—that cop sneer—the one they get when they know you're dirty. "You know what I think, Sam?" McKay said in a barely restrained hiss. "I think you are a Hymie pig who shouldn't be allowed with decent people. Maybe if you bathed more often and learned to speak without profanity, people wouldn't think you were such a kike. And your friend Keith here… he reminds me of someone. Someone I see every day. Every day, over and over again for that matter. Keith"—pointing at me—"you seem to have so much to offer, yet you're just another one of the herd. The herd of greasy-haired punks who fill up the bars in this town night after night. Sleep until afternoon… don't work… all you care about is getting your rocks off and your nose full." He straightened up and tried to regain his composure. "Yes Keith, I'm afraid you remind me of those losers." Staring hard at me: "Those punks who think they're god's gift to the world, doing the world a favor just being alive, when really what they are is soft little parasites—pretty little Nancy boys trying to act tough. Collecting their welfare and their food stamps like the world owes them a living."

"The same people you're getting rich off, Peter?" Sam slurred, scratching his gut.

My stomach tightened up. "I wash my hair every day," I said. "But geeze, Peter, as much as I'd love to continue this philosophical discussion with you, I really must take my leave of this extravaganza. Gotta get up for church in the morning, you know—it's only a few hours away. I never like to miss a good sermon, you know."

McKay's jaw muscle worked overtime and he anxiously rubbed his fist. Mary had her hand to her mouth trying to press down the smile and her eyes held both fear and fascination, like a smart aleck kid facing an angry parent. Sam's face was as red as his eyeballs and he chewed on his finger.

"Peter, my friend, what is this animosity among business associates, now?" Sam said. "One in my position could be hesitant to continue our lucrative transactions, given this recent bent toward unbridled resentment and ethnic slurs you have put on display."

McKay got close and made damn sure we felt his power and his presence. So close I could smell the sour sweat breaking through his anti-perspirant. "The day I depend on the likes of you for anything in my life—"

The Greek captain was suddenly there with us. McKay saw him and shut up. He put his hand on the seaman's back and smiled at us like a snake and then moved away, speaking softly in what's-his-name's ear and gesturing out at the night in an easterly direction.

I looked at Mary and she looked at the door and we both looked at Sam and he was staring at the door. The three of us busted out of there like we were skipping study hall before the teacher came back. We moved as fast as we could, trying not to look scared, back through the rest of the party. About a dozen loaded people were still there. Three overweight women and two short skinny guys stood around the piano singing Beatle songs off-key. We walked past them and the full ashtrays and the empty glasses and the lonely hearts and made our way out the door to the fresh air of the real world. Nether one of us said anything until we hit the pavement at the bottom of the stairs and then we all three burst out in a nervous laugh. Fear pumped through me as we walked down the dark empty street toward our cars.

"Whew Sam," I said, "What's that guys' trip? He seems a little bit on the schizy side of things. We're talking weirdness in the sky with diamonds here."

"Schizy, dizzy—say what you will and you still ain't said shit, kemo sabe. We've been selling the guy some toot, me and Nick. I thought we were getting along all right—even though McKay used to be a cop. Nick and I—"

"Hold it here, goddamn it. Let me get this straight. You been selling blow to the mayor of Hammond's brother who used to be a cop and is now the assistant-mayor? How does that work for Christ' sake? Have you lost all sense of anything?"

"Wise up, Waverly, don't be so naive. Peter McKay runs the streets over here. He's got his people selling stomped-on coke and bad weed and over-priced speed in the bars while the local cops are running all the independent dealers out of town or into jail. It's been that way for about six months now, ever since our friend Petey was given the job. Why do you think they call it *Vice* Mayor, anyway?"

"Oh come on for Christ' sake. The McKay family has been the political power in this town for years, they're not about to let that kind of stuff go on. Jesus fuck, Sam. Did you ever consider the possibility that this guy was some kind of narc?'"

"No way, Jose. There's a lot of scratch to be harvested, Jacko, and this Peter is one greedy mother. Story goes that he's a bastard come from the scrotum of old John McKay Number One and the belly of some German mining camp whore. They say there're probably a few more souls out there with McKay blood that don't know it. I say watch out if there are, but let's be realistic here.... Don't kid yourself about the McKays, they've had their hands in anything they can make a buck on for years. From a building permit to the concrete for the building to the fire inspection to every other fucking thing, the McKays have got their noses in it and have for years. And I'm not sure the government even sends narcs this far north. And if they do, imagine the losers that get sent up to this frozen fucking wasteland. The ones that get sent here are probably the ones who flunked the narc test. That must be a prerequisite to being sent here. You have to flunk the narc test."

"No shit.... But think of how pissed off and mean any poor

fucker that got sent up here would be after a while, man. The guy would become an asshole, even if he wasn't one in the first place. If they sent Southern guys up here, man, it'd be like, 'Billy Bob, your assignment is Hammond, Wisconsin, where it's winter seven months of the year and rains the other five. Good luck, son.' Meanwhile, Billy Bob is thinking of ways to fuck somebody else over as bad as he's getting jacked."

"So how did Peter find out he was a McKay?" Mary asked, taking my arm and snuggling up close and making me feel real good.

"I heard that he was a cop out in Frisco," Sam said, then lit up a Marlboro with a green plastic lighter and put the lighter back in the pocket of his lined Levi jacket.. "Some say he got kicked off the force out there and came back to Hammond. They say he was hanging around the bars drinking himself to death when our poker buddy the mayor found out about him. I guess John knew about his brother from a death-bed conversation with the old man. The family had already been searching for him under the name of Klagen, or Cloggen, or maybe Klege. That's what my brother told me anyway—he and John share a love for antiques and money. That's how the poker games got going. So now you know."

"Now I'm excited," Mary said. "All this intrigue—I could stay up all night. There's a place I know where we can get a drink, just down the road. It's really cool, even at 2:30 in the morning. Who's up for that?"

Sam and I sang "Here, here" in unison, like two young Republicans at a party fundraiser.

We jumped in Sam's old Volvo and got down the road.

The blind pig was about eight blocks from the Castaway on a corner lot across from the railroad tracks. About ten vehicles were parked in front of and adjacent to the three story, wood frame, part Victorian, part Tudor structure that had definitely seen better days but still radiated a certain regal quality in spite of its tawdry surroundings. A boarded-up two story box house covered in shit-brown shingle paper stood next door; an open field and a brick car repair shop filled out the block. Across the avenue was a metal pole building with *American Brands* on a big sign. Blackened mounds of snow were everywhere.

We walked up the icy sidewalk to the porch. The air was crisp. Little stars twinkled in the sky like fresh snow on a moonlit walk. Somewhere in the neighborhood a dog complained with a cold and lonely bark. Even farther away there was a muffled shout, the slam of a door, then silence. Mary pushed the bell. The thudding bass of a stereo massaged my feet. After about thirty seconds the door opened and a guy in a Black Sabbath tee shirt, with biceps the size of tree trunks, stood in front of us.

Mary said: "Hi Bruce sweetie, these are my friends. Can we come in?"

Bruce stepped aside and held the door open and watched us like a disapproving mother mastiff as we passed quickly by.

A short hallway opened into a large living room with a scarred, uneven hardwood floor. Birch log-and-light bulb fake fire glowed inside a hearth on the far wall. Five guys played cards at a round table. Yellowed chandelier soaked up smoke. In the dining room a hawk-nosed guy with blotchy skin and sharp shoulders dealt blackjack to four men at a genuine green-felt casino table. A black vinyl and wood bar angled across another corner of the room. An eight-track player blasted out a Hendrix song. Used-to-be-pretty woman with too much peroxide and too much makeup mingled and hawked coke for ten bucks a spoon. White-shirted business man type who looked vaguely familiar was buying. A real fun place, yes sir.

I went to the bar and spent my last three bucks on a can of Budweiser. They were truly making a killing here, you could get Bud for three bucks a *six-pack* from any grocery store. I was definitely in the wrong business. Even the old days weren't like this; these guys had it going. I watched and stared at the people and wished my penchant for premonitions worked with gambling. Never had the guts or the money to try it. It was easier to cheat if you could make the cards move the way I could. Sam tried to talk me into the poker game in the front room but I wouldn't. Moving the cards on people is a weird thing.

When I wouldn't cooperate Sam dragged Mary into the blackjack game. He backed her. She won. And won again. She kept on winning. A pile of cash built up. We bought more drinks.

Soon we were smoking hash in the kitchen with bikers with names like Big Dog, Studly and Frank. They were good guys— more rebels and outlaws than criminals in the usual sense of the word. The type of guys who never forgot a favor or forgave an injury. They said they were pissed off about the way things had changed in Hammond since Peter McKay took over the streets. These guys—all they wanted was to be left alone to ride their hogs and do their drugs and keep control of the local speed market. But the times they were-a changin'.

Cross tried to make some business connections but instead he ended up buying some coke from Big Dog. I found twenty hits of the red acid in my coat pocket and gave them out to anyone who wanted them—for free. Sam bought more drinks and out came the lines. You knew Cross was really getting loose when he started handing out the toot. Soon I was grinding my teeth and my body was grinding me. Smashing Sam's head into the wall and taking Mary away with me seemed like a good idea. Instead I got the keys and went out to the car. Four-thirty in the morning and the party was almost over. For me it already was. Life was a blur. With biker's coke you usually got a speed chaser and the shit was eating away at my nervous system, you could smell the smoke. I thought about all those fucking people inside with their bad haircuts and big boots and money to burn. Fuck 'em.

I was bent over trying to light a chunk of hash impaled on the tip of a fountain pen when I heard the rumbling of a V-8. When he got out of the big '75 Impala Coupe I didn't really notice who it was. I think I was wishing for a Quaalude or a valium or something when Mary and Sam waltzed arm-in-arm out of the house. Our new guest reached the front steps about the same time they did. He stopped as the couple approached and a start of recognition coursed through his wiry body. He rose up on the balls of his feet and moved forward and bent down into Mary's face. His greasy pompadour touched her frightened forehead. The flaps of his tacky reddish leather topcoat grazed her chest. I realized it wasn't exactly a friendly conversation.

He grabbed Mary's arms; she tried to pull free, screaming at the dude. They did a little dance toward the porch. Sam backed away scared. The newcomer was manhandling her when Bruce burst out the door gripping an unopened beer bottle. He gave the asshole's greasy head a doink and Pompadour's legs buckled. He crumpled to the ground like a dying waterspout.

Bruce the mother mastiff saluted Mary and waved us off with a flip of his massive hand. Black Sabbath never looked so good. He went back inside and closed the door. Pompadour struggled to the porch on his knees, holding his head and groaning, I had a feeling it wouldn't be long before he was swearing. And after that killing us dead.

I cranked the Volvo's ignition. It shrieked—that hideous grinding noise—the engine was already running. I threw it in gear and squealed onto the street. My two companions sprinted to the car. Sam was laughing or blubbering. Mary had her head down. They jumped in and I ripped down the road like Richard Petty, who wouldn't be caught dead in a Volvo. I didn't want to be either. Little jet streams seeped out of the streetlights as we distanced ourselves from trouble. Mary was in the front with me and I could feel her body heat. Her scent engulfed me—sweet intoxication.

"Good thing Bruce came along when he did, eh, Sambo?" I said, "Or you'd be on your knees suckin' that guy's dick, right now."

"What was I supposed to do? He knew her! They were talking. He said she owed him something. Then he grabbed her—what was I supposed to do? Tackle a guy for collecting a debt? And anyway, you'd have come running out to save me before too long."

"Yeah, sure," I said.

Mary kept pushing her hair back behind her ear, over and over. "Look, that guy's just an asshole," she said "Let's leave it at that. Just one of those guys who thinks he has a right to fuck me just because he spends money on drinks and stuffs money down my panties. He doesn't understand that I fuck who I want to fuck. You know, I get that shit all the goddamn time. Most guys eventually leave you alone. This dude, though, thinks he runs the town—won't take no for an answer. Jesus, I saw him bust some poor guy's head open right in the bar the other night. Nobody did a thing. He hit the poor guy with a beer bottle, just like Bruce did to him. Only he deserved it."

"I guess he had bad Karma," I said.

We all laughed. It wasn't the most believable laugh you'll ever hear. Mary wiped away tears and smeared her mascara.

I loved the smeared mascara look.

"No, really…" she said, "he'll kick the shit out of you for looking at him the wrong way. He's bad news, bad shit. My girlfriend told me that nobody messes with him around here because he has some important friends here in town."

"Huh?" Sam said, returning from a trance. "Well all right. You know—all that excitement made me horny. Mary I think you owe us both a blow job for saving you from a fate worse than death."

Mary shot him the bird and said, "Fuck you, Sam."

"I was just kidding," Sam said. "You know how much respect I have for you Mary. Why, you're like my dear old mother to me...."

"You're an asshole Sam," I said.

Mary laughed like a mocking bird high on mountain ash berries.

I drove the Volvo back down to Tony's Cabaret. The streets were empty except for the trash skidding along the sooty ice at curbside. I pulled in behind my sled and threw the Volvo into neutral. I got out. Mary got out. I got in my Olds and reached over to unlock the door for her. Sam drove off in a hurry and we did the same. I searched for the darkest, most deserted street of them all to take us out of there. I got turned around on my way to the old Arrowhead Bridge and we ended up on Billings Drive. I found myself relaxing out there, rolling slowly along the river and the bay on a nice smooth piece of asphalt. Just a half-mile from the North End but another world to be sure. Even my Olds rode like a Caddy out there. There were mansions to the left of me and mansions to the right of me. Mary smoked and stared wide-eyed out the window. She searched through my box of eight tracks and picked out "L. A. Woman" by the Doors.

We came to one particularly lavish mansion: a long, brick three-story with white and green Cape Cod shutters on the many windows and a huge four-pillar entryway with a shingled roof. At the end of a lengthy paved driveway, a large porch light lit up a patch of the night displaying for all to see a brand-new silver-gray Lincoln Continental and a dark blue Pontiac station wagon, the kind with fake wood side panels. The name on the mailbox was McKay, John. My friend the Mayor.

"How do people get houses like that, Keith?"

"Do I look like I know?"

"They say there's blood and lies behind every fortune. Do you believe that? I do."

"You and the Students for a Democratic Society. All I know is that sometimes it seems that the smiling 'civic leaders' of the world are putting the squeeze on everyone else. They get their pictures in the paper on Sunday and on Monday they find another way to ratchet down the wages and jack up the prices. The jobs get tougher and the hours get longer so they can stay longer in the Cayman Islands and live off their tax-free bank accounts. These guys are dealing off the bottom of the deck every chance they get and we just have to take it like an enema."

"You don't have to take it all the time, Keith. There are ways to get satisfaction."

"You mean like the Symbionese Liberation Army?"

She grinned an evil grin and burst out singing: "*Patty Hearst heard the burst of Roland's Thompson gun—and bought it.*"

Her voice wasn't half bad.

I joined in on the butchering of Warren Zevon and together we had a made-for-TV moment:

> *Roland the headless Thompson gunner*
> *Talkin' 'bout the man.*
> *Roland the headless Thompson gunner..."*

Neither one of us knew any more of the words, which was okay, because by that time we were back on track and approaching the rickety old Arrowhead Bridge. I was staring at the amber glow coming from the lights of the abandoned toll booths when a big Impala roared by in the opposite direction, its chassis bouncing wildly on the bumpy potholed pavement.

"Jesus," I said. "That was the tough guy. I guess he recovers fast. I hope Sam is out of there."

"His name is Johnny Wells," she said stoicly. She glanced back nervously at the fading tail lights and chewed on a fingernail. "My friend Stephanie—who's a dancer at the club—she was with me in the cab the other day—she went out with him for a while. He told her all these stories about how he used to rip off bars and drugstores around Minneapolis. He'd burst in with a nylon stocking over his head and a sawed-off shotgun, screaming he was going to blow their heads off. I guess he got busted for something this one time—and when the cops were searching his house looking for evidence—well, they were looking and looking and weren't finding anything and Johnny was getting pretty cocky, I guess. But anyway, Steph said that he always stashed his shit inside the cover of his living room light. And so—when the cops turned on the light—there were these shadows from the pill bottles showing through the glass cover. I guess you could plainly see them there. Dumb fucking Johnny. The shit was from some drugstore in South Dakota—or North— one of them. Johnny swore at the cops—called them assholes and pigs and shit and they beat him up, but he just laughed at them. The worst part is they only got him for that one pharmacy job—and he got out of jail real fast. He's one of the reasons Steph is still stripping—I think she wants to get him back which is a bummer because she's my best friend."

"Good thinking on her part. Sounds like *Taming of the Psycho*."

"Yeah well, she was only trying to piss off her parents by stripping anyway and ah—"

"Do you know that you're coming to Zenith City with me? Can you call some girlfriend or someone to get your stuff from the hotel 'cause he could be after you, you know."

"Yeah, I can do that—I just won three hundred bucks—I can pay for a room, too."

"You won three hundred fucking dollars?"

The lights on the bridge jumped and darted and the ancient wood creaked and groaned with every roll of the cars wheels. Zenith City's hillside beckoned. I tried hard to uncoil the muscles in my shoulders while Mary kept on yakking. She rapped about her ex-husband who tried out for the Packers. She admitted that she was excited by Johnny Wells when she first met him, before she knew what he was like. That one really hurt, I couldn't believe it. Something ached inside me but I was too burned out to figure out what.

I brought her to the Voyageur Motel. Something about the sight of those two bearded beaver-hatted canoe paddlers on that big bright sign that always made me feel safe—just like Kojak did.

I shut off the car and she moved over quickly and grabbed my jacket and pulled me to her and laid on a brief but extremely warm kiss. Her warm hand found its way beneath my shirt and her electric fingers pinched my left nipple. It still twinges when I think about it. It's twinging now.

Mary bounced quickly across the parking lot and walked up the metal stairway to the motel office with her head held high. I knew it was time for me to go home. Just what I wanted to do, go home and sleep. Yeah you bet.

* * *

It took me hours before I finally found sweet Morpheus and when I finally did succumb, eerie tormenting dreams joined me there: There was a poker game at a circular table. Sam Cross and the McKay brothers and my red-headed roommate Mickey were the players. Every once in a while one of those guys would throw paper money on the floor. Then I would crawl out from underneath a table on the other side of the room and go across the floor on my hands and knees to the cash and take it and crawl back out of the picture. From under the table I could see a large window on the wall across from me. On the other side of the glass Nick Cross was pulling levers and studying me while Mary stood behind him weeping—a scarf around her head. I got up and ran out the door in panic and I bumped smack into my ex-wife, who acted like I didn't exist. An empty feeling hit the middle of my gut just as I was jerked awake by the squawking phone.

My eyes struggled to focus on the square plastic alarm clock. Eleven o'clock in the a.m, it said. The real manager of Wabasha Book—my boss—was on the line: "Keith. Keith… is that you?" His weasely voice held a touch of I-gotcha. "You don't sound very good… This is Jim Spurlean. I'm calling to tell you that because of that stunt you pulled the other night at the bookstore, you're fired. Don't bother to come in—I'll have your check sent to you."

"What stunt is that Jim? What are you fucking talking about?"

"That little bit with the Pine-Sol."

"Whattaya mean? I cleaned up the fucking movie booths with the Pine-Sol—just like I'm supposed to do."

"You poured the Pine-Sol directly on the floor. I live upstairs, remember? Linda and I woke up gagging from the overwhelming stench of Pine-Sol, at four a.m.! We had to open all the windows and leave the place—for about eight hours."

"Well, I guess I did use a little too much. I was in a hurry to get out of that fucking pit. I had an important appointment."

"That's another thing. Jimmy LeFave said he saw you in Delaney's at 10:30, which means you closed the store early. That's enough to get you fired right there."

"Fuck Jimmy LeFave. He's a fucking liar. It was at least 10:45 before I got there—the traffic was bad. And while we're at it, fuck you too, you fucking worm. I was getting sick of selling that fucking porno anyway, you fucking asshole. Firing me is a goddamn favor."

Spurlean sputtered on the other end and I hung up and went back to bed.

After what seemed like no time at all but was really an hour later the phone rang again. God I hated the phone. This time it was a conduit to Sam Cross:

"Morning, sunshine boy," he said. "How's every little thing this morning."

"Horseshit. Especially now that I found out you made it back alive. I was hoping the hood had you tied up in his bathroom or something, making you blow him for your supper. So what the hell do you want Sam?" I rubbed the sleep from my eyes. My nose was clogged and my head pounded. The house was cold.

"I have to bring my car in for a brake job this afternoon. I thought maybe you and your Irish prick roomie might want to go out for lunch and then afterwards you can pick me up when at the car shop."

"Yeah I guess. I don't even know if Mickey's here but I could use something in my stomach."

"You want the rest of the acid then? I'll bring it over—the green, I mean."

"Yeah, sure. No problem. Maybe I can find someone to take the whole lot."

"You got the jing for the last batch?"

Sam never talked business when he was partying. He always saved it for the next day when you were sober and able to feel the pressure he put on you.

"Not all of it. I gave the rest of the shit away to those bikers last night. I guess I owe you for those."

"Fucking hippie, Waverly. Maybe all that shit you smoke is draining your ambition, huh."

"What ambition?"

"Fucking hippie freak. Oh well, nothing we can do about you."

He sighed. "I'll bring over the other—we'll see what you can do."

He hung up and I hung up and I thought about a shower.

Forty minutes later when I came out of the steamy bathroom the stereo in the living room was pounding away. I wrapped a towel around me and went out to see what was going on.

Sam and Mickey were drinking bottles of Bud from out of a cardboard case that sat with one flap open in the middle of the empty Minnesota Power wire spool that served as our living room table. I got dressed and brushed my wiry black hair and looked in the mirror. If I stared hard enough I could see my life eating away at me like a giant locust.

Mickey and Sam exchanged unpleasantries in the living room:

"There are no Jewish alcoholics, Mickey. You Irish are the kings of Lush Mountain," Sam said.

"What do you call yourself then, Sam," Mickey said, "a soused sheeny?"

This friendly badgering continued while we drove to the Sunnyside Café; only now the two of them had me for a whipping boy and they took full advantage:

"Did you get your wick wet last night with the exotic dancer, Waverly?" Sam said. "Did she throw you a gratitude fuck?"

"Fuck you Sam."

"Isn't he a beauty Mick? Spends the wee hours with a coked-up stripper and he doesn't get no leg."

"Yep, he's a sweetheart," Mickey said, flashing his oversize teeth and grinning like Howdy Dowdy on steroids.

* * *

We took a booth near the front door of the cafe. Sam ordered a steak sandwich with mashed potatoes and gravy and Mick had a burger and fries. I went for the steak-and-egg special, the Lumberjack Breakfast. A train rumbled by on the tracks outside while we waited. Mick went over by the front window and played the pinball machine with his beer bottle resting on the glass. The skinny old fry cook darted back and forth in front of the order window wiping his hands on his grease stained apron. Smoke floated around the room and conversations hummed along. Sam lit a cigarette and threw down the rest of his beer in one swallow.

After the food came, I bit down on a piece of steak and felt the caving crunch of a filling as it broke free of a bottom molar. Into my hand rolled a black chunk of metal and fragment of jagged tooth.

"Jesus fucking Christ," I said. "Fuck!"

Sam crowed: "Good one, Waverly… that's good. Looks like you're falling apart, my man. You're a real peach. That reminds me… I talked to Nick this morning and he's still pissed off about the poker game. He blames me, and you too, for not giving him an edge. He—"

"I told you before the game I wouldn't cheat for you guys anymore. I'm tired of it. Nick could've given me the boot right then if he didn't want me there."

"You pick a great time to get a conscience, when you're into us for ten big ones. But relax, pal. He mostly blames me—just because I got lucky on a few draws and a last card or two and ended up making a couple coins. He might be thinking you and I had an outside deal going."

"You better tell him different, asshole. What happened to his foolproof scam, anyway?"

"Nick forgot the old signals. Certain subtle signals, like touching a specific part of your face a certain way or holding one shoulder higher than the other. He wasn't doing it right. It's subtle shit. Eyebrows… eyelashes… He lost it when the game got tense."

"But you cleaned up, Sam."

"Yes I did."

"What did he say to you, man?"

"First thing he does is start yelling that I'm a loser and a scumbag…. Says our father would piss on me if he was alive. Then he tells me that I have to start paying rent on my room."

"Big punishment. But, ah—shouldn't you have split your winnings with him?"

"Yeah, maybe, but he's the one that screwed up, not me. I'm not giving him a sheckle. Which reminds me, I need you to drive me somewhere tonight after I drop off my car. Got to see Miko about 'fucking James Bond gun'. His ship is still in port here, getting some repairs. I got to meet him after he gets paid so he can buy back his stuff."

"I thought it was just the gun."

"A nice watch, too. Rolex. I won that throwing the bones after the poker game. Poor Greek douchebag doesn't know when to stop."

"They must pay those bastards pretty good."

"The watch is probably a knock-off. He didn't seem too worried about it. The gun, though, is another story. I'll tell you what, Keith. I'll knock half of what I collect from your tab just for driving me."

"Sounds cool," Mickey said, swallowing beer. "Hey, ah—aren't you guys afraid of getting jumped or something?"

"That's why your big roomie is coming along, Mickey my man. He's-a my muscle."

"Bull-fucking-shit," I said, rubbing my tongue against the emptiness that once was my tooth.

Sam said: "Whatsamatter, you scared, tough guy? No? Forget about it, I'm just kidding. It'll be okay—the ship had some kind of breakdown and most of the sailors are gone. After a paycheck, even the skeleton crew will be in town sucking up the sauce. My guy will probably be the only one on board, who knows. I just need a chauffeur, not a body guard."

"Ah, okay, then," I said. "I need to do something…."

"I speak a little Greek myself, you know," Sam said. "My mother was part Greek."

"Say something in Greek, Sam," Mickey said.

"Fuck me in the ass, Zorba!" Sam howled and then ordered another beer.

We finished our beers and Sam paid the bill and we left. Mickey went home and Sam and I drove over to Zenith City and dropped off his car and then went to C.Z. Wilson Sporting Goods, where Sam charged up a bunch of new equipment for the softball season on the team account: bats, balls, and even a first baseman's mitt. We threw the gear in my trunk and I drove Sam to his basement apartment in the East Hillside.

On my way back home, an incredible longing for summer hit

me hard, followed by a strong premonition that I'd never see summer again.

* * *

Around seven that night I pulled Mickey's Ford station wagon into a spot on the boardwalk near Delaney's Bar. A big white ghost of smoke rose up from the Zenith City Steam Plant. The tall chimney cut a shadow in the light of the full moon. The neon Delaney's sign glowed orange. It was a tough drive over, the steering on that Ford pulled so hard to the right that it was a real struggle. Mickey treated the car like it was a Sherman Tank, always bashing it into shit. I imagine your arms would get strong after awhile, driving a car like this. Mick said he needed to run out into the country to do some kind of deal so we traded cars and I ended up with the death wagon.

Sam and I had a couple drinks at the bar and then hit the road. He was wired out of his gourd.

The side of the highway faded into darkness as we turned off the asphalt onto the gravel strip that led to the Heller Dock. Axle-deep potholes dotted the narrow path. I wrestled past the grain storage terminals that loomed on both sides. Cross reached into his worn black overcoat and brought out a dirty white towel. He unwrapped the towel on the seat, revealing the sweet little Walther PPK. Sweat beaded on his forehead and his eyes were glazed pinholes and he talked way too fast and his jaw kept jerking from side to side.

"Look at this little sweetie," he said, waving the piece around in shaky hands. "I almost hate to give it back. It's even got some German writing on it here…. It's so—" Then he jerked his head suddenly and pointed to a dark slice of gravel angling off to the right. "Take a ralph right there and go down to the big boat—name of the J.R. Ambrozio. You just park and wait for me. I'll go up and get this taken care of and then we can go drink. I won't be long." His eyeballs floated upward inside their sockets.

So I just sat there trying to relax. I stared at the water in the empty slip in front of me and felt glad I didn't have to play bodyguard. The beam of the ship's lone spotlight caught the oil-black surface of the bay as it danced and slid like something haunted. I looked around at the hulking ship and the giant gray towers that soon would be filled to the brim with grain. I lit up a smoke and tried to tune the radio but found only static. When Sam wasn't back in fifteen minutes I got a little antsy so I turned the station wagon around to face out toward the exit in case we had to make a fast getaway. The muffler was a tad loud and that's why I didn't hear the popping sounds coming from inside the J.R. Ambrosia.

Cross was flushed and sweaty when he got back, breathing hard. I wrote it off to his being high or excited from the whole money collection thing.

"How did it go?" I asked him as we bounced down the ruts towards out of there.

"Fine. Fine. Just let's get out of here before the son of a bitch changes his mind."

"What's he gonna do Sam, run after us?"

"He's gotta gun. Remember, dip shit?"

"I think we're safe now," I said as we turned onto U.S. Highway 2 a minute later. "Where to, Mr. Boss man—and how much money did I make?"

"You get your full load plus a tip. But let's get the hell out of here, back over the bridge. I don't feel right in this goddamn town. Let's get back to Delaney's; I'm buying. Goddamn it— I'm going to get fucking wasted. Maybe find a little poontang. I deserve it, for the chrissakes."

Back at Delaney's and drunk. This was getting old. But the booze helped to slow things down in my head and I liked listening to the juke box and remembering the good times. Times from a past that now seemed farther away than ever before. I liked remembering and smoking on those Kool cigarettes and bullshitting with the folks. My words seemed to hold such meaning.

Cross got extremely hammered. I had ever seen him knock it down like that. He had that owl-eyed, night-of-the-living-dead face going. He bought drinks left and right and reeled around the bar like a human pin ball. I sat on a barstool and stared at the rows of pretty bottles. I was doing a lot of that and I was getting pretty good. It takes practice. Nothing like another fun evening at your neighborhood bar, I always say, and if you're miserable you might as well be miserable drunk.

I went to the juke box and searched the titles for "Born to Lose." It wasn't there. I played Dylan's "Girl of the North Country" instead and thought about Mary. I didn't plan on going to see her dance because how in the hell can you date a stripper? How could you watch guys stuff five-dollar bills down your sweetheart's panties? I couldn't come up with an answer.

Linda Ronstadt sang "Dark End of the Street"and Faron Young did "Live Fast; Die Young" (and leave a beautiful corpse). I sat back in my position at the bar and wallowed in the pain as best I could, swallowing alcohol in ever-growing swills. I was reaching some new depth when Cross jostled into me from behind:

"Jesus Christ… Jeesuus Christ…. Keitho, Keitho… we gotta get high man, we gotta get high. Hey… whatsamatter with you, pal? You look like yer dick just fell off or somethin'."

"No, man,that fell off a long time ago. I got one of those implants don't ya know."

"You mean one a-them erector sets?"

"That's it man, that's it. All I have to do is crank this little winch they installed in my hip and voila—hard-on city. It's pretty cool…. It works for me."

His mouth twisted up into a psycho smile.

"Come on Keitho, let's go outside for a toot." he put his arm around my shoulder. "My treat."

"As much as I'd like to partake in anything as rare as you treating, Sam, I'm gonna pass. I'm going home." I took one last swallow of drink and set my glass down on the bar. "I've had enough of this shit."

By the time I hit Wisconsin soil I was worn out from fighting with the steering wheel. Whatever business Mickey had must have been over because, sure enough, there was my Olds parked on a dead end section of John Avenue across the street from the bar. I rolled the wagon into the parking lot and breathed a sigh of relief. I got out quickly and rubbed my arms and went into the bar. A cold wind blew dust in my eyes. Down the street tires squealed.

The Times was about half full and Judy was tending. Mickey sat on a barstool, teetering forward over two half-full Manhattan glasses. I was in no mood for the bar scene I guess because everybody in there seemed dirty and stupid. Mick was seven sails to the sunset and then some. He looked basically incoherent but when he saw me he managed, weak and raspy, to eke out: "Judy darling, get my roomie anything he wants. Anything he so desires—I mean it." His voice trailed off.

I had a beer so as not to offend him but I drank it fast. I couldn't help but think there was something wrong. Mickey kept looking at me with a curious sadness or like maybe there was something that he knew but wasn't telling me. That half-grin half-grimace faded and changed before my eyes as if some force was pulling him up out of his stupor.

"Be careful when you're driving home," I said. "That Ford is like driving a bicycle through a mud hole. How in the hell can you not bang into shit with that fucking piece-of-shit?"

"Don't worry about me, Dad, Judy's gonna drive me home in her car. Besides all I need is a little of this and I'll be just fine." He reached into his shirt pocket and fumbled out a little glassine bag. It tumbled out of his thick fingers and flopped down on the bar next to his drink.

"Put that shit away, you fucking idiot," I said. "Put it in your pocket and keep it there, goddamnit. What the hell is that?"

"Just a little Green Bay Speedball…. Some bikers I know mix it up."

"Green Bay Speedball? …Gimme a fucking break. Is that what you were doing with my car today you fucking asshole?"

"I refuse to answer on the grounds that it may incriminate me."

"Yeah, yeah—fuck you too. I'm leaving."

I slipped out the side door and headed down the dark boulevard towards my Olds. Horns honked and a siren wailed and some guy yelled, JENNY! When I got to the car my front tire was flat and I remembered then that Mickey had borrowed my tire iron a couple weeks back. I walked back over to the Ford and pushed down the door handle and pulled open the tailgate and grabbed the greasy green blanket that held the tools. Then I heard the pavement scrape behind me. I jerked around in time to see a pair of shiny black shoes with a man in them, coming up fast. I grabbed the tire iron but I couldn't use it because a pair of gorilla arms put me in a full-Nelson and sweaty hands were jamming a stinging, stinking cloth over my mouth and nose.

I gagged and passed through nausea on my way to blacked out.

Then I was a pinball dropping down—slowly bouncing—pinging—rolling down to the hole where the bottom drops out and you're out of the game.

I woke up with eyes burning and lips searing and head pounding. Tongue as thick as a barbecued lizard. After a few seconds it dawned on me that I was in Peter McKay's living room and strapped to a straight-backed wood chair. Some kind of weird black leather harness was holding me tight while somewhere in the distant reaches of my fuzzy brain William Tell was aiming an arrow at the apple on my head. Except for the funny green hat, Tell looked just like Peter McKay.

A deep voice resonated through the mist: "Well, sleepyhead, you're finally coming around. I was worried that we had lost you."

When the fog finally cleared, there was McKay in the flesh, sitting in a big leather winged-back chair with brass tacks around the edges. He was dressed in dark blue—the color of a cop's uniform—with black leather boots. He held one arm across his chest and cradled his other at the elbow and stroked his chin thoughtfully. "Those thick-headed bastards can get a little heavy-handed at times. I told them to be careful—not to harm your face. I like to think of you and I as friends."

I was groggy like after a tooth extraction and my teeth vibrated. "Friends? You might have tried a written invitation. What is this shit with the harness anyway? Was I throwing a fit or something? What's going on for Christ sake? What did I do to deserve this?"

"That is for me to determine, Keith. But you were brought here because you were seen entering a station wagon that I have reason to believe was involved in a theft."

"That's my roommate's car—I was just getting my lug wrench…. I couldn't find mine; I've got a flat; you can check on that. Is that a crime nowadays?"

"And who is your friend, then?"

"Mickey Kirby, he bartends at the High Times; but he couldn't have done anything."

"Why is that?"

"Aah—because he's pretty much just a harmless loadie, that's all. What the hell is the problem, anyway?"

"Someone has taken something very valuable of mine. And it is possible that a vehicle much like yours was involved. Someone saw a similar vehicle leaving the scene."

"Do you thing I'd be stupid enough to be hanging out in the bars if I had ripped you off? I'd be the fuck outta here, man. I'm not that dumb, man. And besides, I don't steal."

"But you cheat at cards?"

"No I don't. Not anymore. Not for years…."

He threw me a sharp look and stood up. "So you say, Keith, so you say. But the truth shall be told here, tonight. You will see," he said, hovering over me.

"And I don't know anything about any theft," I said. But a few things were starting to click in my brain while I sweated.

"Tell me, Keith. Have you seen our friend Sam lately?" McKay's jaw muscle pulsed like a strobe light in a disco and his breathing was heavy and labored. I swear I heard him wheeze.

"Sam? No, not since we were in your billiard room, at your party. I haven't seen him since then." I lied, and I was a good liar, ever since I was a kid.

"And do you expect to see him soon?"

"I don't know. He always calls me. I don't go out of my way to see him, believe me. Ah—ah, Peter—can I leave now? What do you think? Whattaya say we at least take off the harness…. I'm not going to run, I promise."

"We'll just have to be patient. Patience is a bitter vine but it yields sweet fruit. You really need to try a little. Right now the boys are looking through the car to see if there is anything of interest to us; you need to relax for a little while longer." He looked down at me and curled his lips in a particularly weird smile. "How about a drink while we wait? Do you like Irish whisky?"

"I've never tried it. But I could use a shot of just about anything right now."

"There is a bottle over in the corner there, in that little cabinet. If I loosen your bonds will you get us each a shot and be a good boy?"

"Yeah, sure—anything you say."

He came behind me and slowly unfastened the metal buckles. His fingers strayed up and lightly brushed my earlobe and as he pulled off the harness his other hand slid down my chest and lingered at the right nipple. What a strange feeling. I got up quickly and scampered to the teak—or mahogany—liquor cabinet and searched anxiously for any large container I could find. Classy guy that he was there were several crystal brandy snifters lined up on the shelf. I knew you weren't supposed to put whisky in a snifter but I prayed Emily Post would allow me this one social faux pas and I poured. A normal shot for him and a half glass for me. My hands shook. I collapsed back down on the couch and took a magnum slosh of the whiskey.

"Smooth," I said.

"You know, Keith," McKay said, rolling the hootch gently around inside the goblet. "I used to be a police officer in San Francisco—just a few years back. I was assigned to the homosexual district, where the little queer boys hang out. I used to patrol the buses. My job was to keep the boys from having sex on the city transit busses, can you imagine that? I'll tell you, I used to catch these guys with their fists up each other's ass—sucking dick—jacking each other off, all kinds of things like that." His eyes grew wider. "One time—I caught two guys actually trying to fuck in the back of the goddamn bus, can you imagine that?" His voice quivered slightly. "You should've seen the size of the cock on this one guy. Heh heh. The way those boys carried on out there…." He sipped his drink for a moment and looked away and then set the glass back down on the table and rubbed his hands on his thighs. "I was born right here in Hammond, Keith—did you know that?"

"Ah, no, I ah—"

"Lived at St. Francis Children's Home for twelve years. You know the place? It's right over by the highway—a museum now."

"Really? I've been to that museum. I've taken my son there." I hoped he'd have mercy on my pitiful paternal self.

"You have a son? You're not doing him much good sitting here, are you? Perhaps he's better off without you."

"Well, I—"

"You know what they used to do to you if you disobeyed at St. Francis, Mr. Waverly?"

"No, I said, but I was sure he was going to tell me.

"They used to put you under the wood stove in the kitchen and make you stay there until they were good and ready to let you out. Which was usually a long time after you started sweating and roasting under there. But that was nothing like what could happen to you later—at night. You ever lived in an orphanage, Mr. Waverly?"

"No. Just a house."

He frowned and stood up. He refilled his glass and began circling the room like I was carrion and he was hungry. "Tell me more about your relationship with Samuel Cross," he said, smiling like Santa Claus at Easter time.

"Like what, for example?"

"How about starting with when you expect to see him next?"

"Like I said, I have no idea. He just calls me when he wants to see me. There's no particular pattern to it." I stared at my whisky.

"And what is it exactly that he talks to you about, when you see him?"

"Dope, of course. Mostly coke. Sometimes a few pills—acid. And the money I owe him, of course. I know some people with some cash to invest and ah…. But I assumed that you knew all of that, um Peter. I mean, the way you and him do business together, I'd expect you talk about me all the time. I bet you've talked about a lot of things with either Sam or Nick Cross. And Sam Cross gets around, if you know what I mean."

"Yes—yes—I see your point." He paused and looked around. "Are you feeling better now?"

The guy was good cop and bad cop all rolled into one.

"Nothing like good Irish whiskey to put a man right. Right, Keith? You got any Irish in you, boy?"

"A little," I said, "on my mother's side." I wondered what was coming next; fear spun in my gut.

"Thank God for the McKays and their Irish sentimentality, eh, son? Where would we, the good people of Hammond, be without it?" He smiled wistfully. "I expect that the boys will have completed their search soon, so why don't you and I stroll into the billiard room and wait for the verdict. It will be easier to relax in there." He stood up and brushed down his suit with the palms of his hands, looking self-satisfied.

I can't say I was too excited about going into the back room with the savior of San Francisco but I figured it was a lot better than getting a knuckle massage from those ham-fisted, raisin-brained tough guys. I knew they were good at ass-kicking and head-shooting from what they did to Harvey Dornan so long, long ago when I was just a simple cab driver and occasional card cheat. Back when times were good.

We walked down the hallway and McKay stayed a step behind me and sucked in deep breaths. I could feel his eyes boring into me.

We got inside the billiard room and the Irishman walked directly over to the bar. I sat on a stool and rubbed my eyes some more and tried to get a grip. Then my esteemed host brought out a black leather briefcase from behind the bar and slid open the thick shiny zipper and out came a big bag of rocky yellowish cocaine. The stuff looked brutish. He dropped a hunk the size of a golf ball onto the shiny wood surface of the bar and then produced a single-edge razor blade and a three-inch silver straw.

"I have this new supply in, that I just acquired. From a new source. I want you to try some… tell me what you think of it. See for yourself. It's the finest—hasn't been cut as of yet."

"Aren't you going to join me?" I said and shaved off some of the soft and sparkly powder. You never could tell what this old duck was going to do. I had a real bad feeling just the same.

"No thank you," McKay said properly, almost mincing. "I only do it on special occasions. And then I smoke it. Deviated septum you see," he said, tapping the bridge of his schnoz with a thick, index finger. Snorting doesn't agree with me—unpleasant habit, really. Too much mucous. "

"Free base, eh?"

"I prefer to think of it as modern man's version of opium smoking."

I sniffed up the stuff.

"Oh yeah? Well, that's an interesting way of looking at it. And say, Peter, you are right—this is some pretty good shit." I put on the fake smile. "And now look, my glass is empty." Jesus, the false bravado.

McKay grabbed the bottle of Hennessy's and set it down in front of me. "Help yourself," he said blankly, strangely out of character.

He walked over to the windows on the far side of the room and gazed out at the street for a while, then pulled the curtains shut and came back to the pool table. His opened hand tapped the cue ball softly into a corner pocket. He seemed to struggle with himself as he poured himself some more whisky.

"This is an unfortunate situation we have here, Keith. I certainly hope that you are not involved."

"Involved in what?"

"Robbery. And murder."

My heartbeat kicked up a notch and my throat constricted.

"I didn't read anything about anything like that in the papers," I said, innocent as a day old lamb.

There was a knock on the door.

McKay walked over and opened it and stood there a moment talking in muffled tones to someone I couldn't see. He closed the door and walked over until he stood above me looking down, his hands on his hips.

"Keith," he said earnestly, with something that passed for happiness. "My men didn't find anything inside the station wagon. Just a lot of fast food garbage and empty beer cans from what I understand. Of course you already knew that— correct? My man also said that you had a tire iron in your hand when they found you, so it seems as if you are telling the truth." He paused and turned away, his hand to his chin. He thought for a bit, then came back hard. "I want you to understand something before you go, Mr. Keith Waverly. I want you to understand completely. This drug culture you are involved in isn't for everyone. There are pitfalls and snares out there that you can't imagine, and even you can get caught in them, don't kid yourself. Someone has to make sure that the right players are in the game and around here that someone is me. One thing I know for sure is that you can't let anybody push you around. You give them an inch, and they'll take everything you have."

"I know you're the boss around here, Mr. McKay. You don't have to worry about me."

"Please, Keith. Call me Peter. I like the way you say it. And before you leave, I insist that you try some of my extra special stuff. I've got just a little left. Let's say it's my way of my apologizing for any inconvenience I may have caused you. This is something I only give to a *very few special* friends."

"Well, geeze—I'm flattered. But what I was really thinking about was leaving—I ah— but I suppose one more wouldn't hurt, uh-huh, as long as you've got the special shit out and all, I mean."

"Good, good," McKay said, smiling and clasping his hands together. He went over to his case and extracted an amber colored vial. Soon there was a new pile of powder and two three-inch lines. "There you are," he said. "I know you will appreciate what this does."

I took the straw and snorted one of the rows. "Whoa," I yipped, feeling the burn. "I never did any toot like this before. It tastes strange."

"Go ahead and have the rest," he said as he dug around in a cabinet in the back of the bar. "You'll be glad you did."

Once again I took the noxious powder into my nostrils. *White powder, white powder, my brain is like chowder.*

"That one didn't taste any different, man—what kind of coke is this, anyway?"

Another knock at the door.

"Special coke," McKay said, as he glided to the door like Plastic Man. He seemed to be fading away a vast distance; then my stomach flew out my ears.

"Say—what was that stuff, anyway? God damn, I never felt like this before.... Anybody here?"

When Johnny Wells strutted into the room I was floating— and falling. Falling backwards into a long dark tunnel where my head was already waiting.

Bottom of the Slide

Lying on my back on an isolated beach—hot and humid. The sun feels good after a long winter.

She giggles beside me and puts her hand on me down low where I like it.

Her body is beautiful and tan.

She has no face.

I jerked awake, choking back a silent scream.

I was lying on my back all right but on some kind of bench in a large dark steam room—jaybird fucking naked. Four other nude men hovered over me and stared down at me like vultures at a dead bird potluck. A bearded fat guy knelt over my crotch. I snapped to an upright position and nausea rushed to my head and I gagged.

"Get the fuck away from there," I snarled.

The vultures stepped back a little but kept on staring. I got to my feet and stumbled for the aisle.

I was on the middle level of a rising set of benches and could see the door across the room, so I made for it. My foot slipped on the second step and I started to fall headlong for a face-to-face with the concrete floor but at the last instant a silver-haired guy with a hairy chest and a towel around his waist stood up and caught me. He held on firmly and looked thoughtfully into my eyes.

"Be careful young man," he said, his deep voice bouncing around inside the sauna. "You might get hurt."

He let me go.

I waded through the steam and burst through the door into a

small room filled with wood lockers and benches. I franticly opened the lockers and looked for my clothes. At about the twentieth try I found my pants and shirt but no shoes or under- wear. I kept trying the locker doors and found a nice old gray and black Harris Tweed overcoat inside one. It fit. A pair of brown wingtips and rubber zippered boots in another. The shoes were too small but the boots slid easily over my bare feet.

Beyond the locker room was an open area with three or four hallways. One led to the stairway going up and the others went to some small rooms. The door of one of the rooms was partially open and inside two guys were fucking and grunting on top of a small cot. I looked away and climbed toward the light at the top of the carpeted stairs and stared down at the faded floral patterns. The fuck dudes grunted and groaned behind me. Big red flowers on the dark green wallpaper.

Behind the desk in the old-fashioned, fern-filled lobby sat a fifty-ish guy with thinning red hair who looked like he'd seen too much of one kind of life.. I went over to him and leaned forward and put one hand on his nice brown desk to steady myself. There was a fan on the desk, but it wasn't spinning. I was. Look at me, the Prince of Dizzy. "Say, ah, kind sir," I said, "I was wondering if I—how I—what the—ah, hell… never mind."

"You wondering how you got here, by any chance?" He said knowingly. "I wouldn't be surprised." He drummed his thick short fingers on the desk and looked up at me with empty eyes.

"Yeah, I guess. Whattaya mean by that?"

"I mean, your buddies brought you in a little after ten this morning. You were pretty drunk. They thought the steam would sober you up, they said. Why you could hardly walk, but you were singing. Once in awhile, anyway, so I figured you'd be all right."

"Singing, eh? No shit. Ya don't say. What song?"

"It's a long way to Tipperary."

Suddenly there was a big hole in my head and some horrible voice was chanting a Hindu curse loud enough to make me scream. I had to get out of there. "See ya," I said. Beads of sweat broke out on my forehead as I shuffled through the door.

As soon as I hit the street I knew I was in downtown Zenith City: Zenith City Sauna hanging above my head on a gray plastic sign. No memory of getting here. I couldn't remember anything after that funny-tasting coke in McKay's billiard room. Twelve or fourteen hours later I'm across the bridge naked and unconscious in a steam bath with an acrid medicinal taste lingering in the back of my mouth.

My head started to throb.

It was only a few blocks to the Blue and White office so I hoofed it up the hill in my new-found galoshes. Wet snow hit my face and revived me a little. I watched the tiny flakes melt on the pavement and spaced out. The ice was back in the harbor and my bones were hollow and frozen. I was thankful I had stolen the coat.

* * *

Al the dispatcher rasped into his microphone and looked at me like someone whom he'd just caught pissing on his basement windows. "Jesus fucking Christ, Waverly," he snorted like a rat guarding a cheese wheel, "you look like death warmed over." And then he yukked: "Yuk, yuk, yuk. What the fuck have you been up to, college boy?"

You go to college for less than two years and you're a fucking college boy. "Just having a good time, Al. Just having a good time. You know us light-hearted types…. Say, ah—I need a ride over to Hammond, Al,—on credit—can I do that? I can pay the driver when I get to my house."

"Not when I'm dispatching, you can't. You know how Minnie is about credit for her drivers. And you're not even one of them anymore. You quit so you could sell god damn porno. So if you think I'm gonna take responsibility for your fare, you're wrong." By the time he was finished, he was wheezing.

"Ah Jesus, Al, I didn't quit; I only took a little vacation. Can't you see my tan here? Come on—you know I'm good for the fare. I never gave Minnie any trouble. I'm just asking this one fucking time; I need to get home real bad."

"Sorry, Waverly, I can't do it."

"Well, then, fuck you, you fuckin' asshole. I hope you die of fucking lung cancer you piece of shit."

Al writhed in his chair like a salted leech. I thought for a second that he might swallow his tongue but no such luck. I flipped him a hard bird and walked out and spit bloody on the sidewalk.

Across the street in the laundromat two bums sat on the floor with their backs up against the washers, watching the dryers spin around. One of them tipped a brown paper bag to his lips. Then a blue and white Checker crossed in front of me and turned into the garage driveway: it was Tommy Morrison, or Morrie, as a lot of us called him.

Shit, I knew he'd give me ride over the bridge; he was a good old boy for sure. Good softball catcher and hitter when he wasn't drunk.

Crossing the bridge, you could see low clouds jockeying for position: gray and black and brown globs pissing out cold rain. They had us surrounded. Ice floated in the bay like chunks of vomit in a toilet bowl. My stomach dished out doses of acid and my head throbbed. Nature was about to make all her calls at one time. I concentrated on sitting in the back of the cab and keeping quiet. Stared out the window and tried to clear my head. I felt like frozen dogshit; Montezuma, Leinenkugel and Bacardi were having their collective revenge. And that fucking McKay, the nerve of that cocksucker. What the hell had he given me?

I had Morrie drive through the residential sections so we could come around to my place from the south while I slumped down in the seat and tried to remember. The hole burned like a flashbulb behind my eyes. I had to warn Sam. What had he pulled? Robbery? Murder? That's what the man said. What the fuck would he do that for? Must have been something valuable. Maybe it was a mistake; maybe the Irishman was playing some kind of a con. But he knew about the wagon, or at least had an idea about it. It was something about that boat and Miko and big money….

We got near my house and I was checking things out in all directions:

"Turn left there, by the Clark station, Morrie, and then a right in the alley. I'm the fourth building in, that shitty looking yellow place. Y'know, man, I've been kind of out of touch the past few days. Anything exciting happening around here lately? Any good stuff on the news or anything?"

"Nah, not that I've heard," Morrie said, fingering a tuft of red nose hair. 'Course I hardly ever read the newspaper, and I never watch the news on TV. I haven't heard of anything, though, nothing exciting on the street. Pretty much the same old shit, you know, for this time of the year—few suicides, few missing people, some bar brawls. Same old, same old."

"Suicides, man, are you serious?"

"Well, I really didn't hear about any, but I'm sure there a few going down. It's this weather; it gets to everybody." He took a flask out of his jacket, flicked his eyeballs around furtively and took a pull.

"Here we are, man," I said, "it's that driveway right there. Just pull in. We can go upstairs and get your fare." Morrie got on the radio and checked in; I could hear Al snarling on the other end.

We went into the house.

A note from Mickey—dated the previous evening—looked up at me from the telephone table: *Hey, Keith, how are you doing old man. Judy and I came home only to find you absent. If you come back before Monday, meet us out at the farm. Check you later—Mick.*

* * *

I paid Morrie, including a nice tip, and watched the rusty Checker drive away. Then I went into the bathroom and shit blood. That really makes you feel good. Must have been the booze, the bad food, drugs, fear, depression, anxiety, lack of sleep—or maybe something in that weird coke.

I sprawled out on the bed and fell into another restless drug-coated sleep of weird dreams: green stuff—a few inches in front of my eyes—like a wall or something, right there, directly in my face. Sometimes it was thick and impenetrable, other times gauzy. Fuzzy images moved behind it. Lights flashed; incomplete black and white images bounced around. Then McKay stood there in a Nazi officer's uniform, holding up a snifter of whisky as if to make a toast. His fellow toaster was my father. The father who had given up on me a long time ago. Together they turned to admire a fine painting on the wall. I looked closer and discovered it was a glossy shot from a fag mag. McKay and Dad turned and pointed at me with long boney fingers and then they kissed; tongues going nuts.

I woke up gasping and short of breath and looked around at my room. I wiped the sweat of my face with the sheet and fell back down into the pillow.

*   *   *

About seven that evening I crawled out of bed and weakly went in search of food. Mickey had left some cold Shamrock pizza in the fridge and I tried to choke it down as best I could. I had to get a hold of Sam Cross somehow; that much I knew. But he would probably just lie to me. I could call Nick to see if he knew what his little brother was up to but I wasn't sure what good that would do so I just sat there and stewed for a while and stared down at the cold spongy cheese and the grease stained pizza box and wondered how I could get my ass out of trouble. Nick Cross was the only answer I came up with. I would have to fill in the blanks as I went along. I craved a beer and a can of brain plaster—something to fill in the cracks and holes. My stomach cried out for a carton of Rolaids and a blue valium but I settled for some baking soda in a glass of water and another hunk of cold pizza.

Nick was home when I called.

"Nick," I said. "This is Keith Waverly. How are you doing?" We exchanged mindless pleasantries. "Have you seen your brother around lately?"

Nick said he hadn't seen Sam for a few days. Any more insincerity, he might be the president.

I told Nick as much of the story as I could remember—leaving out the steam bath part—telling him only that I had been detained against whatever will I still had left.

He acted shocked by the possibilities but was noncommittal until I mentioned murder and then he started talking real fast. Hadn't seen anything in the papers or heard anything on TV, he said. I should watch my tongue, he also said.

I said maybe it was too soon. Too soon to read it in the papers and too soon to keep my mouth shut. But how can you suspect your own brother of wrong doing? Easy I guess, if he's Sam Cross.

Nick fended me off again and again until I threatened to spread it around about his little cheating scam at the big shot's poker game.

"Do you think anyone would believe I was cheating, given all the money I lost?"

"I think they would believe you were trying, after I gave them all the asinine details."

He started spilling like a broken piggy bank:

"You don't know how dangerous those people are," he said, obviously shaken, tough guy composure turned to jelly. "Even his brother the mayor is afraid of Peter McKay. I've heard Dick say that Peter was getting out of control—didn't know what he was going to do about him. Peter's a fucking *faigelah*,… did you know that? And from what I hear, Johnny Wells is also on the payroll. That guy is one crazy motherfucker; I went to high school with him."

"You went to school with Johnny Wells?"

"Yeah, you must have heard of him back then, even though you were just a young pup. He was somewhat of a local legend among us kids. His name used to be Klazuewski. Johnny Klazuewski, but his father changed the family name to Wells so his sons could feel more American. Johnny has always been mean and nasty; he used to run a shoplifting ring in Zenith City in the old days—he was seventeen, I think. Had all these kids stealing for him, and if they balked at all, he'd beat the shit out of them. He's a legendary tough guy. One time he and Billy Marsden fought out at the Lester River railroad bridge to see who was the toughest guy in town. Marsden beat and kicked on Wells for hours and hours and couldn't put him away. They had to call it a draw because Johnny wouldn't quit. The guy scares me because he's crazy; he'll do anything. And now I hear he has a sizable drug habit to go along with everything else. If Wells is after my brother, that is trouble. We'll just have to wait and see."

"Look, Nick. Your goddamn brother dragged me into this goddamn mess, and I didn't even know what he was up to. I was trying to work off some of my tab by helping him; at least you ought to suspend my debt, considering what I've been through. And also considering that your attempted poker scam might possibly ruin more than your good name—if the news got out, that is. Neither of us would want that to happen. You may be the only one who can save little Sammy's ass, so you'd better stay righteous."

"Yeah, yeah—you are right—we have to get him out of this. I'll do what I can… I'll stay in touch."

"Do that," I said and hung up.

Time passed. Another week started up. I still hadn't seen Mary since the night of the party and I didn't have whatever it took to look her up. Most of the time I just sat around the house and drank beer and watched a lot of horseshit TV and smoked whatever weed I could find. My main concern was getting rid of the daytime nightmares I was having.

No crimes of note in the newspapers. I was beginning to think the whole murder and robbery thing might be bullshit. Just a ruse cooked up by McKay—an excuse to get at me. I must've had KICK ME stenciled on my ass.

But what about those new guys in town?

Dusky, curly-haired guys wearing fancy leather jackets and expensive looking shirts were suddenly all over Hammond. They were driving big American sedans and making themselves known. They stood out like a drunk's red nose. You could hear them talking in a foreign language if you listened. You could see they spent a lot of money if you looked. You could smell Brut if you sniffed. They were hard to miss; you didn't see many guys with wide-open shirts and gold medallions in Tugtown, except maybe on Saturday night when the Travolta wannabees swarmed in. There wasn't much flash in Hammond, it was a shoplifting-welfare kind of berg. The regular citizens kept their eyes on their shoes and minded their own business for the most part.

What the hell were those guys doing in a town like this? I had no answer but I had a strange feeling that I was connected somehow.

Sam was still not around and Nick was unreachable. Every time I called Nick's house I was greeted by the sound of his brand new answering machine: "You have reached such-and-such and such-and-such... Please leave your message at the sound of the tone."

Yeah, well—fuck you, too.

At the antique store some woman said Nick was "on vacation." After a couple days of that I was ready to give up but then I got a call from Mickey. I hadn't heard from him in a few days but I hadn't worried. If he was shacking up with Judy out at the farm I knew he'd be safe until he came up for air.

He said he was calling from Sam Cross's apartment. Sam was coming back into town that night, he said, and he and Nick and Sam were going to meet somewhere. Mick didn't know where yet.

I screamed into the phone: "Stay the fuck out of this, Mickey goddamn it. You go fucking around with the Crosses, you'll get your ass in a sling in a hurry. I'm telling you for your own good. Nick and Sam will just be using you no matter what it is they're offering. Christ, you ought to know that by now."

"Nah," he said. "I won't let 'em get over on my ass. You can't con an Irishman."

"Mick—listen to me—I got jumped the other night when I left the bar."

"Who jumped you?" His voice turned angry.

"Three big goons—I don't know. But it was your fucking car they were interested in, not me, you fuckhead. And correspondingly, they will most certainly be looking for you. They might be over there in Sam's backyard right now. I think this has something to do with him. The other night when you had my Olds, Sam and I went to the docks in your wagon. So you figure it out. They doped me with something and held me until they searched the wagon, that's what I'm trying to tell you. When they didn't find anything they let me go. I mean they knew it wasn't my car—and I think McKay believed my story anyway. If you've got any brains at all you'll stay the hell away from Peter McKay."

"You mean the mayor's fag brother? Runs the dope, gambling and sex trade in town there? What has he got to do with it?"

"He's the big boss. Those guys work for him."

"Never met him. Only seen him once or twice. He's a flamer, they say. How do you know him, anyway? What are we talking about here?"

"Never mind about that. It's not important. What matters is that you help me on this or stay the fuck out of it. Are you sure you don't know anything about this?"

"I'm not going to take on anything that I can't handle, you know me...."

"Yeah, for sure Mick, for sure. I know all about your legendary control. Is that why you've spent so much time in the slam, because you're so fucking in control and on top of things? This is serious, you asshole. You have to keep me on touch on this shit, man. My ass is on the line here. Believe me, I know what I'm talking about."

"Yeah, yeah, yeah. I'll call you when I find out—I swear. Now leave me alone so I can watch Green Acres."

He clicked off. I stared at the receiver.

Mickey was a frustrating guy at times: stubborn pig-headed and arrogant but sometimes good-hearted, generous and friendly. With too much liquor in him he could be violent and greedy. But he'd always been straight with me in the past—at least until his demons took hold of the wheel—which was way too fucking often, come to think of it.

I decided to walk the almost two blocks to Jack's Bar: a tiny street-corner tavern built back when the cathouses outnumbered the grocery stores. I hoped Jack's would be one place I could avoid trouble while I softened up my head with alcohol.

Dirt and dampness swirled around me and my shoes crunched the gravel on the sidewalk. The sky was overcast and the wind blew a gale. Bad weather, frayed nerves, and the floating sensation... I wasn't feeling too bad. I didn't know why.

Was the bartender's name Jack? I never asked him but I know he wore a white shirt with the sleeves rolled up and the collar open and he had an anchor tattoo on his forearm. What was left of his dark brown hair was greased straight back over the top of his head.

I surveyed the room: Camped at the end of the bar was a silver-haired hag nodding off with a cigarette in her hand, the burning coal creeping dangerously close to her wrinkled flesh. A middle-aged couple who looked like they drank for a living occupied one of the two round Formica tables near the front of the bedroom-sized tavern. A blowzy peroxide blonde in a dress two sizes too small and her skinny Elvis-haired boyfriend sat grinning up at the TV that hung from the wall.

These people were going to be my friends for a while. Inside of Jack's Bar we were going to spend a little part of our precious lives together.

I ordered a Budweiser and a shot of Smirnov on ice. I smiled to myself because I had that feeling you get when everything seems right with the world. This life, I thought, it just can't be real.

I drank some more.

We had a good time—me and my new friends. You know, you can meet some really nice people in a bar. Buy them a few drinks and they'll listen to you all night long and talk about anything you want. It's a damn good thing that they have taverns everywhere in this town, I was thinking. Then I ran out of money and it wasn't so much fun anymore, so I left.

Out on Tower Avenue the nightlife traffic busied-up. The world was strange and painful even with a buzz on. Walked home. Got some dust in my eye.

I went in through the front door of my house so I could check the mail. The downstairs neighbor's mailbox was jammed to overflowing and a few days worth of newspapers lay on the cracked linoleum floor of the vestibule. I was expecting my final check from the porn store, and it was there along with an bill for the electricity and a large manilla envelope that had been forwarded along from Wabasha Book. There was no return address and it bore a Zenith City postmark.

I picked up the current issue of the *Hammond Evening Times* from the pile on the floor and moved unsteadily up the stairs. I went in and sat down in the green easy chair and felt the broken spring against my ass. I tore open the envelope and looked at the check. The amount was correct: $142. Second thing I did was tear off the tape on the large manilla envelope.

At first I thought someone had sent me some cheap porn from the Wabasha as a joke. Maybe some kind of commentary on my firing or something.

It didn't take long to see how wrong I was.

The pictures were of men. Men engaged in anal intercourse on a pool table. And it was me that was clearly being the recipient of some anonymous donor's dick. Another naked male body—whose head didn't make the picture—gripped my hair with his hands and pointed my face toward the camera. There was a silver ring of intertwined snakes on his right hand. My eyes were half-shut and vacant like the motel was open but the clerk was on break.

My knees turned to jelly and I started to shake. Fucked in the ass. Buggered. Cornholed. All those words you've been sniggering about since junior high. Now it was me.

I started to remember; pictures in my head began to fill themselves in. The hole in my brain closed slowly, creaking—memories coming in shuttering spasms: Cruel laughter, shrieks of pleasure and the smell and taste of the green felt pool table caromed around inside the vacuum that was now my head.

I sat there limp and stunned, my gut twisting. I wouldn't cry but tears came anyway, angry bitter tears. I tried to squeeze them back but I couldn't. My hands were shaking and I was dizzy as I pulled a small piece of paper from the envelope:

Dear Keith,

Wanted you to have a keepsake of our evening together. Maybe you can display these on the shelves of your book store. I'm sure they would make a fine seller. Maybe your son or your ex-wife would like a copy. Enjoy.

It was unsigned.

I squeezed the paper and dug my fingernails into the palms of my hands. Bile rose up until I could taste it: bitter and burning and sick. My brain writhed around inside my skull trying to figure shit out. Something had to be done. What? What was it any way? Why should I care about this thing? I guess I did care. Caring hurt. My brain spun. If no one found out then no one would know… My son could never see these pictures. It was that simple. Loathing filled my gut as I stumbled into the bathroom and had the dry heaves. I came out of the bathroom and that burning sour taste was in my mouth and I punched a hole in the paper thin wall with my fist. Damn it felt good. I thought about smashing up the whole apartment but I didn't have the energy.

EVERYBODY SING:

Well you can't let one Mick dick keep you down, no oh,
No you can't let just one prick keep you down, oh yeah,
You got to find a way to get back on top, uh huh,
No matter what it is that you have to dooo, ew-ew.

* * *

It was suddenly very lonely and empty inside of that apartment. And way too quiet. Friends and lights and warmth was what I needed. Jack's joint was the place for me. I moved on rubber legs down the stairs and back out into the cold night.

A brown Lincoln Town Car was parked alongside the curb in front of my house. The darkly-tinted passenger side window slid down as I approached. An ugly, pock-marked face with a bad case of five o'clock shadow popped out at me like a cheap wine nightmare. "Hi-ya, Waverly," the face croaked. Then in a clipped, Chicago white-trash accent: "Mr. McKay would like to talk to you. Whattaya say you be a good boy and come along quietly, so we don't have to get all worked up here. The man just wants to discuss a few things—you know how it is."

"Yeah, and you stink like fucking garbage you fucking pig."

He sprung out of the car and jolted me with an uppercut to the midsection and I doubled over from the shot. I turned away and put up my left forearm in defense and tried to run but my legs were filled with lead. He punched me twice in the kidney and shoved me to the ground.

"Okay okay," I wheezed. "I'm coming. Leave me alone. I'm coming. No need to get rough."

He cuffed me around a little and dragged me into the back seat of the Lincoln and we took the proverbial ride downtown.

The boys escorted me up the backstairs of McKay's place. They brought me into the billiard room and threw me down on the couch and waited. More memories came rushing back as I stared at the pool table and then he made one of his dramatic entrances, bursting in through the side door; and my body got rigid without my consent.

He was dressed in his green ensemble, just like the first time ever I saw his face. He motioned to the goons to leave; smiled a sick, arrogant smile and walked over to me and put his fingers on my cheek. Nausea was my middle name.

"Keith, my friend. Here you are back again. How good it is to see you. You mustn't stay away so long the next time." The guy must have really thought he was cute. "Did you get the memento that I sent over to you?"

"Yes I did, Peter. That was really good work. How you spliced my head onto that picture to make it look like it was me there on that pool table—that was good work."

He smiled thinly. "Let me assure you that those photos are genuine. Next time you look at them just take a look at that mole on your lower back. I believe it is quite visible."

I had to stay in control and not let him get to me. Not let him know….

"I'll have to take your word for it, because I can't remember a thing about that night—not after I snorted that weird coke. What was that shit you poisoned me with?"

"It was cocaine. Isn't that what you like? I thought that was what the young men liked. Isn't that what all the people want these days? Oh, there was a small adjunct—an insignificant little additive. A little something I get from one of our local veterinarians. I believe it is called Rhohypnathyelene. It's used for operating on animals. That's appropriate, don't you think? You were such a beast. Would you care for some more?"

"Ah gee, no thanks, Pete, I like to remember."

Pretty soon I was going to start screaming and never stop. *Straight Jacket City here I come.*

"As much as I would enjoy lingering on our past encounter, Keith," he said, clasping his palms together. "I'm afraid I don't have the luxury of time at this moment. I—"

"What did you bring me here for, then—if were not going to have any time together?"

"Don't interrupt me, you little punk. I had a good long talk with your red-haired Irish friend. He was—"

"Then you know he didn't rip you off."

He walked over and slapped me hard across the face. The little smile told me he enjoyed it. I sat there pretty much motionless and felt the sting and the rising heat in my cheek.

"You wait until I'm through speaking before you open your sorry mouth, hippie boy—or you'll end up just like your friend."

I wanted to ask him what that meant but I kept my sorry mouth shut for a change. I didn't want to think about poor Mick and I was sick to my stomach.

"As I was saying, Mickey was kind enough to elaborate on his business activities, and it seems as though you are in a little deeper than you told me, Keith. Now I don't begrudge a man making a few bucks here and there, even perhaps on my streets.... But, you see, now, there has been a theft. A theft of something that I am responsible for, the loss of which puts me in an extremely dangerous situation. A situation that must be rectified. You see, there was evidence pointing to your friend, he was involved. Him and the jewboy. He said you were clean. Either he was telling the truth, or he was one mighty tough kid. Yep, one tough kid. As for you Keith, I can't think of anything more you can do for me."

"What if I can help you get your stolen property back?"

"Are you telling me that you know something?"

"No, but I have a way of finding things out. I hear things. I know lots of people who aren't afraid to talk around me. Usually, a few nights hanging out in the right places, and talking to the right people, you can know everything about everything that's going on around here. I bet I could find your stuff—if I knew what it was, that is. I can do good things for you, I swear."

He looked at me kind of strangely, almost softly. He put his hand to his face and stroked thoughtfully underneath his chin. He smiled. Then he sighed and looked toward the windows. "It's time for you to go now, Keith. And before you go, here is something from Mickey." He took a small envelope out of his inside coat pocket came over and stuffed it in my jacket. "He wanted you to have this," he said faintly, then got up and walked over to the door where he came in and pushed a buzzer on the wall. My chaperones came into the room and hustled me down the stairs and out to the Lincoln. The envelope burned in my jacket.

One of the big dufusses drove and the other one sat in the back seat with me. Camaraderie was thick. The envelope was still unopened in my pocket and I was thinking it was going to be my last ride anywhere. "Hey, do you guys mind if I open this envelope that your boss gave me? I think he wanted me to open it."

The dufus in the back grunted, "Yeah, asshole, go ahead."

I tore open one end of the envelope and shook it. Two bloody teeth: roots, rotting flesh and all, dropped into my palm. Mickey's extra-large front teeth, complete with gold-backed caps. A strange noise jerked out of my throat and my gut locked up against my spine. I flipped the teeth onto the floor like a handful of stinging scorpions and fought hard against the nausea. I could barely draw a breath.

The two goons enjoyed the biggest laugh they'd had since Martin Luther King got shot.

"Whatsamatter, sweetie, you don't want those gold nuggets?" The driver kept laughing his pig laugh.

The more I stared at those guys, the more they looked like pigs. Or maybe decaying wild boars. I slumped back into the seat. Mickey was dead. Fucking Mickey. Fucking dead. And now it was my turn. Those boys must have had an eye for beauty because they were taking the scenic route.

We drove past abandoned houses—their gutted windows like black staring vacuums. Past sooty gray factories with phallic chimneys spewing vaporous jizz that fertilized nothing. Snow tires whined beneath rusty frozen bridges that lead to nowhere you'd ever want to go. Here and there dark metal mounds that once were shiny new automobiles decayed slowly like steel carcasses. We went past the hospital and the airport and the fairgrounds and the Town of South Hammond—featuring Les Birds Bar—and the South End bowling alley. Then the cold empty darkness. My time was running short.

About ten miles farther down the desolate highway the craggy-faced driver slowed the big car and turned right onto a narrow tree-lined road and I knew we weren't there to make out. We rolled slowly down the lonely lane for about a mile or so and then turned into a small service road of some sort and stopped at the edge of the woods. The guy in the backseat slid over next to me and the putrid exhaust of his dinner washed hot against the side of my face.

The driver was coming around to open my door.

"We're going out nice and easy honey, so just relax," said the guy next to me.

The driver began to pull open the door. I threw my shoulder into it and it smashed into his knees. Then I leaped out and took three quick steps and dove headlong into the ditch and rolled forward on my shoulder. I came up running and zigzagging and staying low to avoid the bullets. They never came. The only sound that I heard was the two bozos' loud laughter as they climbed back into the Lincoln and drove away, honking the horn. I must have been about a block into the woods when their tail lights disappeared from sight. Let me tell you, I was glad to be alive. But my shoes were soaked through from running through patches of snow and I was in the middle of the deep dark woods. Without the lights of the Lincoln for per-spective, I couldn't see shit. I stumbled back in what I thought was the direction of the road. My feet got numb and pine branches slapped my face.

It was at least an hour before I finally found the highway. Just as I broke free of the trees a big rabbit burst out and ran past me in the ditch. Scared the shit out of me.

I danced and hopped on the pavement and tried to get the feeling back in my feet. I tried hitchhiking: A couple of cars drove by but kept right on going. I begged and pleaded to those lights. I screamed, "Stop, stop… come on you bastards, stop, STOP." That's probably why they all sped up.   But after fifteen minutes I got lucky. A guy and his girlfriend in a pick-up truck with a snowmobile in the box pulled over. I had to prance ten yards on numb feet but when I opened the truck door the warmth from the heater greeted me like a pretty girl's smile. *Praise the rural party-goer, for he is God.*

The driver reminded me of the singer from Dr. Hook: oily, shoulder-length hair, trim beard, straw hat but no eyepatch. His large-headed girlfriend had a friendly face. Her dark brown hair was pulled back in pigtails and she smiled a lot. I wiggled my toes but couldn't feel them.

Dr. Hook said: "Geeze, what are you doing all the way out here, man?   Car break down or something?"

"Nah. I just had a little disagreement with my sweetie. She kicked me out of the car and left me here to freeze."

"She must have been a pretty strong chick, to throw some-one like you out of the car," said the girl, a horsey grin on her face.

"She was—take my word for it."

"Man, you oughta come with us to the keg party," the driver said as we passed a slow-moving VW van. "There'll be lots of chicks there—you should come." .

"That sounds like lots of fun, but my feet are all wet from stepping in snow, and I really need to clean up before I go out anywhere. But my house is right along the way here, pretty soon…. You can just drop me off by Jack's Bar; it's not too much farther."

"Yeah, okay, no problem, man. I'll give you the address, in case you change your mind. There'll be lots of chicks… you'd like Anna Marie…. Don'tcha think, Julie?"

"Could be, Frank."

Julie searched in her large knit purse for a pencil while I stared out the window at the nothingness and furiously wiggled my frozen toes inside my thin Dingo boots.

It was after midnight when I turned the key in my lock of my house. I got a beer from the porch and started up the bath and made sure it was good and hot. I threw my clothes in a pile on the bathroom floor and I sat down in the tub and the heat soaked through me. Water gurgled from the faucet, crooning a special song: "*They killed Mickey but not you… They killed Mickey but not you… they killed Mickey but not you…*"

I got out of the bath feeling like a zombie and got dressed in a clean pair of jeans and a nice old charcoal v-neck sweater that I still had from my college days, and started to search through Mickey's shit. I found nine hundred dollars in cash and a cheap-looking little hand gun, probably a thirty-eight. Those were the only things of interest besides the full carton of Trojans.

The situation was dangerous but somehow it all seemed like a dream. Mick was dead and that was real. But he should have known better. My own life seemed like nothing. As I climbed out of the tub and reached for a towel I heard the shriek of the phone and felt my life tear further apart, like someone was pounding the last nail in the cross. But I wasn't Jesus, I was the thief next door.

Stephanie Ricci was on the horn, Mary's friend and fellow dancer. What did she call me for? To fuck up my life. To drag me into something that I should have been running far away from. She cried to me about Mary, how she was dancing downtown at a place called Beaner's Bar. "Whore Central," Stephanie called it.

I said: "Am I supposed to get all worked up about that? I mean, taking off her clothes is her chosen profession. I'm sure she's good at it. Besides, I like strippers." I felt like I was reading a script.

She said, "She's working for Johnny Wells. He's a secret partner in the bar, on account of he can't own a bar of his own because of his felonies. You should worry about that."

"I should worry because Wells can't own a bar?"

"No—because of Mary being with him. She told me that she'd found somebody to love. That was you, honey."

"Oh come on. I've got enough to worry about, you don't even know…. Mary's a big girl, I guess she can take care of herself. It's none of my business what she does…. When did she say that about me?"

"Last time I saw her—last weekend. I used to go out with him, you know—Johnny. I can handle him most of the time. I talked to his parole officer once—he warned me. Said Johnny liked to rape little girls and for that matter, just about anything that moves. Said I should keep him away from my kids if I had any. But I don't—I almost had Johnny's kid about eight months ago, but he made me— "

"Do I need to hear this right now? What about Mary and Wells?"

She choked up a little and her voice got a little cloudy, but she kept on. "He had this thing with Mary going on in his head, and he wouldn't let up—some shit about getting hit with a beer bottle."

"Yeah, I'm familiar with that situation. But what did he do to her?"

"Nothing. I mean, he won't hit her hard enough to bruise the merchandise, but Johnny's got ways…. It's just that he found out about the fire, and he's holding that over her head. He's got a lot of drugs, too, y'know. Sometimes Mary just has to be where the drugs are."

"Drugs, yeah, I s'pose. Fire you say? What fire is that?"

"You didn't know? I would have thought she'd have told you everything—the way she was talking about you, well—"

"She didn't."

"She probably thought you'd hate her if you found out. It's all about this trailer down in Wisconsin that burned down at the same time that she split town. There's a warrant out for her back there, and Johnny found out about it."

"Yeah, but what did he do to her?"

"He threatened to have her arrested unless she did what he said."

"Which consisted of?"

"Dancing exclusively at Beaner's for one thing. He knew she'd be a big draw. Johnny thinks he's some kind of slick promoter—he cooked up this big production thing for her."

"Any other things?"

"Dating him, I suppose…."

"Dating him? And what kind of dates do you have with Johnny I wonder? Never mind, don't say anything. Stephanie, here's a question for you, dear…. How did you get my number?"

"I found it on a piece of paper that Mary left at my house. Your name and number were inside a heart she drew on my phone pad."

A heart… Jesus fucking Christ. I was getting dragged back in, something rude was going down.

"Listen Keith, there's more—but I can't talk about it on this phone. You should come over here tonight, so we can talk. You don't know how much Mary cares about you." Her voice was sweet and child-like.

"I don't know what I can do for her."

"You can talk to her. She wants you to talk to her. She told me to call you, don't you understand? You have to get her out of there! You come out to 336 East Water Street tonight, out in Allouez, and I'll tell you the whole story."

She hung up and the dial tone rang hollow in my ear. The voice in my head was screaming that I owed something to someone but it never said who. I chewed on the phone cord for a little while. Biting on that thing felt good, strangely satisfying.

I waited until dark and then I made the drive to Allouez.

Sitting at the foot of a hulking rusty railroad bridge, 336 Water Street was the last house on a dead-end street: A faded two-story white box with a broken sidewalk and a peeling front porch that sagged in the middle like a wino's lower lip. The yellowed front shade was drawn down and a dim light showed through.

I knocked and a porch light came on above the door. Two minutes later I was still shuffling around on the rotting porch and getting pretty cold, when Stephanie slowly opened the inside door and invited me into her living room. I could tell she had just done a fast but imperfect clean-up job because the plunger end of a syringe peeked out from under the couch skirt. Twenty-something Stephanie was looking thirty-nine and not holding. I tried to get a read on what kind of drugs she was ripped on.

She sat down in a sagging overstuffed maroon chair and lit a cigarette with a tarnished silver table lighter and blew out the smoke before she had time to taste it. Her hands trembled and her eyelids were sinking fast. I sank down in a couch that matched her chair and gave her the evil eye. She laid the cig on the edge of a large, green ceramic ashtray, clasped her hands around her arms and held on tight.

"Keith—shit, Jesus—I didn't think you'd come. Jesus, you know… forgive the mess, would you please? I haven't been feeling well lately—the lousy weather and all. But, can I get you something? Beer? Vodka?" She waved her hands in the air and looked at me with pain-filled eyes.

"No, nothing for me, thanks. What's this shit that you couldn't tell me over the phone—now what's all that about?"

She blew out a thin puff of smoke, leaned back in the chair and crossed her legs. Her tight denim skirt hiked up, revealing a hunk of creamy white thigh. "Johnny just committed another robbery, you know, down in Minneapolis."

"I think I read about it in the paper. It sounded like his style. But I imagine the cops will think the same thing."

"Maybe they will, but they'll never ID him—he wore a fencing mask. A fencing mask that he took off of my fucking wall. I bought the goddamn thing at a fucking rummage sale, y'know, because I thought it looked classy—like an old Tony Curtis movie or something…. That prick Johnny, he does anything he wants around here."

"I can't believe that the cops in town would let him get away with all that."

"Do you see him in fucking jail?! Do you see anybody doing anything?! I'm tellin' you, Keith, he does whatever he fucking wants— and now he's getting Mary hooked on all those pills and hard drugs. He's trying to make her his sex slave, that fucking bastard. Then after he gets tired of her he might trade her to one of those Southern biker gangs for a couple ounces of coke. I betcha I heard that threat a million goddamn times, and I always believed it… cause Johnny would do it."

"Excuse me darling, but you didn't shove your needle far enough under the couch here. Do you mind if I?" I shoved the syringe under the cover with my heel.

She pushed back a sob, her voice cracked: "Yeah sure, that's me. Dumb freak Steph, who could never do anything quite right… the wrong boyfriends… the wrong jobs…. It's me, dumb bastard Stephanie, who could never please any man, any time. It didn't matter who they were, y'know I al—"

"Wait a minute; hold on here. Let's not travel down the river of regret right now. How about you tell me how I can get in touch with our friend Mary. And if you have any suggestions on how I should handle this, keep them to yourself."

"She's worth saving, Keith, she's got a head on her shoulders—not like me. Me who thinks she can be a dancer—five feet two, with an appendix scar—I just never get it right…"

"I'm sure you looked pretty good up there. I wouldn't mind the scar. Course, I got one of my own."

"Really, Keith. You liked the way I look? You said you liked exotic dancers…. Do you like it when they shake their pussies?" She uncrossed her legs, reached down and slid her skirt up, exposing the satiny crotch of lacy white panties. "Do you like my pussy?" she was moving it. "Do you like it when I do this?" She put her hands down there and got down to business.

"Yes I do," I said. Then I got up and walked out the door. I didn't need to put up with her anymore. Beaner's Bar was on my mind.

I drove around thinking. Just drove around and around that rotten town and came up with nothing. You had to be either dumb, numb, crooked or rich to live here. But I guess that goes for anywhere. Then the voice said, *Run you coward, run.*

"I've heard that before," I said back.

I shoved *The Best of Jimi Hendrix* into the eight track and listened to the "Wind Cries Mary" over and over. After an hour of aimless driving and senseless thinking I stopped at one of several Dew Drop Inns to be found in the area. Inside in the sweet darkness, shots of Smirnov and glasses of Old Milwaukee got me feeling at home with the aromatic mix of urine and sweat and stale beer and cheap perfume and blood that is truly the essence of saloon. Old geezer sat down by me who looked like he washed his face with coal dust just to get in the mood. Hamm's Beer sign behind the bar grabbed my eyes: Canoe beached on a sandy point with a beautiful stream bubbling alongside. Water in the stream on the sign actually moved. Grizzly Adams lookalike crouched by a perfect campfire with a large brown bear at his side. I wanted to join him there and roll a joint and stare at the fire. Forever.

After a round or two my shakes and my fear gave way to a worldly and weary philosophical outlook. The glint in my eye returned and cocaine craving commenced. The desire for dope overrode everything. I sat and remembered how good it used to feel to lock the door behind a big load of blow. But if I hadn't ever started up with that shit I would not be in this mess, that's the one thing that I knew for sure. Seems like the dope will take your good sense and hide it from you. Geeze, the booze was loosening me up. I wasn't chicken shit anymore. But the voice kept saying all sorts of nasty things, so I burned down another shot of vodka to keep it silent. It was time for action. But what? I didn't even know where to score any coke. So I drank some more….

Second trip to the men's room I noticed a bulletin board on the wall with a bright orange poster tacked to it. Ink drawing of a veiled belly dancer smiled out at me:

NOW FEATURED AT BEANER'S BAR: PRINCESS MARY— PAGAN PRIESTESS from L.A. and her Coven of Sexy Witches. Backed by the raging live rock and roll of the Zenith City Gloom Band. Admission: $2. Drink Specials all nite long. 9:00 P. M till Close Thurs. thru Sun.

The clock on the wall was mounted next to a sign that said: Sorry No Credit. Don't Ask. I got up to leave because it was 10:45.

"You ought to change that sign, asshole," I said to the bewildered bartender. He was bald and stumpy and his ears had been boxed a few too many times.

"What the fuck are you talking about, mister?" he said, squinting and frowning.

"It says there that you're sorry you don't give out credit. You're not sorry. There's nobody here sorry but the poor drunk you just bled of all his money and now you won't even extend a man a little credit after he's broke and can't go home. You're a fucking leech, that's what you are. You trade blood for alcohol and turn it into cash. You—"

He said: "Get the fuck out of my bar you crazy sonofabitch," and bent over like he was fetching his bludgeon stick from behind the bar.

I got my besotted ass out of there.

* * *

There were cars parked everywhere.

I slid the Olds into a spot about two blocks away from the

club. Behind me waves of red light pulsed from a giant neon LIQUOR sign and bounced off my rear-view mirror like warning beacons.

I pulled open the red upholstered door and entered the hazy world of Beaner's Boulevard Lounge. I paid my two bucks and got my hand stamped and moved slowly through the crowd. I was reeling drunk. An amply endowed black chick gyrated in a G-string on the single stage; baying hounds at knee level paid money to stick fingers up her snatch. She squeezed her tits together and ground her pelvis against the intruding digits while over to stage right the band played a loud sloppy version of "Born to be Wild." I ordered a double shot of Smirnov on the rocks.

"Bartender," I asked, "What time does Queen Mary do her thing?"

"She comes on around midnight. The last show's at two."

"Well, I guess it's worth waiting for—Queen Mary and all."

"Yeah," he said. "Some nights she really puts on a show."

Squirming, squirming, squirming inside. You can't do anything about it when you got that kind of squirm going. I gritted my teeth and poured down the booze. My head was heavy and discretion took flight. The baying continued. Voices got louder; sweat beaded on my forehead. After what seemed like forever the hands on the clock finally joined together at the number twelve.

The band started up a grinding version of Dylan's "Just Like a Woman." At the chorus, the pale and sunken-eyed lead singer would rasp: "*She sucks just like a woman. She fucks just like a woman. But she tastes just like a little girl.*"

Surely the devil was in the building.

The hounds hooted like it was 'coon season.

Then Mary strutted out on the stage, rocking in red stiletto heels with sexy little straps around the ankles. The place exploded with applause and whistles and rebel yells. Red, red roses sparkled on her shiny lavender robe, little stars glittered in her hair. My Queen of the May. The feeling was indescribable—so much mixed together. I was breathing heavily—swaying back and forth and staring—like a stageside lunatic at Altamount.

The band jumped crisply into "Season of the Witch." Mary undid the robe and slid it off her bare shoulders and tossed it to the crowd it and shimmied inside lingerie the color of blood. She danced. She glided. She shook it. She unhooked her bra and let her delicious round breasts hang above the crowd. The junkie singer hissed those familiar words about rabbits in the ditch and hippies trying to make it rich. Then it was truly the season of the witch: Mary lip-synched and played the hounds like a ringmaster. Waving hands with bills clutched tightly in anxious fingers swayed at her feet like a brood of praying mantis.

I couldn't take much more—that I knew right then and there. I was aroused—watching her move—but I felt real funny.

Pushing my way through the crowd toward the stage, I had second thoughts. I sat down in a vacant chair at a table near the stage so I could think. A fat guy sat across from me, his huge forearms resting on the table. He looked at me like he was King Shit.

"I'm just taking a little rest," I said.

"Yeah, well, rest your fucking ass somewhere else, faggot. That's my buddy's chair."

"Fuck you, fat ass." I jumped up and jostled back into the crowd and started weaving my way toward the alley-side door. I expected the fat guy to be hot on my trail but he never moved. I went outside and headed for my car, but a half block before I got there I turned around and went back the way I came. Back to Beaner's to face the music.

This time I moved directly to the foot of the stage. Men grabbed and shouted at Princess Mary but she stayed an inch beyond their reach—thrusting and tantalizing—occasionally coming close enough to touch and then darting backward. The room rose to a fever pitch. The band hit the crescendo and crashed to a halt. Mary bent over at the waist with her back to the audience and pulled down those crimson panties and shivers shot up and down my spine. The mob roared approval; something in my head went SPROING. I was squeezed in between two guys in suits when the next song started up. Mary looked down at me, her face like a mask. She saw me but I couldn't read her. Was it love? Disgust? Pain or embarrassment? Now I was just one of the pack. I wanted so badly to taste her.

She came close to me and leaned over slightly and said something but I couldn't hear through the noise. I grabbed her ankle and squeezed it—softly at first. It was so warm and smooth. I couldn't make myself look up; I stared down at the stage. I squeezed a little harder; she tried to pull away.

"No, Keith, don't, please stop," she barked. "You don't know what you're doing. Let go."

Then a fifty-pound bee stung my right ear and a horse kicked my left kidney. The next thing I knew I was saying hello to everybody's shoes. I tried to scramble away on my knees; a boot popped out of nowhere and collided with my ribs. THUNK—another stung my mouth. I kissed the ground. Star showers everywhere, man, funny electric shocks in my neck. Two guys pulled me off the floor and shuffled me away. Spitting blood and not fighting back. They dragged me across the room. One bouncer slapped me across the back of the head. I struggled free and made a dash for the door, scattering tables in my path. No bum's rush for this kid. I burst out the door and hit the sidewalk running and headed for darkness. Shouts and laughter were soon behind me. I turned into a dark alley, walked down a half a block and stopped and listened. It was quiet, street lights reflected on the rainwater in the puddles. I walked another little bit and listened some more. Still quiet. I leaned against the side of a house and pushed my hair back off my forehead. I bent over at the waist and blew out bloody snot. At the end of the alley a neon-bathed rat scurried by.

After a moment of reconnaissance, I cut through several back yards of garbage cans and rusty autos and moved quickly across the street, doubling back to my car. Beaten and kicked—kicked and beaten. *Needles and pins-a.*

I couldn't make myself drive so I sat there and squeezed the steering wheel and my head reeled and whirled. Eventually I settled down a little. I found a long butt in the ashtray and fired it up. Nicotine narcosis, baby, let's have it.

Violated and dominated and kicked around like a diseased rodent—not to mention getting fucked in the ass—that shit will linger with you for awhile. That's the shit I couldn't take. That and about five hundred other things that were struggling to the surface like a thousand pissed-off rattlesnakes. I just couldn't stand for anymore abuse. Time to get even, before the game got over. Time to stop running. You can only run so far, before you realize that what you're running from is yourself.

I still had the stamp on my hand from the bar....

I tried in vain to figure it all out. What the hell do I get for trying to help somebody? My fucking ass kicked. I should've gone to Jamaica. *Yeah you shoulda, asshole, but it's too late for that now. You're in too deep.*

Maybe I could live in my car for awhile, I thought. After all, the automobile is like a rolling womb. You got wheels. You got door locks. You got the radio, heater—storage space in the trunk You can sleep in your car and eat in your car and fuck in your car. Americans learned how to live out of their cars as teenagers. Why couldn't I do it? Shit, I could park wherever I wanted. Go wherever I wanted. If anything hassled me I could just drive away. Just me and my womb on wheels.

A man needs something to drink if he's going to live in his car.

I walked over to the now painfully throbbing Viking Liquor sign, went in the store and bought a pint of Windsor Canadian and a pack of Kools from the thick-headed clerk. I didn't even like brown liquor and I was trying to quit smoking so it must have been some kind of self-destructive urge like the cool rock stars all had. The clerk gave me a funny look for a second, like maybe I smelled bad, which I probably did. I looked like hell, too.

Back in the womb, I started it up and drove around until I found a street lonely enough and dark enough. I stopped next to a big black oak tree whose branches seemed to point at me accusingly. Across the street was a vacant lot and a row of small dark houses with their shades down and lights on. I took a blast on the bottle and the whisky swirled into the bottom of my gut, both hot and shivery. I felt myself sinking down, giving up. I needed a smoke. A man needs a smoke. My match book said "Relax and Enjoy" but it was empty. I flipped open the glove box and rummaged for matches because the car lighter didn't work. A sheet of green pyramid fell out onto the torn rubber floor mat in front of me. What the hell? I thought. Why not do some right now. Could it make things any worse? Always sick, always in trouble, always guilty… it don't get no worse.

I tore off a strip of the acid, sixteen hits at least. Washed them down with Windsor and laughed a bitter laugh like everybody's fool. Then me and my friends Whisky Man and Mr. Cig went for a little walk, or stumble as it were, around the empty streets. I could no longer feel the cold. Icy rain soothed the wounds on my face. *But could I save face up in outer space without a trace—of sanity….*

In a time that seemed like an hour but could have been ten minutes, I came upon a boarded up-church: a small, white clapboard building with a bogus steeple on the roof.

As I walked toward the rear of the building to relieve myself there was a strange metallic taste in my throat and the glands in my neck were going squirrelly. Brain was shifting gears like a sixteen-wheeler rolling down hill in a snowstorm. Putrid smoke from factories thick in my nostrils. Cars on the bridge whined in my ears. The universe vibrated through me in intermittent waves. Lights on the hill—miles away—hurt my eyes. Pain always there to remind me.

Bad thoughts tumbled out with the rushing urine: The High Bridge would be a good place to end it all. It'd be a big deal—women would cry. What a rush just walking up to the middle… cars zipping by like you're not even there. You not caring about jackshit. Every time they whoosh by your heart just about explodes and a chill of fear grabs your balls. Imagine: Up on top, the wind would be blowing. You'd look down at the dark, icy water below and the voice would be screaming:*Jump. Jump you miserable coward. Jump.* You'd just go numb—it wouldn't be that bad. *Come on, what are you waiting for? Take the plunge… You're outta here… Gone Johnson.* People'd be yelling… horns'd be honking… when Johnny comes marching home again, hurrah, hurrah… the lights… the water…. All around me it swirled. Inside me it swirled. On the ground in front of me it swirled.

It was a long piss.

I zipped up and pulled out the bottle and sucked hard on the whisky. *Take me back to my daddy's knee sweet whisky, take me back….* I knew if I stayed there much longer they'd have to change my name to Catatonic State. *Maybe I could dye my hair.*

"Can't be pissing yourself away like a child," said a deep voice in the darkness.

I looked up and saw a tough-looking old man frowning at me from ten yards away. He crossed his arms against his old-fashioned clothes: a bowler hat and a thick wool topcoat, round collar shirt and tie, navy blue wool suit.

A bolt of lightning popped inside my temple like a soundless firecracker. "What'd you say to me? What the fuck are you laughing at old man?" I waved the old codge away: "Get the fuck out of here you old bastard." I scraped some mud off the ground and threw it at him. He moved aside before it got half way there. The laughter got louder—now it was inside my head.

Then I recognized him: James Wallace Waverly, a grandfather I had never known. His picture was on the wall when I was a kid. According to the stories I had heard, he was a tough son-of-a-bitch: a hard-bitten Englishman who was bouncer on the trains in upper Michigan during the Depression. Had to disarm and disembark freeloaders all the time. But he died before I was born... and he was standing right there in front of me. *This was some good fucking acid.*

"What are you doing here, old man? This isn't fucking Halloween. Why don't you leave me alone? Everyone else sees Jesus, and I get you for the chrissakes!"

"Fuck Jesus!" snapped old Jim. "Jesus was a martyr. You have to be dead to be a martyr. You want to be dead like me?"

Suddenly his face was a skull, worms wriggling from the empty eye sockets.

I freaked and rubbed my eyes and looked again. This time he had a face. A face that was giving me the look. The look you see on the pioneers' faces in the photos in the museums. I always admired that look but I never understood what was behind it.

"Are you trying to tell me that I'm a coward—taking the easy way out? Look at me, I've been beaten to fucking shit.

Knocked every which way AND loose. My marriage is long in the trash barrel and now Mary is playing house with a psycho and the big fagaroo killed my friend. These other guys, they— ah fuck it. It's just not worth it anymore. I don't see the point of life…."

Again the laughter in my ears.

"What's the point of death, son? Anything worth having is worth suffering for. Unless you'd rather give up. In that case, it is your choice."

"That is funny. And fucking trite. Do you like that word— trite? I went to college y'know. I know a lot of words and they're all about to come spilling out here on the ground any moment. What do you want with me, anyway? Welcoming me to the graveyard? Introducing me to the family?"

All I got was The Look.

I was close to him. I took a swing at his head, a looping overhand right.

He disappeared.

Bad acid, probably. Indigestion, maybe. *Fucking chemicals in the booze. Bad lifestyle, hormones in the hamburger—could be anything.*

Then the world jumped to the left. Then back to the right. *Stand up, sit down, fight, fight, fight. Whattsa matter, can't you see straight?* My stomach lurched; loins itched. Some kind of crazy energy came up from the ground. Felt it in my legs—then everywhere: Nostrils the size of Mason jars, breath rushing like a hurricane. Ready to run with the wild dogs. Then the laughing again—no longer in my head maybe but I really couldn't tell. Then I saw him across the street encircled by a million pulsating raindrops.

"No sex in the grave, boy," he shouted as he toe danced in front of a boarded-up theater across the street. I couldn't remember ever seeing the building before. Today's feature was written in bold but fading letters on the peeling marquee: Waverly's Demise .

More laughing seemed to come from behind me but when I turned there was no one there. A strange, electric buzzing—like from a recording—reverberated off the deserted asphalt and empty buildings. Then I heard a wailing sound, at first getting stronger and increasingly mournful and finally fading.

A harsh whisper: "The beast is on a short tether, boy."

I looked everywhere. No Gramps. When I turned back around the theater began to crumble before my eyes. Before long it was an empty lot with an old tire and a broken concrete block in the middle. The distant wailing sound came back again—as a siren this time—getting louder and coming my way. I ducked into the darkness and ran and until my legs stretched out. Suddenly everything was clear. Ever clear ever true. Running was good. You just had to have direction.

I got back to the car all ready to go.

I drove to a spot on Fifth Street, right across the boulevard from Beaner's, walked across the street and started searching for Johnny Wells' big Chevy. It was in the back parking lot—nose up to the rear door of the bar—in a spot marked: Management Only Violators will be Towed. The blood pounded in my head.

I thought about going back in but I put the kibosh on that. I was too fucked up. I thought about standing outside by the back door but it was raining—a cold, relentless, freezing drizzle—and even I knew enough to stay out of the rain. I had to talk to Mary and say my piece. That was what Stephanie wanted. What the fuck did I care what Stephanie wanted? I owed Mary. *Why is that? Because she said she loved me. Did she show any love on that stage in there? I don't know. She's doing hard drugs. There's a warrant out on her. She can't be trusted.What am I doing here? I don't know. I should leave.*

There she was.

Out came a steady stream of people and Mary peeled off to the side and told some guy to leave her alone, then stopped alongside Wells' car. She leaned against the bricks and pulled a cig from the pocket of her most likely new black leather jacket and fired up it up. Took a big drag and blew smoke into the rain. Took a deep pull of fresh air and held it in for a few seconds, her head tilted back. I followed her gaze up to the street light: shining, blinding raindrops fell.

I was almost to her before she saw me. Shock and wry, groggy amusement played over her tired features but she still looked sexy in her black stockings and burgundy, thigh-high skirt. I tried to say something but she beat me to the punch:

"You fucking loser. What are you doing here? You didn't want anything to do with me. I'm a stripper and you're just so damn good. Isn't that the same old story. Ain't that how it is." Her voice was metallic like a spoon rapping on a counter top. "Now I got a real man, so why don't you split before he comes out and kicks your ass. I don't want him thinking I'd have anything to do with someone like you." She pawed the ground with the toe of her knee-high black boot and looked away.

"What the fuck are you talking about? Do you expect me to believe that shit, Mary? Or is this some weird way of punishing me for your delusions?" Coherence didn't come easy for either of us right then.

Mary crossed her arms in front of her, scowled and spit out her words: "You don't have to have anything to do with me if you want—that's fine." There was moisture in the edges of her eyes—my chest was about to explode. "But this place— why did you come here? Why did you do that to me in there?" Her voice cracked at the end.

"I don't know. Something came over me. I was drunk. The band was weird. My brain broke. Why do we need a reason? How about this thing with you and Wells? What about all those things you said about him before, they're not true anymore? Stephanie told me a few things about Johnny, like he's a baby raper, for one. Or maybe you knew that. Did you know that?"

"Steph's just making that up. She wants Johnny back."

"Popular guy for a grease ball…. Why don't you split, Mary? Get out of this town for good."

Who was saying these words? I wondered. Who was making this body move? Surely not me. *I can't move anymore by myself for Christ sake.*

"Steph is just saying that, because she wants to be where I am, but I'm tired of running. Johnny gives me things—things I like. And I make good money here. Everywhere—everyplace else—I always have to leave."

"That's such fucking bullshit. How can you even say that? Can't you see what Wells is trying to—"

"Somebody looking for me?"

He was standing right there, sneering at the both of us, his narrow eyes locked on me. He flashed that thin and viciously gleeful grin I had seen once before. He was wearing the same jacket and the same pointy-toed boots as that time at the Castaway. Screw baby raper, this guy was a killer. Crazy Harvey Dornan knew that but he could no longer tell anyone about it.

I stared in Wells' face like a drunken fifteen-year old defending his first love from the neighborhood bully. "Yeah, me," I said, with as much bluster as I could muster.

His gloved left hand flashed out like a snake's tongue and crushed my nose. My knees slammed down on the wet gravel. I spit blood and tried to clear my head. I'd been expecting the *right* hand. His fists were like lead.

A boot crashed up into my chin and everything went fuzzy. Too fucked up to beg for mercy, gang.

Goodbye, goodbye, I'm diving into this puddle.

Sounds and voices then—lots of voices—and scuffling in the gravel. Johnny was yelling; Mary cried hysterically.

Out of my one good eye I watched as some bikers dragged Wells back toward the door of the bar. It was Big Dog and Frank and some pals. They formed a ring around Wells and wouldn't let him get to me. A kind-eyed man in a light colored golfing jacket helped me up off the ground and held me steady. He tried to keep from getting blood on his jacket but I think a little got on there.

"You're in rough shape," he said, studying me with concern. "Maybe you should go to the hospital."

"No, man, I'm all right," I said, wiping away blood and mud and bits of gravel with my sleeve. "That asshole just straightened out my crooked nose for me, that's all." I was about to puke on the guy's nice jacket.

Pain of a different kind surged through when I caught sight of those hurting brown eyes staring out at me from behind a row of cars. I saw tears through the rain.

"Why won't you leave Johnny and I alone?" she yelled out, with just the first hint of panic or maybe hysteria lingering at the back of her throat. "You know how it is. Why don't you go away, you fucking weirdo." She gave me one last sad look that made me think that this wasn't over yet and turned and walked quickly into the club.

The show must go on.

Farewell Redemption

I worked loose from the crowd and made it back to my car. It was still raining. Little gray pencils of rain that sparkled when the lights caught them and made you shiver. All of us were just waiting, that I knew. We were all waiting for everything to play itself out like everyone in the universe knew it had to.

The world inside the womb would seem normal for a while and then a wave of madness would wash in and slam into my brain and make everything go whack. All I had to do was wait. Good things come to those who wait. Whisky tried to keep the heavy edge away. I guess I was dreaming but I was awake. Really awake. I had never been awake like this before. My ghost never came back and I was kind of hoping he would because I could've used the company while I waited.

I know I was getting close to some secrets of the universe— maybe the next Dianetics—when Johnny, Mary and a beefy red-faced guy came stagger-swaggering out of the door. The men's faces were flush with alcohol and aggression and an evil glow lingered at the edges of their empty eyeballs. The little clock on the dash read five to two and now it was really time to get even. Or have I said that before?

Before he got into his Chev Wells took a leisurely piss on the door of a pink Cadillac parked next to him. Mary waited outside in the rain while he shook off his dick. Johnny's hairy goon friend guffawed and got into a shiny white Galaxy 500 and drove off toward the bridge.

Wells motored off and I followed but not too close.

We cruised slowly down Fifth Street; the rain was starting to freeze on the roads. I let him get a couple blocks ahead of me. It was slippery but my trunk was filled with two one-hundred pound bags of sand, a bag of softball equipment, two sledge-hammers, some heavy house jacks and an old truck rim. Finlander four-wheel drive.

Out to South Hammond and turning toward Allouez, street lights fluttered and grew tails. Noises darted in and out . Radio played cacophony. I hummed "Onward Christian Soldiers". I got too close to them and the beam of my headlights caught the dark shadow of Wells' hand as it snapped across the seat at his companion. The loving couple must've been having a small tiff. Hatred ran bitter in the back of my throat. Just past the snow-patched Nemadji Golf Course we started winding our way downhill, following the curves of the Nemadji River. The road undulated. My brain percolated. About a mile down, the road straightened out for a bit, then came to an abrupt halt at a T shaped intersection. Wells would have to stop before turning either left or right.

The Chev skidded and slid sideways, braking for the approaching stop sign, cherry red stars for tail lights. My mind blew; my chest pumped up... *king of the apes—testosterone of a thousand ancestors coursing through.* As I came around the final curve I turned off the headlights and stepped on the throttle. It was plenty dark.

Just aim for the glowing red cherry candy stars.

I was fifty yards behind and closing when Wells began a slow left turn. At twenty yards, I flipped the headlights on high beam and jammed on the brakes and all four wheels locked. Sliding fast, the heavy Olds rear end was catching up to the front. Ten yards. Pulled my foot off the brake pedal and jerked violently back to the right. Floored it. WHUMPH!! Crashed in hard, front bumper to his rear half. Both cars slid toward the ditch. His wild face caught in bitter surprise. The Chev teetered at the snow bank on the shoulder for an endless moment and then slid over the edge and came to rest at a slight side-hill lie. The Oldsmobile's massive bumper was pushed up tight against the Impala's rear door but my back wheels were still on the pavement.

Johnny swore and cursed in both English and his other tongue: "I'll kill you, you fuck! I'll rip out your balls!"

He struggled against the weight of the car door; he didn't look so good. Mary's head rocked and bounced like a panfish bobber in a slight chop. With my left hand, I opened the door just enough so the latch was unhooked, making sure the interior light didn't go on. My right hand squeezed the rubber grip of my favorite new Easton aluminum softball bat that Sam Cross had been kind enough to purchase for his old pal Keith, the best hitter on the club. I sat still like dead meat. Johnny moved slowly, limping a little, a cut on his forehead. I waited. He drooled with hate. When he got close enough—breathing hard and wheezing angrily, kind of growling—I shouldered open the door and danced out like a homicidal Nureyev, whipping the bat back and forth through the gray drizzle like a scimitar. Someone clicked on the slo-mo cam. A look of dull surprise crossed Wells' face and he tried to scramble backwards on the slippery pavement. Tried to dig in the narrow heels of his boots while he grasped desperately for his piece. His hand was coming out. I took two quick steps and launched the Easton with a line-drive swing. Felt his wrist crack. Gun skidded and bounced across the road. Wells howled and grabbed his forearm. With some effort he struggled up to one knee.

"I'll kill you fucking faggot," he half whined. Fear and pain sat on top of his words. He let go his broken wing and his good hand dove back down into his jacket. I came back swinging from the left side and tried to drive his evil melon into the bleachers but he put his arms up in front of his face to block. I checked the swing and shuffled my feet and brought the Easton down hard on his kneecap. He wailed like a weasel in a trap. It was supposed to be quiet in the country. I didn't like noise in the country. I spun around behind him and let him feel the meat of the stick on his spine. Vertebrae crunched like dry turkey bones. Hands fell down away from his head and shouts turned to desperate gurgling. I took him out with one sweet shot to the back of the skull. His face hit the black-top with a dull sort of smack that sounded like the time I was a kid and I blasted my dad's prize souvenir coconut with a pitching wedge. Gore spray like dark red velvet lay there on the glazed pavement, wriggling with escaping life. Rain diluted it. *Strawberry ices: 50 cents....*

"You should've worn your seatbelt Johnny," I said to the battered corpse. I couldn't take my eyes off him. He didn't look so scary anymore. Huge clouds of steam hovered about. Around Johnny it was rising. Mary struggled out of the ditch and walked slowly across the road in shock. She looked at me and then at Wells and spit on Wells and then turned away and vomited on the glazed pavement.

"Get in the car," I snapped. "Get back in the car. We have to get out of here." She just stood there staring at the freezing bodily fluids and laughing hysterically.

I wiped the bloody bat on my jeans before I opened up the trunk and carefully wrapped it in an old, green plastic rain poncho. Then I picked Johnny's magnum off the road and put it in my jacket. Mary was still standing there hugging herself and shivering. I had to take hold of her with both hands and walk her around to the passenger door of the Olds and push her in. Her condition had as much to do with heavy drugs as shock. After I took care of her I slid Johnny across the icy road and lifted up his head and shoulders and set his torso against the rear bumper of the Chev while I crept back around through the ditch and popped the trunk button.

Johnny went into the trunk all loose-necked and pulpy and easier than I thought. I was pushing his hand down inside the trunk when I saw the snake ring on his finger. Well well—one of my butt buddies— and now he was gone. *That wasn't so bad now was it.*

I closed the trunk on the hood named Wells.

I climbed in the Olds and tried to back out but the tires spun and slid down toward the shoulder and I couldn't move forward. Mary held her index finger sideways between her teeth and chewed, mascara smeared again.

I turned the wheel full lock to the right and tried again, rocking as best I could with my front end flush against the Impala. Still no go. My heart pounded, I felt the first hint of panic rising in my gut. Fear and guilt and rational thought and common sense were trying to crawl up to my brain where I might hear them scolding but I couldn't let them get there. With some effort, I held them all together in a knot where they belonged. I opened the glove box and punched the trunk button and then I ran back and grabbed sand from the trunk and threw it underneath the rear tires. I got back behind the wheel. Still no cars to be seen or heard.

The Olds moved off the Chev in two swings at it.

Now I needed Mary.

"We have to get rid of Johnny's car," I growled, feeling wild with fear. "I need you to wake up, Mary. I need you to pull it together. You have to drive my car and follow me. That's all you have to do, just follow me. It's either that or someone comes along and finds us— and we try to explain how it was that the party took such a horrible turn."

One look at her and I almost abandoned hope. I wanted to say ahahimammaya. But it would be too easy to connect me with Wells because of the incident behind the club, I had to make the evidence disappear.

She glanced at me sideways with her smudged, half-awake— half-asleep eyes, made a try at the old wry smile and creaked: "Okay captain."

I jumped into the tilted Impala and cranked on the starter. It fired right up—those boats could take a punch. I backed it up carefully for a few feet, scraping against the Olds bumper, then put the floor shift in second gear and slowly let out the clutch. The thing bucked a little bit then chugged right on out of there and up onto the road. I took a last look behind me—my heart heavy like fucking LBJ—and drove away through the darkness and the rain. *Because it's one, two, three strikes you're dead at the old ballgame.*

Then came the laughing. A chuckle at first—coming from I don't know where—then uncontrollable, stomach-hurting laughter. But Johnny's smell was in the car—and Mary's. Suddenly nausea gripped my gut, followed by waves of tears and then sobs. Draining, chest heaving sobs. A tornado of emotion twisted in my head: Shutters. Amazing laughter and then the tears—then the laughs—then sobs.... laughs... sobs... laughs... over and over and over and over.... My brain spun in a big circle and I couldn't stop it. Struggling against darkness and ice and wind and fear, twenty minutes of driving felt like twenty years. And then I saw the turn. I flicked on the blinker and hoped Mary would follow and not decide to keep going and leave me and Johnny to ourselves. Thankfully, she turned behind me. Suddenly I was calm. I prayed most of all that nobody saw us. You could drive down that same road a hundred times and never see a sign of life but as soon as you start fucking with the cosmic status quo, everything changes. The odds change like when the dealing's from the bottom of the deck.

Five minutes down the iced-over gravel and our grim caravan came to the road leading to the water: two narrow ruts down a small snow-patched hill to a muddy back bay of the Nemadji River. There was a concrete fishing pier on the bank and a short cast from the end of the pier was twenty-five feet deep of cold brown water. I knew that because I'd fished there with my son on more than one occasion. Caught a few catfish and a decent northern onetime.

I turned down into the ruts and stopped and threw the Chev in park and got out and walked back to the Olds. Spikes of rain crashed against the crusty snow and glazed trees and made an eerie sound like gravel hitting a window screen. Mary had a cigarette between her dark red lips and a modicum of composure on her face. She shook just a little when she rolled down the window.

"You stay here," I said "Don't move, shut the lights off. I'm going to put down a new fish crib." I shuttered, like the gods didn't think that was funny. Suddenly I felt weak and the smell of death engulfed me. The air was poison and darkness and hell. Then it passed. I rolled the Chev to the bottom of the hill—about thirty yards away from the pier—and stopped. I wanted to tie my shirt to the steering wheel so the car would roll straight but I couldn't figure out how to do it. No matter how I tried, my mind would not give an answer. The car would just have to go straight, held in line by my intense will.

I folded up the floor mat and wedged it in between the gas pedal and the driveshaft hump and pushed the throttle down to wide open. The engine raced and roared; bouncing lifters clicked. But it was a fucking four-speed and I couldn't throw it into gear without pushing in the clutch. I couldn't push in the clutch without sitting in the seat... *I couldn't think without my thumb up my ass.* I jerked out the floor mat and the engine returned to idle. I would have to ride it to the edge like James Dean in *Rebel Without a Cause.*

I backed up a few yards, popped the clutch and put the hammer down. Just before the pier I bumped the door and rolled out. My jacket didn't catch on the handle like in the movie but the ground did jump up and smack me hard on the shoulder and the hip. I rolled and rolled. Waited for the big splash but when the Chev hit there was only a sickening thud and a light splash and a deep cracking sound.

Ice was still there. Fuck.

I squinted out at the shadow and it seemed like the beast was slowly sinking. I'd look away for a moment and then stare back out there and it seemed like it was sinking lower. *Maybe wishful thinking*....

I couldn't afford to appreciate nature right then so I turned and started up the hill. The pain in my shoulder wasn't bad except for the weird, psychedelic, throbbing sensations. My jeans clung to my legs and pulled like a ball and chain. Sing it Janis, please. Blood and mud mixed and turned black. All I could think about was getting back in the warm car and driving out of there. Then everything would be all right. As soon as I got home again, things would be all right. Home.

When I reached the upper road I could barely move. But what's this? The Olds was on the opposite side from where I left it, with one rear tire in the ditch. Mary hunched over the steering wheel with her head flung backward and her wild eyes searching the darkness in panic. In vain she spun the tires. Whine, whine, whine they went. Smoke and rubber stink filled my head. Hands and feet were numb and snot and blood and tears crusted on my face. Rain drove down clean and sharp and loud.

"CUT IT OUT!" I pounded on the window. "TAKE YOUR FOOT OFF THE GAS!"

The tires stopped spinning. She looked at me. I opened the door. "Mary," I gasped "you'll have to wait. You're just spinning the tires deeper into the mud. I'm going to have to jack it up. Maybe I can push us out, but you can't be flooring it. It has got to be smooth or you'll just get stuck again. Hold on while I jack it up."

I moved aside the plastic wrapped bat and the spare rims and pulled out the tire jack. I cranked up the rear bumper. Chinka-chinka-chinka. I got the rusty beast leaning forward and got my hands on the bumper and prepared for a push. I shouted for Mary and put the muscle to it. The Olds leaped forward and the tires caught a piece of hard turf. The jack snapped off the bumper, flew back into my knee and bounced into my nuts. I screamed GODDAMN IT and fell into the fetal position in the mud—hands between my legs—turning white and thinking the world was coming an end.

Back behind me in the emptiness there was a flicker of light. Then a flash. A car.

I crawled on my hands and knees and climbed into the front seat and pulled Mary to me and fell on top of her.

The big sedan rolled up and I could hear it slowing down, then it stopped. Our heads popped up like parked lovers too cheap or too poor to find a motel.

The old lady in the white parka who was looking at us got embarrassed and told her husband to drive off.

Before we left I took one last look down the hill. I couldn't see a thing but blackness.

I took the wheel and pointed in the direction we needed to go. We got back out to Highway 2 and I rolled down the window. The surf of Lake Superior thundered in my ear like the wrath of god. The winds smelled fresh and full of life but felt as cold as death. I shivered. Seemed like I'd been shivering for days. Cold was only a state of mind, I told myself. My life was just a state of mind. *Everything was just a state of mind.* But the car heater sure did feel good.

We got to my place and parked in the back. Before we went up the stairs I inspected the car for damage: The front end hardly showed a sign. The bumper was still wedged in slightly toward the middle from last spring when Loraine smashed into a bridge on Lake Avenue after catching me with another woman but the only sign of any new impact was some reddish paint scrapings on the bumperettes. I scratched at them a bit with my fingernails, got the poncho and the bat from the trunk, and went up the stairs with Mary moving sullenly at my side as if she was wrestling with demons of her own.

We walked into the kitchen and I flicked on the light and sat down at the table and got hung up staring at the brown swirls in the linoleum. My mouth was open and my lungs grabbed for big hunks of oxygen and Mary circled around the room and casually picked up a Green Bay Packers cap off the counter top. She put it on her head and it slipped down to just above her eyes.

"Is this your hat?" she asked.

"No, that's my roommate's," I said, then I remembered: "He's dead."

I started to cry, no stopping it this time. No fight left in me. I let my head fall down on my arms and sobbed into the table. Next thing I knew her warm hands were stroking my head and her soothing voice was saying it was going to be all right. I gave in to it all and let her take care of me. She dragged me into the bathroom and washed the crap off my face with one of my threadbare towels while I ran warm water and soap on my hands in the sink and tried to avoid looking at the pathetic wild creature in the mirror.

She was drying my face and I was sitting on the toilet seat with my shoulders slumped forward. She stood up and put her thumb beneath her chin and studied me, her eyes narrowed. Then she ordered me to take off the muddy, bloody clothes and throw them in the tub. I shivered uncontrollably while she dried me off and stumbled into the bedroom and crawled underneath the covers of my bed and she undressed and spooned up close to me from behind. She put her arms around my chest until I stopped shaking and fell asleep.

I slept fitfully at first, waking up several times covered in sweat. Each time, a smothering feeling lingered behind as a reminder of the oppressive night terror. Then I was comforted by the warmth of Mary's body and fell back to sleep. *Safe and restful, sleep, sleep, sleep...*

I dreamt that I was walking naked through a dark and treeless cemetery, whacking the crosses off the tops of gravestones with my softball bat. Next I was the emcee of a quiz show standing behind a red silk pulpit instead of a lectern. The contestants were a bloody-faced Johnny Wells and a nameless, toothless junkie wearing baggy pajamas. Question Number One: How do you mend a broken heart? Question Number Two: How can a loser ever win?

The next morning, halfway between dreams and awake, I reached over to find more of the reassuring warmth. I was feeling like it might be time for something more but all I found was empty sheet. Weakly, I called her name and got no answer. No surprise if she was gone. Gone to the cops or the mayor or the fucking F.B.I. to fry my ass for murder and kidnapping and littering a scenic waterway. They were going to hang me with a spiked noose and put a picture in the newspaper.

Suddenly I had to take a leak.

When I popped open the bathroom door the first thing that registered was the foam, the bubbles.

She smiled at me sweetly. Her arms were beautiful, streaked with little wisps of white foam. A candle burned slowly on the window sill above the tub. All the bloody clothing was gone and the place even smelled nice, like soap.

I said, "I'm glad to see you made yourself at home," and tried to soak it all in without seeming like too much of a geek.

Her hair was pulled back into careless pigtails; creamy bubbles melted into the braids. "I hope you don't mind," she said, sounding slightly groggy. "I thought sure it would be all right. I feel so much better now. I love this bathtub."

"Oh, it's okay all right. You deserve it.   It's beautiful… you're beautiful. Just don't look while I piss…"

When I turned back around Mary slid her hands away from her eyes, leaving more bubbles on her cheek and forehead. "Come here, Keith," she said. "Take my hand. I just want to thank you for taking such good care of me.".

When our lips met it was so hot: warm water, bubbles, and sweet, sweet flesh.

* * *

When the bath water turned cold we both got out and shyly dried off, our backs turned. I was always shy like that, but you would think a stripper would just walk around nude and not worry about it. Sometimes people surprise you, I guess. Mary asked if there was anything she could put on that was clean so we took a walk into my bedroom. The paint spotted wood floor was littered with dirty clothes. I found a clean T-shirt with a picture of a bearded guy and the words *Mr. Floods Party* on the front. On her it was a perfect fit. She got the last clean pair of sweat socks. I put on an old terrycloth robe with a brown scorch mark in the shape of an iron under the left front pocket. Then I cooked up a breakfast of eggs and toast and the last six pieces of bacon. Even made a pot of instant coffee—Maxim. The two of us ate together at the kitchen table like newlyweds. Newlyweds who didn't do laundry. I overcooked the bacon a little and I wondered if she liked it. The egg yolks were hard too. Usually I'm a better cook than that. After breakfast we smoked a few cigarettes and a joint and sucked down a pot of coffee. The talk was small talk, like about my wife and kid. My legs were as heavy as tree trunks and my weariness was eternal. I was a killer now. Still, all things considered, I was feeling pretty good—just a little uneasy about the future. *Meet me in hell won't you please… Jesus, that bacon tastes good. The joint ain't bad either.*

After we finished eating and smoking Mary started to pick up the dishes.

"You don't have to do that," I said; "Mickey will—ah—goddamn it," A wave of nausea ran through me. "Mary, what are we doing?"

"Cleaning up the kitchen?"

"You know what I mean."

She carried the dishes to the big old-fashioned sink.

"I'm not sure that I do, " she said.

"Well, Jesus fucking Christ, we can't just play house here and ignore the fact that Johnny's dead and that I'm going to get killed by McKay for stolen property that I didn't steal. That's what happened to Mickey, in case you were wondering…. They killed him. Oh, that's right, you missed out on that little twist while you were so very busy shaking your ass and getting numb. I forgot about that. Jesus…."

"You just wait a minute, smart boy. I'm not the one who killed Johnny. I was only getting high and 'shaking my ass', as you so delicately put it. How long did you think I was going to wait—while you brooded and felt sorry for yourself."

"Yeah, what you did takes a lot of courage, all right… and Johnny was such an honorable guy…. I forgot—you were do-ing what's best for both of us. I'm glad you're so fucking thoughtful."

"Fuck you," she snarled, moving closer, the curl in her lip growing ever cuter.

"How come you never told me about the fire, Mary? And the warrant? "

"What fire? What do you mean?"

I got so hard that I was busting out of the robe. She saw it and her eyes turned mischievous and instead of taking a swing at me she grabbed my dick and gripped it tight like shaking hands with a frozen trout. I pulled her down to me on the chair and our mouths came together in hot, wet heat. She led me into the bedroom and we did the bone boogie like two little devils who were late for a train.

The afterglow: We were lying there in it, kind of staring at the ceiling. I was struggling to push back mental images of Johnny and Mary together that kept coming up after me like green flies from the basement. That kind of shit comes to you after you've blown your wad.

Mary said: "So what do we do now, Mr. Pornography Salesman?"

"That's supposed to be my question. I don't have an answer. If I only knew what it was that McKay is looking for I might have a chance. Otherwise my ass is grass."

"What does it have to do with you, this missing property?"

"He thinks I copped it. Or at least he did. He had Mickey killed trying to get him to talk, and now he's real interested in our friend Sam. I think Sam stole whatever it was… maybe off a boat that I drove him to. Whatever it was is about the only thing that's going to keep me alive. Probably coke or money, but Jesus, could be a dozen things. Sounds like the McKay brothers are into anything that—"

"Heroin. Heroin. Smack, junk, scag, boy, brown sugar…. That's what McKay lost. A kilo of heroin. I heard Johnny talking about it with that fat fuck Milo Korski. Somebody stole it off one of the boats, and now there's a bunch of pissed-off Greeks in town wanting their money. And Johnny mentioned a big finders fee."

"No shit, so that's it. Fucking Sam just never knew when to draw the line. He's gotten so fucking cocky he thinks he's invincible."

I got out of bed right away and put on my black jeans and my work boots and an almost clean tee shirt and my charcoal v-neck sweater.

"You got a nice butt, Waverly," Mary said. "You ought to be a stripper—we could work together. I can see it now, up there in lights. Maybe we could do a Sonny and Cher thing…."

"I'll think about it. But right now I've got some work to do. So if you want to finish the dishes, it'll be all right. Mickey won't be doing them."

I got the bat and the poncho and washed them off in the tub along with my dirty clothes. I hung the poncho on a hook by the backdoor and took the plastic garbage bag full of balled-up clothes and the bat and put them in the trunk of the Olds.

I cleaned off the front bumper with some steel wool. The day was just as gray as ever. Blue-steel clouds weaved together in a dark tapestry, holding down the sour industrial stench for all to enjoy.

Then there was the problem of Mary: She couldn't stay for long. I had to find somewhere safe and out of the way for her. Somewhere where she would stay out of trouble. Somewhere like Charlene and Carla's Last Fall Inn. Out there on the far reaches of County Road E where Charlene and her late professional wrestler husband had made their last stand. Had it good out there for a while, too, until hubby died of a heart attack and left the two of them there to fend for themselves. Carla just a young teenager then. Now they do enough business to pay an extra bartender; they can get out once in a while and shake their booties like everyone else.

The cops could be looking for Mary to answer some questions about Johnny, like how he got inside the trunk of his car on a hunk of ice floating by Wisconsin Point. Being out there in the country away from everything would be good for my girl.

When I got back inside the house, she was gone, just a note left behind:

Dear Keith,

Had some things to take care of. I'll be out at Charlene's bar in the county tonight if you want to talk or anything. Don't feel obligated—you have done enough for me already.

All my love,

Mary

She was out the front door and headed for who knows where. Suddenly I had that lonely, empty Sunday feeling. It was only Saturday but I was still alone and feeling like it. Like I was an island.

All I could do was lay around and think about shit and smoke and sleep. My mind kept traveling back to my childhood home against my will. It was another bad break having a family like mine....

When I was a little kid I could do no wrong in my mother's eyes. "My beautiful darling boy," she used to say. And she always stuck up for me against the old man, whose cold eyes were always telling me how fucked up I was. But by the time I was in junior high the old lady had a new routine: valium at night, bitching during the day. The Wicked Witch of the North for sure. Then she got a brace on her leg because of bone weakness and started drinking all day on top of everything else. She'd have a Salem in her mouth and a Rob Roy in her hand: "I always dreamed of a man like Rob Roy… she'd say, "that's why I like this drink so much." She was always trying to make me feel guilty for something or other, and it worked for a while. I spent most of my life trying to get her out of my head. I used to wish that she could be more like the other guys' mothers, but the more I thought about it, I realized that they were all pretty screwy, too. When she finally died I didn't cry much—just a little—and only for the mother I used to have. Before the pills and the bills and the long spells in bed turned her into someone that drove you crazy. Sometimes she'd be up there pounding on the floor with her broomstick and I'd just ignore her. Let her hobble around with that piece of iron on her leg. I wasn't going to be her servant for Christ sake. Then she'd cry to the old boy about how cruel I was and he'd jump in my shit for it and lay on the muscle. He'd teach me that I wasn't going to treat him like the people at the office did, giving him ulcers with their disrespect.

"She thinks you don't love her," he'd say to me, always squeezing my arm and digging his fingers into the muscle. "She's crying about it. She says she can't understand why you treat her that way." Then he'd poke his hand into my chest and maybe slap me one. If I mouthed off it was the fist. He'd say that she was hard enough to deal with without me causing trouble. Later we'd just kind of let it ride and not mention it. Everything would return to normal and I'd feel sick.

The End of the Beginning

Easter Sunday, 1978: I had risen at nine o'clock and gone forth to the front vestibule for the morning paper. And yea verily it was another suck-ass day so I turned around and went back to bed. I still had some thinking to do but it was hard to get things straight in my head. I browsed through the paper and found nothing about nothing or nobody. I fell asleep.

Blue Monday morning: I paid a visit to the precious Antique Shoppe of one Nicholas J. Cross, hoping to catch him there counting his money. As I pulled up to the curb I could see him standing inside the store behind a glass display case, fussing with a tray of something. He didn't look as tough as he used to, somehow. He was getting old and soft and fat and becoming an antique in his own right. Story on him was that he could never take a punch. I was hoping it was true.

He stood up and shuffled his feet nervously. "Hello, Keith, he said, not looking in my eyes. "What can I do for you?" His white shirt was open at the collar, revealing a jumble of black wiry hair. He should have some of it transplanted to the top of his head, I was thinking.

"You know, Nick," I said, pointing at the glass case in front of me, "I've always had a strong urge lingering inside me—left-over from my twisted childhood—to run my arm across a display of precious and fragile antiques just so I could watch them break apart on the floor. And you know, I don't even care if you tell me where Sam is, because I'd really enjoy busting up some of this dainty overpriced shit you sell, any fucking way."

He looked at me funny like he was seeing me for the first

time then flashed that peculiar fake smile of his where he kind of tensed up his upper lip, lifting it slightly.

"Keith my friend, are you all right? What happened to your face?" he said, lips pasted to his teeth.

"I slipped on the ice and fell on a hunk of frozen dog piss, pudge ball."

I moved next to a table full of china plates and crystal drinking vessels and raked my arm across the top like a topspin forehand. The delicate little numbers crunched and tinkled against the far wall like your parents' old Christmas tree balls when you dropped them on the kitchen floor.

Cross was still sticking out his lower lip, distaste was in his eyes: "Settle down, Keith. There's no need for this senseless destruction. I'm sure we can work something out. What if we just erase your tab, like you suggested. Maybe you want in on this deal I've got going—it's big money."

"Listen, you fucking flab bag. All I want is the heroin your brother murdered to get. I wanna save—"

"Murdered? What are you saying?"

"What's the matter asshole, he didn't tell you? Your trustworthy little brother left that little detail out of your fucking big deal?"

"Well, I never heard anything about any murder…. I didn't hear anything on the news about any murder."

"Well," I said, mocking him, "let me ask you something, you fucking gas bag. Where do you think Sam got all the smack, the bingo parlor? That is your big deal isn't it? You two got your thick little fingers in someone else's smack pie. Look me in the eye and tell me I'm wrong."

East Hammond.... You think they would be interested? But maybe you *should* call in the cops—the Zenith City cops. You can explain to them about your brother and the Greek sailor he met at your house. Maybe you should call the fucking IRS, too, I got a few things I feel like sharing with them. Just to cleanse my soul, you understand."

"How do you know about the pharmacy? Sam, I suppose...."

"You are right there, fat boy. Your little brother talks a bit when he's got a buzz on. But I bet you knew that already, eh?"

"You don't have to remind me. I know my brother's weaknesses better than anybody. Lay off the fat boy shit and I might help you out...."

"Yeah, sure. But you seem to be forgetting about the danger your dear sibling is in. Those Greeks find him before I do, somebody will be eating his ground-up dick in a Gyros fucking sandwich. So I'd appreciate it if you'd tell me where he is, so I can finish my good deed to the world and catch a little rest before fishing season starts. I just might cut myself if I half to kick out some more of this glass. I do love the sound, though."

"Okay, okay!" He was doing that thing with his lip again. "He's hiding out in one of my properties. Nine West Fifth, upstairs. In Zenith. He's probably there passed out right now. Use the alley-side door."

"Thanks, Nick. One more thing—you got a phone, here? I need to make a call before I go."

"Yeah, in the back. In my office. Help yourself."

I went back there and ripped the receiver off the phone and put it in my jacket pocket.

"See ya, Nick. Thanks much."

I walked outside into the wet of a lake-effect snow shower but it was a fine day indeed.

* * *

I parked in the alley behind the rundown shingle-board duplex. I got out and moved cautiously across the wood walkway that lead to the back door of the upper unit. Halfway there I noticed a circular key ring, the paper kind realtors and car dealers use, hanging from the lock. Being close to a fortune hadn't changed Sam's attention for detail or his lack of caution.

Nick had been correct in his assumption: Sam was sprawled across a discolored mattress and box spring combo on the bedroom floor, a pool of drool underneath his gaping mouth. Resplendent in tee shirt and red-striped boxers with a brown blanket coiled and knotted around him like a polyester python. The deadly little Walther rested on the warped linoleum, a forearm's length away from the mattress.

Sam opened one eye as I entered but it didn't seem to register right away. He closed his eyes again. I moved over quietly, bent over and lifted up the handgun. I pressed the barrel firmly into his oily temple. His eyes opened. He cleared his throat. His breath damn near gagged me.

"Well, hi, Keith—ah…. Good morning to you, too," he said warily, eyeballs straining at the gun barrel. "What can I do for your young ass this morning."

"You can start by getting me all that smack you stole from the boat the other night, so I can return it to its original owners."

"So you figured things out, Keith."

"Yeah, but I'm a little slow…. Because of that Mickey is dead. Now it's your turn if McKay gets a hold of you. "

Sam only blinked a little. He rubbed his eyes and pushed back his hair with his fingers. "That fucking queer. He killed Mickey…. He's not going to get me." He yawned. "My brother knows a few people who can do some damage of their own."

"Nick is not going to help you on this one, Sammy boy, he'll be too busy covering his own fat ass. The only answer is to give it up to me so I can give it back to McKay."

"Give it back? Are you on chemicals?" He rubbed his eyes some more. "Now that would be a goyishe thing to do. Ease off a little, why don't you? Don't be such a schmuck. We can all get a little fat here if you loosen up your ass. Why don't you mellow out a bit; latch onto a good thing when it presents itself. Come on now Keitho my man… let's use the old bean here."

"What's the matter with you Sam, you got yourself a smack habit already?"

"Fuck you. I never touched the stuff. That shit is for niggers and losers like Mickey. That's why he's dead, 'cause he was snorting the shit and lost all his sense—of what little he had. You and me though, we could make ourselves enough to retire to Florida. Think of the women you could have with that kind of money, big boy."

I aimed the Walther at the top of his head.

"I oughtta do to you what you did to that poor fucker Miko, Sam. Blow a hole in your head, right here. Shit, if I put a pillow over the gun, the neighbors won't hear a thing. I could put the piece in your hand and Zenith City would have a drug-related suicide to gossip about. I think I've seen it all written on your Karmic tablet, asshole breath."

"Don't give me that poor fucker Miko bullshit. The fucker was smuggling heroin for god's sake. He was trying to sell me some that night. Trying to cut himself a deal on the side. I wouldn't have killed him, but he grabbed for the gun and it went off—in his chest. I mean, the shit was right there... of course I took it. Opportunity missed is opportunity lost."

"You're a fucking liar, Sam. I think you got Miko drunk and all coked up and he blabbed about the deal and you saw a chance to make out and took it. You didn't give a shit who got hurt as long as it wasn't you. You spell 'soul' with a fucking dollar sign. I've got a thousand fucking reasons to shoot you, not the least of which is that you set me up for a fall, thinking it would be my car we'd be taking to the docks. Fucking people been chasing after me and punching me out and god knows what all because of you, asshole." His face was blank of emotion, maybe just a hint of a resentful smile, like I was the dumbfuck, not him. "Don't you think the reason nothing broke to the press about Miko was that somebody covered it up? And do you think those guys would hesitate to kill you—and me—because we're such cool guys? They don't give a fuck, Sam. They'll sink us in Lake Superior for the chrissakes.... We'll wash ashore one day all preserved, looking exactly like the day we went in. You don't know how lucky you are—just being alive."

"Nobody's gonna know it was me who stole the junk—"

"They already know, you fucking douchebag. You're fucking crazy."

"Hey—I'm making out-of-town deals— they have no proof. Now—"

"Proof? These people don't need proof. You have been tasting the shit."

"Why don't you put away that gun before someone gets hurt."

I stuck the piece next to Sam's head and squeezed the trigger; the muzzle banged loud and sharp. Acrid smoke hung in the stale air; there was big hole in the mattress.

Cross rolled off the other side of the bed holding his ear and screaming in a high-pitched shriek: "God damn you Waverly! God damn you, you crazy bastard! What's the matter with you?" He went down on his knees. "I can't fucking hear! I'm goddamn deaf! You fucking asshole. I can't fucking hear. You fucking cocksucker!" Blood dripped out of his ear and ran down his hand.

"Do some lip-reading then, fuckhead. Get me the goddamn smack! People are dead all over the place because of that shit. And you and I might be the next ones. We have to get out of this before it's too late. I feel like a fucking recording or something. You're making me just nuts enough to put one in your brain pan, motherfucker. Brain pan… yes indeed."

"Oh pu-lease don't give me that shit. This is big money, a chance to break out. Come on, let's do up some of this shit. It'll wash our troubles away." He wiped his hand on the mattress, moaning softly.

When I readied the gun a second time, the fight went out of

him. He seemed to shrink down into the mattress. "Oh for the Christ sake," he said, wearily and thin-voiced, rubbing his temples and blinking. "Why am I wasting my breath on a pisshead like you? It feels like it's my big chance and I'm blowing it because of you, you cunt." He paused for a few seconds. The light came back in his eyes. "How about if I cut just a small tad out of it? I've already got some deals set up. Come on, Keitho, just a little. Fifty percent for you, fifty for me. Who's going to know?"

"You using Mickey's connections?"

"Yeah, a jeweler from Madison. Mick was going to do the legwork. I'm sure I can still pull it off. I'm not stupid."

"That's all you care about, isn't it Cross? Just the fucking deals and the scratch. Fill your pockets, empty your head. You've got the soul of a garbage-sucking seagull for fucking Christ sake. You and your goddamn brother.... Forget about any fucking deals. Just let's go get that dope before I get the urge to touch off this piece again. I never knew it was so much fun. "

Probably the hardest words he ever said in his short, greedy life: "It's in the fridge. In a brown paper bag." He bit his lower lip and stared vacantly at a stain on the mattress.

"In the fucking refrigerator? What, you drag the shit around with you?"

"No—ah, yes—I've been coming here for a while, only at night. Parking a few blocks away and all that. I figured if worse came to worse and the cops busted in I could say I was just crashing here and I didn't know what was in the fridge.

Maybe I could blame it on the shvartzes in the neighborhood. I could probably get away with it in this town."

"That's a good one. How long did you work on that gem? I suppose Mick helped you out with that—maybe after a gram or two up your noses."

"Fuck you. Why don't you just take the dope and get out of here. I can't stand looking at a sucker."

And that's what I did.

Grabbed the grocery bag with the Zip Lock of powder inside and left without another word. Cross was still sitting there on the mattress and moaning. Smeared with blood and wrinkled, he looked like a used tampon.

Now what do I do with the junk was the big question? Chances were good that my place was being watched. A cheap motel? Maybe, but bad shit seems to happen at cheap motels. The answer: The Last Fall Inn. The three girls and I could have a party while I planned the next step. And I don't mean a party with heroin. Something told me it would be a mistake to tell anyone about the white horse in the trunk.

* * *

Step One of the plan Mary and I came up with after I told her about the smack against my better judgement: Keith calls Peter McKay from a payphone.

Step Two of the plan Mary came up with: "Tell him you got a line on his missing package. Tell him you need a reward. You need a bunch of coke and some money for your efforts. And most of all, you need a chance to talk to him alone. If he threatens you you're going to split for somewhere warm and disappear; sell the shit to someone down South; let the junkies have their poison."

What the hell do I care, anyway, once you think about it, Peter? What do I have to lose?

Step Three of the plan: Tell him you're going to return his stolen shit and he's going to be so happy. Then lie low for a while and let McKay sweat. Let him think and wonder. Let him bounce between hope and despair for a few nights. Let him feel the heat from those angry Greek motherfuckers. Then when he's nervous and probably drunk, deal one from the bottom—his lucky card—and your ace in the hole.

* * *

Step Four: I pulled up my collar against the wind and put a nickel in the slot of an outdoor phone mounted on a pole at the edge of a Spur station along Highway 2. Charlene's white Ford pickup idled smoothly in front of me. Mary smiled from behind the blue-tinted windows. Tires hissed by on the wet pavement. Behind me the angry surf roared. Headlights and taillights had stars around them.

After a few rings he picked up. "Hello," he said, querulously.

"Hello, Peter? Is this Peter?"

"Yes it is. Who is this?"

"Keith… Keith Waverly, I'm calling from a pay phone out on the road…."

He sputtered, cleared his throat. His voice was reedy, constricted; his breathing, labored. "Is your little game coming to an end, Keith? Are you calling to tell me it was all a mistake, some kind of false hope tossed my way to tantalize and torment? To keep me awake nights—"

"Peter, I got your fucking shit for you, man…. Easy, big pony… just listen to me: This isn't easy, you know, nothing in life works for me anymore—I've pretty much given up on things. I—"

"You've really got the product?"

"Yes, Peter, I do, really. I just want to get this over with, I can't take it anymore. I'm all coked up and I can't stop thinking about everything. The road just leads back to it and I know now that I want to go back down that road. Oh god—listen to me babble. I need some more coke, Peter. I need it bad. I'm ready to do the deal. I'm leaving town tomorrow. I'll come by your place at seven-thirty."

"If you're lying about this I—"

"I'm not lying. But there is something else… something I forgot to mention. It's about those pictures."

"You want the negatives? Well certainly you can have them in exchange. Unfortunate circumstances I'm afraid… I—"

"Of course I want the negatives. But there is something else… this is the funny part… I want to make more of them."

A strange sound came from McKay's end of the line, like there was something caught in his throat.

"Exactly what do you mean by that?"

"Are you going to make me spell it out? Can't you see? I started thinking about those pictures you sent me…. You probably won't believe this, but I still have them; I couldn't throw them away, it was so strange. I was thinking about them today after I did a bunch of coke; I couldn't stop myself. I got out the pictures and looked at them and I got the biggest baddest hard-on of my life. I couldn't believe that thing. I took it out and stared at it. It's so fucking weird, you know: I sit here snorting this blow and drinking my Bacardi, and I can feel my dick in your mouth and your big cock in my ass. I can see now that my life has been a big funnel, with you waiting at the tip. Truly this was fated. I want to make more photos like that, maybe a film. I want to get into the adult film business. Working at the Wabasha has allowed me to see the tremendous amount of money to be made by a guy like me. You can help me—those pictures will be a start, ah, ah, kind of a resume or something . I think I might try some of the junk, too. That way there will be sort of an other worldly quality to my acting."

"The package better be intact, Keith," his voice was thin, higher than normal and quivering slightly. "This is truly good news. As I said before, I've been waiting anxiously for you to come around." He swallowed heavily. "In more ways than one. Yes.... I sensed something about you that first night. That's why I took an interest in you. That's why you are still alive; you can thank me for your life—and now I must thank you. Doesn't it seem strange.... I've been thinking about you, fondly, as a matter of fact."

"I'm jacking off right now, Peter. And I'll be there at seven-thirty ready to celebrate, celebrate, dance to the musak. Have everything ready, I will. Invite some other friends if you like. Instant Karma's gonna get ya, bye bye...."

* * *

My jaw was locked tight as I climbed the stairs to O'Toole's apartment. I was stone cold sober, riding the adrenaline Winnebago. A cold damp wind from out of the east bounced off me like bullets off Superman. Inside the right-hand pocket of my newly purchased cashmere topcoat (eight dollars at St. Vincent DePaul's salvage store), my fingers sweated against the butt of Johnny Wells' Smith and Wesson 357 Magnum. The other coat pocket swelled with a kilo of top shelf smack. I was thinking it might have been a better idea to take off with the shit and have a run at it out on the road. One time for the roses and then out. But it seemed like that one time could ripple around me a thousand-fold, like a pebble thrown into a pool, ruining many lives as well as my own. *But what did I care what other people put in their bodies?* It was four-thirty in the a.m. and McKay had been waiting for nine hours. The guy should be ready.

At the top of the stairs I was surprised to find the thick front door slightly ajar. I looked all around and listened and tried to feel any bad vibes in the air. I pushed open the door and slipped quietly in, then I locked it behind me.

"Peter, are you here?"

No answer.

The smell of cigarette smoke hung thick in the air, Brut lingered sickly on the edge. I started down the hallway towards the billiard room, the gold, brown and red floral pattern rug softened my steps. What seemed to be the peaceful glow of a television seeped from a half-open doorway up ahead. I had been filled with resolve but I was beginning to lose it. Images and feelings and paranoia called to me from somewhere I'd never been. I gripped the gun for support. *Happiness is a warm gun, momma.* The grim reaper's whip cracked above me, driving me faster down hellfire highway. Somewhere in my head the ghostly voice of Frankie Lane sang "Ghost Riders in the Sky.."

McKay had said it himself: "If you let people push you around they'll take everything you have."

I learned quick.

I pushed open the heavy door of McKay's bedroom: an 8mm movie flickered on the white wall. In the ghostly light, four naked guys performed group fellatio, daisy-chain style, in the middle of the desert. The room smelled of something heavy and bitter and primal with an overlay of free-base smoke. Peter lay naked on his back on his large four poster bed. Piles of porn mags surrounded his lifeless body. His hands rested on his chest and gripped a glass pipe.

His heart must have gone from too much of the shit. Maybe he got too excited about me coming over. I can be cute sometimes. I got down real close to check him out, just to make sure. From a certain angle he almost looked alive—almost. He seemed shocked by his predicament. He didn't do anything when I slapped him across the face, so I did it again. I felt ashamed. I got down close to see if he was breathing and I noticed a little red dot of freshly dried blood on the loose flesh above his huge Adam's-apple. I didn't know what to think of that—so I didn't think about it.

Standing up, I saw my reflection in the mirror across from the bed. Who was that strange character inside that cloudy world on top of the cherry wood dresser? Nice coat. I tried to sit down and think but my heart was pounding like a speed freak drummer in a punk band and my insides were rising. I had to get up and move around the room in starts and stops, my hand cupped on my chin like that statue, The Thinker.

I wiped off Johnny's gun with the bed sheet and pressed it into McKay's right hand. I wrapped his fingers around the grip and put the index finger on the trigger. It was so easy it made me nervous. Then I put the gun in the top drawer of the fancy wood dresser where it would be easy to find. I looked closer in the mirror: red, white and blue streaks ran down the glass like watercolors. I thought I saw gray hairs. My eyes were blood-shot, wild.

I searched the dresser but all I found was clothes, a studded dog collar with a leash, a shit-caked dildo wrapped in a hand-kerchief and a bull whip. The negatives weren't there, so I went on a treasure hunt.

There was a small blonde armoire by the closet and I started there. Copies of my pictures and other gay porn occupied the top drawer but the negatives were noticeably absent. I wondered if he had a safe. Somewhere in the apartment there had to be a stash for money and drugs, probably behind the bar in the billiard room. But it was a big place and I was getting anxious to leave before any new visitors showed up.

I went back to the little table by the bed on a whim. McKay's skin was turning yellow. The little envelope with the negatives was inside the table drawer, right on top. Kind old Peter had them there all ready for me, maybe—or maybe he was going to taunt me with them until I handed over the product. There was no cash or dope in the drawer but I was thinking there was a lot more to find around there. Must be some money—lots of dope—who knew what else? But the overwhelming instinct was to run. Shit, I had what I wanted. Wells and McKay were dead and I had the negatives back; no sense in risking everything for a little unfettered greed.

Still, I went into the billiard room.

He had two cameras set up in there. Empty glasses on the bar, half full ashtrays on the tables. His mates had all gone home. Then I noticed the empty wall safe behind the bar. It looked like Mr. McKay had been ripped off at some point in the evening. Maybe the perpetrators were here when he died and they cleaned out the family jewels on their way out. Just a little souvenir of the late great Mayor of Vice. I got the hell out of there. When I got outside I crept softly down the back stairs, hoping I was invisible.

Everything was quiet. The air was mild and calm. I moved slowly to Carla's little Chevy Nova and drove slowly away. I didn't see anything else moving out there but me as I skulked down Banks Avenue like a deer-chasing dog. I worked my way out to County Road A, hung a right and blew down the lonely asphalt toward the Last Fall Inn. Light snow began to fall, whirling and dancing in the headlight beams. I pulled over to the side of the road, tore up the negatives and scattered them to the white wind. I started to think my troubles were almost over. Just a few more plays to make and everything was gonna be all right this morning, whoa yeah. I was crazy, you see—the drugs and all…. And I was starting to like being crazy. Certain people thinking it, anyway. You got treated politely if they didn't know what to expect. Just like it used to be when I played hockey: nobody fucked with you if they har-bored even the slightest suspicion that you might flip out and chop them up with your stick. That was a better kind of re-spect than the phony shit that guys like Nick Cross handed out to people for "business reasons."

I had no idea how the Greek contingent or the police and the mayor for that matter were going to react to McKay's death. I assumed it was the Greeks who had emptied the safe, and they weren't going to say anything to the authorities, that much I was pretty sure of. I also assumed it wouldn't be long before someone came upon the body. I hoped that Johnny Wells' dis-appearance would put some odd spin on the situation in the eyes of the law.

To me, it was an open and shut case that only a lard-veined cretin could not see: McKay killed Wells over some unsettled grievance, disposed of the body, then took Johnny's pistol home for a souvenir, knowing full well that he stood no chance of getting any heat for the killing. He was so happy about finally getting rid of the low-ball thorn in his side that he celebrated just a little bit too hard and his ravaged old heart stopped beat-ing. Like I said, an open and shut case. But then, there was that little red sore on McKay's neck.... The authorities could deal with that one if they so chose.

But there was still one little catch; I was in sole possession of a kilo of probably uncut heroin. I had no idea what it was worth except that the numbers would be HUGE when you considered cutting it and all that. Do you think I was tempted? You bet your sweet ass I was. I started shaking just thinking about it. I needed to get back to my sweetheart for some moral support and advice. By god it was sure nice to have a pretty woman who adored me again.

I grabbed Mary from the Last Fall and we drove across the Arrowhead Bridge to the Sunrise Motel, just outside of Zenith City, to put our heads together.

The next day, the papers in both towns were running the story of the tragic and sudden death of Hammond's assistant mayor. There was no mention of foul play and I got a big charge out of the quote from John McKay: "The tragic loss of my brother Peter will be felt deeply by many in our region. It is truly sad and to have him leave us so soon after being reunited. Our time together was short but productive…. My family is grieving."

After I stopped choking, I called in an old marker. Tommy Boudreau—a part Chippewa, part French Canadian former associate—owed me for three pounds of Mexican weed I had fronted him a few years back. Tommy had, in turn, given it out on credit to a member of a rival Indian tribe, who then vamoosed with the bundle and never came back. Tommy and I had been pretty close friends at one point but after that little incident we hardly saw each other.

He was a Vietnam veteran—a Marine, no less. Also an accomplished but pretty much reformed car thief who was currently living a life of golf and pool hustling, house painting, dope smoking and screwing nutso women. I asked him over the phone if he could find me a nice vehicle I could use for an ultra-low profile outing. You need the practice anyway, I told him. You're probably losing your edge, I said. He sniffed a bunch and cleared his throat, took a couple deep breaths, and said he'd see what he could do.

Then I called Nick Cross and had him set up a meeting between me and John McKay.

The final phase of the plan was in motion.

* * *

Motoring slowly down River Road towards Mayor McKay's mansion and bathing in the multi-colored glow of the jumbo dashboard, it seemed the white '75 Lincoln was my own personal space vehicle. Somewhere, Tommy was smoking a joint and laughing his ass off.

I looked over at Mary for an instant and she seemed determined as she gripped the wheel of the big car. Her chin jutted out and her jaw worked the muscles in her cheek. The black turtleneck underneath the black Levi jacket was a nice touch. The black eye makeup, also nice.

I hoped she was up to the task.

She dropped me off about a hundred yards or so past the mansion at the bottom of a small hollow. She was grinning and I could see where her teeth were just the slightest bit crooked. I was entranced. The flint-like spark in her eyes only added to her beauty.

I moved quickly into the darkness at the side of the road. Soon I was creeping along through the soggy yards of the mayor's wealthy neighbors and praying that I didn't stumble over any sleeping Dobermans. When I got to the stucco Tudor next to the McKay house, I surveyed the surroundings: a dark dry night and the air was cool but not cold. It felt good on my face; I had energy. I couldn't see anyone else around but visuals were shadowy at best. A dark station wagon parked down the road from McKay's driveway made me nervous. I was thinking that if I made it into the house, I'd be okay, because the mayor couldn't afford any kind of ruckus inside his own fine digs, such as they were.

I crept out of the shadows and walked slowly across the front lawn toward the door. Warm yellow light filtered out a den window. I saw my shadow bouncing up the front steps of the mayoral palace and pushing on the doorbell. There was a big brass knocker on the white door and I really wanted to give it a few raps, but I resisted. A chill raked the back of my neck. Don't turn around, I said to myself, which was pretty stupid. I pushed on the button again and fought the urge to turn.

The big door opened and the Mayor of Hammond stood there in front of me in black formal attire—the only thing missing was the black tie. In the golden light from a crystal chandelier that hung from the high white ceiling behind him, he looked pissed off. He was a big man but not as big as his dead half-brother. They shared some of the same features but the mayor was more refined-looking and had a smaller nose and reddish hair.

"Evening, John," I said, keeping my hands in my jacket pockets.

"Mr. Waverly..." he said politely, as usual.

"Sorry about your brother, John," I said, "terrible thing, death."

His eyes narrowed: "Yes it is. Most especially when it's yours, wouldn't you say. Please—come in, but I thought we agreed that you were to use the back door. What the fuck are you trying to pull?" All this with a plastered on smile.

"Oh, man… I just have a hard time with directions, Mr. Mayor," I said, still standing there. "You know how it is… just can't seem to follow them." I looked him in the eye.

McKay looked nervously around the darkness behind me. "Come on in then, quickly," he rasped. "We can't stand here in the doorway all night."

"Sure Mr. Mayor, sure, anything you say. I aim to please."

Old Richard had quite a place: shiny hardwood floors, lots of dark woodwork, oriental rugs, fancy art on the walls, fireplaces in the dining room and the living room, beautiful furniture, and much, much, more….

I was impressed. "Nice place you got here, John. Who do I have to kill to get a place like this?"

"What are you implying?"

"Just kidding, John boy, just kidding. Now, whattaya say we go someplace we can talk."

"Did you bring the stuff?"

"Now, hold your horses, big fellow…. Don't forget that I'm the one directing the arrows here."

He looked at me like I was seagull shit on his shoe, frowned and turned toward the back of the house. "All right, then. We can go to the den, it's this way. Come along won't you?"

"You sure you haven't got the Gyros brothers back there waiting for me, boss?"

"You can be assured of that. I find them as distasteful as you do. They were Peter's associates, not mine. It's extremely unfortunate that I must deal with them at all but it is now a fact of life. Part of settling my late brother's estate you might say."

"And saving your own crooked ass."

"I think this meeting will go a lot easier for both of us, if you cut out the smart ass bullshit."

I ignored him: "You're to be commended for your effort at the rehabilitation of Peter, John. You did some real good for the world—most especially your hometown here. I guess I never really grasped the nature of your relationship with your brother—friend John. I'm afraid that as close and Peter and I got to each other, he never shared that aspect of his personal life with me. It was always an area of great disappointment to me."

"Fuck you," said the mayor.

The den was a beautifully dark and leathery room at the back of the house, with large windows facing the river. McKay pulled the green curtains shut and invited me to sit down. I chose a big brown chair with brass tacks around the edge of the leather-coated padding, much like one I remembered from Peter's apartment. I guess you just never know when you'll go nostalgic. John sat down across from me in a straight-back wooden chair with leather on the seat and back.

"You see that man in the portrait over there?" John said, pointing at an impressive oil painting inside an ornate frame. A wild-eyed, silver-haired man in a dark blue suit stared out at us from the past. "He was my father. Peter's, too. He started everything for us here, shortly after moving here from Chicago after the repeal of prohibition. You see—"

"The old boy doesn't look like the friendly type, John. Say, speaking of prohibition, got any booze? I could use a drink."

McKay frowned: "As I was saying, our father had somewhat of a drinking problem, which occasionally led to adulterous liaisons. One of which was his dalliance with a German whore, name of Kleig, a stripper at one of my family's clubs around here many years ago. One night, shortly before he died, my father was extremely intoxicated and he told me the story of his bastard son Peter. After his mother died of TB, the boy was placed in a children's home. It seems that dad was feeling guilty in his old age. Or maybe he was just boasting in some twisted way. After father died, my stupid bleeding-heart younger brother Steven felt it was his duty to track our sibling down and offer him his birthright. Allowing it to happen was the biggest mistake I ever made. I suspect that it may have ended everything the McKay's have accomplished here in Hammond."

"How about that drink? Peter, for all his faults, at least had some Irish whiskey for his guests. You look like you could use one yourself," I said.

"I'm afraid I don't look upon this as a social occasion."

"Yeah, I suppose not. You just want me to believe that you had nothing to do with any of Peter's doings."

"Believe what you want. The truth is, that Peter was bringing in a lot of money at first. And I was getting sick of this little town. All the dirt, the long winters—the ignorant fucking people. I saw a way to escape with enough cash to live out my life in comfort. Isn't that what it's all about?"

"No… well, maybe…. You were going to leave all this behind?" I waved my hand slowly at my surroundings.

"So the trappings of wealth and power impress you, Mr. Waverly. These things come with a price tag attached, you understand. It became clear to me, sometime after Peter's machinations were fully realized, that I no longer wished to play the game of politics. And realistically, as I became aware of how out of control everything was getting, I knew the end was soon coming. To use your vernacular, it was time to split. Now, if you don't mind, I'd like to get that terrible package of yours, so I can return it to the original owners and relieve at least some of the pressure. I'm—"

"Peter's friends got their baklavas in a bundle?"

If looks could kill….

"As I was saying, I'm already late for a fundraising dinner, and I'm afraid that my unbearable wife will become even more so if I keep her waiting there much longer."

"All right, boss. All right. But first, one thing. The money. And let's not forget that I've got everything written down that happened and I'm not the only one who knows. Anything happens to me… well, you know the routine. And don't think I haven't done it, because I have—all that's necessary. But if you don't say anything; I won't say anything. Kind of like a political deal, eh John? Kind of like the arrangement you and your brother had, I bet. You don't tell; I don't tell; nobody asks.

"I told you, I never soiled myself with drugs. I leave that up to people like you."

"You're really trying hard with that holier-than-thou routine, aren't you. You think I don't know how this town works? I think you and your brother were as thick as thieves at a political convention. I think you two hit it off real well because you shared the family propensity for greed, and you're only trying to whiten your image now because your leavings are finally starting to stink. Shit doesn't go well with tuxedoes, does it, Sunny Jim."

"Listen, you sanctimonious little prick. I've taken about as much of your impudence as I can tolerate. Either pony up the junk or get the fuck out of my house. I'll let the Greeks deal with you."

"Easy big fellow, easy. A man your age has to watch his blood pressure. Look what happened to old Pete. Or did somebody named Zorba jam a lamb chop up your bro's ass? Serve him right after what he did to Mickey. But you are right about one thing—this conversation definitely has its limits. I do have a few more questions, if you'll be kind enough to humor me just a little while longer. Then I'll take flight on gossamer wings."

"Very well, then," he flustered. "What is it?"

"Two things. One, what did you people think you were going to do with that much smack around a depressed area like this? I mean, you could sell a little of it around here, but it would like take you forever to get rid of that much horse around here."

"Well, you're right about that. The stuff was never meant for here. It was headed for the negroes of Chicago. If it hadn't been for that scum bag Wells, there would never have been a grain to hit the streets of Hammond."

"Johnny's got a way about him, doesn't he?" I almost slipped up and used the past tense there. Couldn't have old John suspecting about poor young Johnny Wells now, could we? "One more question, Ace. Why was Mickey offed? He didn't steal the shit. There was no need for him to be killed."

"He was just unlucky, I suppose. I know nothing but what I heard—after the fact. I was totally against that kind of behavior from the start. Peter had these peculiarities that seemed to have risen in his later years. These family things have a way of getting sticky, at times; it's a blessing that he's gone. Truly the hand of God has intervened."

"Sticky, you say... now that's a politician talking, all right. Hand of God, eh.... I think you've got your own hand so far into the cookie jar that the red ants call you mama, John boy. Sticky for sure."

The phone rang in the other room. The mayor looked at me for a second as if I should answer it. On the third ring he got up and walked down the hall to a low table with a formal chair on each end and a shiny black phone in the middle. He picked up the receiver and turned away from me for a moment, mumbling something and bobbing his head. I went over to one of the large windows pulled open the curtain and stared out at the shadows in the yard.

McKay came back to me with a red face and an armload of attitude. He went over to his big black desk with the thick hunk of glass on the top and pulled open a side drawer. Instead of a gun, he lifted out an envelope and flipped it over to me. I caught it two-handed, basket style. It was "say-hey" all over again.

"Well, John," I said, inching my way toward the front door, "it's time for me to take my leave. Come and walk with me to the door so we can savor our final moments together. Then, and only then, I'll tell you where the shit is."

"Not so fast," came a thick-accented voice from inside the darkened dining room. Before I moved another step, two big swarthy guys in fancy clothes and shiny pointed boots stepped out in front of me.

"You're not leaving here until we see the product," a guy with a thick black moustache said. "How are we to know if it is not baking soda?"

I whipped out Mickey's cheap little handgun from my pocket and pointed it at the talkative one's chest. The other one made a move but stopped when I swung on him. "Because I don't lie and I don't do heroin," I said. "Your going to have to accept that. Now me and the mayor are going to walk outside to that nice arbor vitae tree at the corner of the house there, and John is going to bend down and pick up the bag. Then he's going to walk back here and hand it to you guys while I boogie. Enjoy…. Be seeing you…"

"Stop Mr. Waverly," said a voice behind me that I'd heard somewhere before but couldn't place, "I don't want to shoot you, but I certainly will, given the stakes."

It was the captain of the Greek ship, Mr. Unpronounceable, and he was aiming a very dangerous-looking semi-automatic pistol somewhere near my loudly beating heart. I wasn't even sure if Mickey's gun worked but even if it did it was no match for that piece of iron. I didn't know what to do so I didn't do anything. Just stood there and kept waving the gun from goon to goon, sweating bullets instead of firing them.

"Please, please," pleaded John McKay, "no gunfire, please. This is my house. There are neighbors. I am the goddamn mayor of this town, in case anybody has forgotten."

"I don't think these boys care about your house or your neighbors, John," I said. "But I bet if you went outside and got that stuff for the gentlemen, everything would turn out fine. Do you think you can do that? Does that meet with everybody's approval?"

Everyone nodded and mumbled and McKay started for the door. I had to move out of the way a little to let him pass and the two muscle guys chose that time to jump for me. The first guy grabbed my gun hand and held it while the other one got set to break my ribs. I squeezed the trigger on the grab-bag piece but nothing happened. Then from the hallway, came the loud ka-chink of a twelve-gauge pump and the piercing sound of a chick yelling: "NOBODY MOVE! MOVE AND I'LL BLOW YOUR MOTHERFUCKING DICKS OFF! PUT THE GUN DOWN CAPTAIN! AND YOU DISCO DUDES BACK OFF AND GO INTO THE LIVING ROOM. I WANT YOU ALL ON THE COUCH LIKE THE THREE MOUSSAKA-TEERS." Mary, looking like Faye Dunaway in *Bonnie and Clyde*— sans the beret—was cradling my old J.C. Higgins bird gun in her arms like it was a Browning Automatic Rifle. She stared those guys down until they let go of me and stood up and stared.   After a few nervous seconds every-one turned to the mayor.

"John…" said the captain, "why don't you do what he sug-gests. I think it would be best."

By the time McKay came back in from the great outdoors we were all settled in the living room. The only thing missing was a crackling fire and some fine brandy, maybe a cheese fondue. Instead, we got a kilo of heroin.

"Let's take it with us, Keith," Mary said, sneering and squeez-ing the stock of the shotgun. "These assholes were looking to fuck you over, anyway. Just think what we could buy with that stuff."

"Nah, no thanks. It's theirs, they can have it and all that comes with it. I've got our money, let's go."

"We better hurry then, honey."

We backed out of there with our guns trained on the men. As soon as we hit the outdoors we started running. Back through the yards until we reached the dark quiet hollow where the enormous white Lincoln idled softly.

I said: "Let's go. Let's get the fuck out of here."

Mary turned and gave me a strange smile: "Where to, sir?"

"Let's try getting out of town. South Hammond sounds good for a direction. We can get lost on those county roads and make our way somewhere. I'll drive."

"Now that's decisive thinking. Somewhere, he says…. Should we go back to the Last Fall Inn? Carla and Charlene were sure nice to me while I was there."

"Nah… I think we should try and work our way toward the lake. Nobody drives those roads at night this time of year.

Maybe we can get to somewhere with Greyhound service if we play it cool."

Suddenly, a tremendous explosion ripped through the night air and the sky behind us lit up like the Fourth of July. I jerked around and looked: The rear of the mayor's house was all of a sudden a billow of yellow, orange, blue and red flames. It was cool.

I said: "Jesus, what the fuck was that?"

"Sorry, I must have miscalculated, I thought we'd be farther along when it blew. But I didn't plan on all that fuss."

"What the fuck are you doing, Mary? We were almost home free."

"We'll be all right, honey. That ought to keep the cops and everyone busy for a while."

"I sure as fuck hope the mayor wasn't hurt. He was our only buffer between the powers that be."

"Fuck him. Just another rich asshole who doesn't deserve your concern. Reminds me of my father's old boss from the mining company—red hair and everything. Fucker was always coming by the house when my dad was away on company business, getting my ma drunk and trying to screw her."

"Uh huh... What did you do back there, plant a fucking bomb?"

"I blew out the pilot light on the gas stove while you were in shooting the shit with Mr. Pig. Then I used the old cherry bomb-on-the-end-of-a-cigarette trick. One of the finer things I learned at my high school. One of Johnny's old cherry bombs and a half of a dry old Phillie's Cheroot—worked, didn't it.

Would you like one, I've got a couple whole ones left? Cheroots, I mean."

"Ah… no thanks, not right now, but I'll have a cig if you've got one."

She handed one over and I torched it on the car lighter with shaky hands.

"I put the lit cigar and the cherry bomb on top of the oven door and hoped we would be out of there in time." She smiled like a kid. "I didn't know we were going to dance with the boys in the hall before we left."

"Cutting it kind of close…."

"Winter gets boring sometimes, you know…."

"Uh huh." *Jesus.*

"Besides, when did you start getting holy? I mean, you fucking killed John Wells. All I did is blow up some rich pig's castle."

"Uh huh…." *Fucking Christ.*

*   *   *

We made it out to the country okay. I stopped for a moment to put the shotgun in the trunk. It was dark as the devil's heart. I took a deep breath and felt better. It was quiet as a cemetery.

I started weaving my way east along the South Shore of Lake Superior. Mary snuggled up next to me, content as I'd ever seen her. We were cruising in the direction of Ashland— probably what they were calling the mayor's place by now.

After a few miles, Mary leaned over and opened the glove box. She pulled out a bindle of cocaine, one that I didn't know was there. Imagine my surprise…. "Let's have a toot, Keith, to celebrate," she said, then broke into song: "Ooh, ooh... the witch is dead. The wicked witch is dead."

Beware, shit storm approaching.

"I'm not sure I feel like celebrating much at the moment," I said. "I'm hoping for a space ship to come down and beam us up."

"Oh, come on, you old poop. Just look at us, here. You and me together in this big fancy car. We've got drugs and wheels. I think I could get used to this. Let's just keep going—all the way to Florida. Just me and you and a dog named Blue."

Oh my god....

She had me sweating: "I don't know about that, this car is hot. Like a lot of things right now. It won't be too long before somebody spots us if we stay in this baby. Look, ah—why don't you close your eyes for a second. I've got a little surprise for you." I pulled the envelope out of my jacket and set it on her lap.

She opened her eyes and examined the contents: "Keith, oooh, heh heh—look at all this money.... We're rich."

"Half of it's yours, like we agreed. Personally, I need a new car. I'm afraid mine has taken a beating lately."

"Now we've got drugs, wheels—and MONEY honey," she said, settling back into the pillowy, white upholstery and clutching the bills in her lap. "Put the petal to the metal dreamboat."

Something terrible was wrong. Fear and anxiety and depression were riding a merry-go-round in my solar plexus. *Don't get stuck with this one*, said the voice. *You'll be sorry*, went the echo.

"I can't, I'm going back," I said. "Back to town for a while… I need to tie up a few loose ends." Staring straight ahead at the emptiness: "If there's anyone after us, they'll be looking for a couple. You'd have a better chance alone."

She bit her lip and her eyelids drooped: "Why won't you come with me, Keith? We make a great team; you can see that. You have to come with me… they'll be looking for you back there in Hammond. You can't go back."

"That all depends on a few things, like if the Greeks got out of that house alive with the junk. If they escaped, they would split town instead of hanging around for the brouhaha. That's what I would do in their shoes. And the mayor—he'll just lie like he always does. He's good enough to figure something out. Last thing he wants is to have me involved. For now I'll ride along until we dump this boat and find you a way out of here. Get some old clothes at a Goodwill store somewhere— cover your hair… wear some glasses or something…. You know. Send me a card when you get settled down South and I'll get there."

"Yeah… and maybe someday the sky will fall. Where have I heard this before…. This is so lame." A dark fire burned in her eyes.

"This isn't easy for me either, you know. You take your share of the money and have a good life. Find some nice guy…."

"Please don't start with that fucking shit, you sound like my father." She pouted for a second, looking out at the black trees. Then she shook her head and came back smiling, a glint in her eye and a twisted little grin on her lips. "Are you ready for a toot of this coke then, being that it's our final farewell and all?"

"Ah, I don't know… that shit… suppose it wouldn't hurt… I guess…. You've gone and twisted my arm."

She laughed a short little laugh, opened the packet and snorted up some powder with a tiny straw. She poured some on the back of her hand behind the first knuckle and put it under my nose. I sucked it in. She closed up the bindle and put it in her purse in the backseat and counted out the cash. Five grand for me and five grand for her. I took mine and stuck it in my jacket. She put hers inside her purse along with the cocaine and turned back around, sniffing. She went to work on the radio.

The drug was twisting up my head, the scent of her hand lingering sweetly behind, when all of a sudden the radio and everything else got real quiet. I got this terrible urge to start crying and I didn't know why. We just kept rolling along and looking pie-eyed at the moon over Lake Superior. All of a sudden Mary slid over close and put her burning-hot hands between my legs and eased down my zipper. Her eyes were cloudy. I didn't resist.

"I'm going to give you a little thank you, honey, for being the sweetest, kindest, bravest man I've ever known."

"Oh yeah," I gulped. "Uh huh…."

I tried to relax and enjoy.

My stomach was up inside my throat and all a-flutter. The radio got louder again—way louder—drowning out the world. Pink Floyd was on. Her silky-soft hands held my balls off the seat and her wet tongue made me crazy. The road ahead was black, headlights the only light around.

Ecstasy….

That's what we're all looking for I guess. And for a moment there, I had it. Climbing, climbing, climbing the ladder of love. Mary's sweet warm mouth did its wonderful work. I must have closed my eyes there for a second. Suddenly gravel crunched beneath the tires. Then we hit something and bounced upward. A horrible weightlessness and the headlights shining into black and empty space. The piggy white Lincoln hurtled off the bank toward the dark cold waters of Gitchee Gummi with the two of us wide-eyed and helpless. I braced for the impact. Mary jerked her head up, bewildered. The water cushioned the fall but the big splash chilled me to the bone with fear. The huge sled stayed afloat for a bit, wallowing. I pushed the buttons and the front windows went about three-quarters down before they conked. Freezing, burning rush of black water hit me like a ton of ice cubes. I gasped and choked for breath. I had all I could do to wiggle out my side. A panicked Mary made it out her window okay and then I never saw her again. I could hear her calling my name—her voice had bubbles in it— I'll never forget. I looked around madly in the blackness. Nothing. All I heard was the deadly swish, swish, swish of the waves. Maybe she was struggling out there, I don't know; we were on opposite sides of the sinking hunk of iron. My limbs grew numb and the lake pulled me down, begged me to stop fighting. I was never much of a swimmer; used to stand on the bottom of the pool during those Red Cross survival tests in junior high. I slashed away for a few yards and then miracu-lously it was shallow enough to touch bottom. I barely made it to shore. I stood there and screamed her name into the black-ness. Shivering—deep and uncontrollable. *Frozen-solid com-ing up soon.*

I knew I was going to die of hypothermia if I stayed there, so I clawed my way up the bank and started running down the road, hands and face bleeding. I ran and ran until I couldn't run anymore, frozen and sweating at the same time. Lying in the middle of the blacktop I pulled up into the fetal position. Closed my eyes. Inside my head I was swinging the bat at Johnny Wells as he lay prone on the icy road. Ready to surrender and die right there on that lonely hunk of asphalt.... Who? Me? Him?

My wet clothes were stiffening; I could no longer feel my feet.

Then in the distance there was an ever growing roar.

I opened my eyes in time to see a hopped-up Plymouth Bar-racuda skidding to a stop. Three drunken kids scrambled ex-citedly out of the doors and ran to my side.

"Man, you all right?" asked a booze-smelling teenager kneel-ing down over me. "What the fuck you been doing tonight, dude?" There were two guys and one girl. She was cute, chewing gum.

"Just a little too much partying," I think I said. I could barely hear my voice. "I'm afraid I'm freezing to death."

They helped me into the back seat and got my wet clothes off, put a smelly blanket around me and gave me a blast of their lime vodka. The girl sat in back with me and rubbed the blood back into my neck and shoulders. She wore a red ski parka and had cheeks to match. When they asked me again what happened, I told them I'd been tripping on some acid and fallen into the lake by accident. They seemed to understand, nodding and saying "Bummer."

We drove to my front door. They dropped me off and said I could keep the blanket. The driver smoked a cigarette and had black hair down over his forehead and pimples. He laughed when I walked away. The girl said bye bye, and I waved back at them before I turned and walked toward my building. I heard some kids yelling in the alley behind the house. I couldn't tell if they were playing or arguing. My neighbor's television was tuned in real loud to some action movie and whenever the soundtrack hit a bass note the walls would buzz. I walked up the stairs and unlocked the door of my apartment. Everything stunk of decay and sadness and stupidity—also the garbage.

I started putting my valuables on top of the bed. Threw in some clothes and my tennis racket and a few pictures of my kid and my Beatles and Stones albums and wrapped everything up inside the bed sheet and tied together the ends to form a nice rucksack. Everything I could think of that I might need was in that sheet. Everything but the water soaked money in the zippered inside pocket of my old jacket. I got the cash and put it in my tattered army surplus field jacket and grabbed the bundle and left by the back door. I threw the stuff in the back of my Olds and got the hell out of that dirty old town. I was going to miss little Mike but he was probably better off without me.

To say that I left town a broken man would be true. To say that I was shattered, the same. But there is a certain resiliency that comes with youth and a high level of denial as well and I was gifted with ample supplies of both.

I dumped the evidence in a dark ditch just south of Eau Claire and shaved my moustache in the bathroom of a freeway truck stop in northern Illinois. The oil pump on the Olds blew outside of Marietta, Georgia. The engine seized up and I had to leave it at a gas station where all the parked cars had bullet holes in them. The attendant was a red-headed southern boy who reminded me of Mickey, except not as smart. But at least the cracker was alive. He was a nice enough guy and he gave me ride to the bus station in town. I had to sleep all night on a wood bench with my tied-up sheet on the floor next to me. The next day I got a bus to the white sands of Clearwater, Florida, where limes grow in people's back yards. I made a vow to myself to stay away from cocaine and wild women and drug deals and card cheating. But the best laid plans oft go awry....

I was in South Florida for the chrissakes.